Gracie Goodbye

Charlotte S. Snead

Jan-Carol
Publishing, Inc

"every story needs a book"

Gracie Goodbye
Hope House Girls Series
Book 4
Charlotte S. Snead

Published July 2019
Little Creek Books
Imprint of Jan-Carol Publishing, Inc.
All rights reserved
Copyright © 2019 Charlotte S. Snead

ISBN: 978-1-950895-06-9
Library of Congress Control Number: 2019944515

You may contact the publisher:
Jan-Carol Publishing, Inc.
PO Box 701
Johnson City, TN 37605
publisher@jancarolpublishing.com
jancarolpublishing.com

This book is dedicated to every birth mother who makes choices for her baby. Whether the child is placed for adoption or the mother chooses to single parent, each choice is fraught with difficulties. God bless them and give them victory.

Dear Reader

I have been in crisis pregnancy ministry since 1985, and I still stand in awe at the bravery and dedication of every birth mother who walks through our doors. I have seen the choice ease in these years, enabling more birth moms to choose life for their babies. We counsel each mother about the dangers and side effects of abortion, encouraging them to carry their babies and offering them the blessing of placing for adoption or raising their babies. God never fails to undertake for them and we continue to support them as long as they need, providing clothing, diapers, and encouragement.

Acknowledgments

I would like to acknowledge and thank the volunteers and over-worked staff at the Central West Virginia Center for Pregnancy Care.

Chapter One

IN THE BEGINNING

Missy and Julie returned home late Friday night from their jobs at McDonald's. In a small town like Beverly, West Virginia, the two teenagers were happy to have a job in nearby Elkins. Missy's best friend, Julie, dropped her off, but Missy groaned as she reached for the car handle.

"Troubles?" Julie asked.

"See that ratty black truck over there?" She pointed. "That worthless, piece-of-trash guy is always trouble. I wish Jimmy would stay away from him—he's a pot-smoking jerk."

Julie had known Missy all her life, and she never criticized anyone. "You want to come home with me?"

Missy jerked the door open. "No. I'd better go chase them out and clean up so Mom doesn't see it when she comes in."

"Okay, I'd better run. Dad gets in a twist if I'm not home at a certain time."

"Thanks, Julie." Missy closed the door, shuddering as she looked at the truck. She felt a cold chill. Coming home to the house where her grandparents once lived always lifted her spirits. Her refuge was filled with warm memories of Thanksgiving and Christmas, birthdays, and warm summer nights. Tonight, as she picked her way around the broken stairs, the throbbing, acid rock music slammed against her body.

The stench of stale beer and marijuana assailed her nostrils as soon as she opened the door. The air was a haze of smoke, and empty twelve packs were strewn around the living room.

"Look at this mess! What would Mom say? You guys better clean this up." Missy's black-as-night eyes flashed with anger as they swept the room.

A powerful arm reached up from the easy chair and grabbed her. "Relax, beautiful," a big man-boy said, pulling her into his lap.

"Let me go, you creep!" Missy struggled, and he rose easily out of the chair, twisting her arm around behind her back and holding her firmly in his grip. "Jimmy, get this guy off me."

Jimmy glanced over with a goofy grin and dull eyes. "Hey, man, she's my sister. Leave her alone."

The three boys laughed. "Cool it. Have another puff." One boy put a joint up to Jimmy's lips and turned to offer it to Missy. "Why don't you join us, sweetcakes? We've got more."

"I'm not that desperate," Missy replied coldly, jerking away and heading toward the hall.

In two quick strides, the largest boy stood in her path. "Come on. Give us a break. We want to have a little fun." His arm blocked the hallway.

"I want you to leave me alone." Missy looked over to Jimmy for help as she tried to duck under his arm.

Jimmy regarded her carelessly, with a languid grin on his face.

"I've got something really nice for you," said Jimmy's supposed friend, pulling a joint out of his pocket, sticking it in his mouth, and lighting it with one hand. When Missy tried to avoid the offer, he drew her firmly toward himself. She twisted her head, knowing if she opened her mouth to speak, he'd shove the joint into it. The others thought that was funny and laughed as she turned toward Jimmy.

Her brother struggled to get up but flopped back on the couch.

"Give him a few more drags," the bully ordered. "He'll be out awhile, flying while we're riding."

Missy began to panic and screamed as she struggled harder to get away.

"Who's going to hear you, doll? 'Mom' is gone for the night. We're going to have more fun than we thought, guys. She's little, but she's feisty. I like

2

'em feisty." Picking her up and throwing her over his shoulder, he carried her back to her bedroom.

While Missy kicked and screamed, he laughed and threw her on the bed, tearing off her uniform slacks. When he was through, he held her down and let the others take their turns. When they were through, they left, laughing and slamming the door behind them.

Hearing the truck kick up gravel as it sped into the night, Missy ran down the hall and knelt beside Jimmy. "Get up, Jimmy. Please, please get up." She frantically shook him.

"What, Missy?" he muttered, and still in his haze, he fell back on the couch. "What? Leave me alone."

"Please, Jimmy, take me to the hospital, please. Help me, Jimmy."

"Carburetor's down. Truck won't go."

Unable to get him on his feet, Missy sank into a chair. Running her fingers through her long, dark hair, she looked at him and trembled, realizing how much he looked like their father right now. How many times had they seen him passed out on the same couch? Tears trickled down her cheeks as she remembered Jimmy swearing he would never be a drunk like his old man. He was fast becoming what he'd always hated.

"Oh, Jimmy," she sobbed. "Where has my big brother gone?" He looked at her, cock-eyed and grinning. Missy knelt beside him, and he nodded off. She ran her fingers through his beautiful, thick, red curls. They'd always been close. He was only eighteen months older than she was, and they were inseparable as kids, creating their own happy world of childish play in a confusing and sometimes violent world. When Jimmy went to first grade, nothing would console her until she saw the yellow school bus stop at the end of their long driveway. She pedaled to it as fast as she could, and he never fussed at her or acted embarrassed like some brothers do. He was big for his age, and he'd scoop her tiny frame into his arms for a huge hug before he set her back on her tricycle and walked back to the house while she pedaled furiously to keep up with his long strides, plowing determinedly through the rocks. He was a big lout, and she was a petite girl, different as night and day, but they were as close as any brother and sister could be.

Where had Jimmy gone, and what was she going to do without him? Her head fell on the couch beside him, and she sobbed. She unfolded her legs and walked to the bathroom. She turned the water to scalding hot and scrubbed, harder and harder, hating the sight of her body, noticing the blood running down her legs and the bruises already spreading across her thighs. She leaned against the shower stall, her tears mingling with the water that flowed down her face.

Oh, God, what am I going to do? Stumbling into her room, she saw the blood on her sheets. Remembering the boys' laughter as she'd bled, she began crying again, but resolve strengthened in her. Her mom had gotten this job at the hospital. She was an LPN now and proud to be independent after struggling through school on government hand-outs. She hated taking assistance after Missy's daddy left. Maybe it was better this way. If she didn't go to the hospital, her mom never had to know and Missy wouldn't risk her mom's job or cause her to worry. Her dad, and now Jimmy, had already broken her mom's heart.

In a daze, Missy gathered the sheets. "Oh, God, help me to get through this," she moaned. Remembering her mother's trick, she first poured per-oxide on the bloodstains—to save on her mom's uniforms, they learned that one early. Missy started the washer, stuffed her ruined slacks into a garbage bag, and tied it up with a vicious tug. Trudging up the basement stairs, she walked to her bedroom and mechanically made up the bed. She wanted to throw herself onto it and cry herself to sleep, but first she had to get rid of the stench. Wrapping a warm robe around herself, she turned on the attic fan. She opened several windows, and cool air swept through the house. She covered Jimmy with a blanket and sprayed air freshener everywhere. She tried to tidy up, but tears blinded her. She stumbled back to her room and fell on her bed. When all the tears were wrung out of her, she fell into an exhausted sleep.

The brightness of the sun coming through her eastern window hurt Missy's swollen eyes. Hearing her mother in the kitchen, the teen pulled on her jeans. Jimmy had gotten to his room, but the house was trashed. Missy splashed cold water on her face, holding a cloth to her eyes. She went through the living room to the kitchen.

"Exactly what went on here last night?" Alice asked. "This house was freezing when I arrived. I turned off the attic fan. Are you sick, Missy? Where's my early bird?"

Missy pretended not to see her mother's attempt to hug her and poured herself a glass of orange juice. Choking back the threatening tears, Missy took a deep breath and averted her head, mumbling something about being too tired to clean up when she came home.

"Jimmy had a few guys over to work on the truck. Uh, they got a little drunk. I'm sorry I didn't pick up."

Alice walked over to the Formica table where Missy sat and patted her hand as she sat beside her. "You've been crying. What are we going to do with Jimmy? He worries me to death. He's fallen into a million pieces when I need him most." Putting her hand on Missy's forehead, she asked, "Are you feeling all right. You look awful, hon. What's wrong?"

"I had an argument with my boss. He said my uniforms are all shabby, so I need to buy new pants. I told him we couldn't afford it right now. And then I walked into this mess. I'll help you clean it up. I must be coming down with a cold. I have such a headache." Missy avoided her mother's eyes as she told one lie after another.

Alice sighed. "You've got that right. I can't afford tires for the car. Did you see Jimmy's truck? What are your plans for your paycheck?"

Missy knew her mother was tired when her conversation became disjointed, but she couldn't stop herself from asking, "Why did you let him talk you into buying that heap of junk? It's going to cost even more fixing it up."

"Maybe if he gets involved in a project, it'll be good for him. Can you buy uniforms with your check?"

"I have to give Julie gas money. I planned to put some down on my class ring, but I'll put it off till next payday and buy the slacks to get Mr. Conner off my back." Missy felt guilty for maligning her boss, but she had to have an excuse for buying the slacks.

"Honey, I'm so sorry."

"It's okay, Mom." Missy was sure she'd break down when her mom hugged her. *Now's the time to tell her,* but Missy couldn't put another burden on those frail shoulders. She was as tall as her mother now, and she wouldn't grow anymore. They were both tiny women—Missy's daddy used to call them his little, brown, Indian girls.

"God knows, I don't know what I'd do without you, Missy. You've been such a strength to me. I don't know what to do to get Jimmy through this funk he's in."

Such strength. Yeah, well, right now I'm dying inside, and he's lying on his bed. His 'funk' has cost me big time. Missy took a deep breath, deciding again that she had to put that horrible night behind her. She stepped back from her mother's embrace.

"Mom, you've been great. Look at you. You're a nurse. Jimmy's a dope. He doesn't appreciate a thing."

"Let's not talk like that, honey. We need to pray for him—something will break for him soon. Do you want some coffee?"

"Mom, think about asking him to get his own place. Maybe he'd have to find a job then. It isn't good for him to keep lying around."

Alice responded with a smile. "He does keep my car running. I can't get over what he can do with that old clunker. I wish he'd take the mechanics program at the Vocational Center. He plans to fix up that truck and sell it, or he might use it to get to work."

"Good grief, Mom, you need new tires. Yours are completely bald. They aren't safe to drive. What's he thinking? He doesn't even have a job."

"If he gets his mind engaged on this project—I thought he needed to know I trust him."

"Don't mind me, but I think your trust is misplaced. Shouldn't trust be earned? I mean, after it's been betrayed so often?" Missy stopped, seeing her mother's worried frown, and she sighed. "I'm sorry, Mom. You need a good sleep. I didn't get your breakfast ready this morning. I'll be glad when you get another shift and we can see you more."

"New hires don't have much choice about their schedule. I'm low on the totem pole. That's part of Jimmy's problem. He resents that I have to be gone."

"Jimmy needs to get over it. He's a man now—maybe he should join the military or something. Get out on his own. Contribute."

Alice smiled and leaned over to put a quick kiss on her daughter's fore-head. "Then who'd keep my car running? Now, both of us have to go to work later today." She headed back to her bedroom, and Missy washed the dishes and picked up the living room. She felt even worse for not fixing her mom's breakfast when she realized Alice hadn't even nibbled at her toast. If she'd prepared something, her mother would've eaten every bite so she wouldn't hurt Missy's feelings. They enjoyed sitting in the quiet morning hours, after Alice got off from night shift and before Missy went to school, while Jimmy slept.

Missy tried to go back to bed, but her mind wouldn't let her. She was furious and wanted to haul Jimmy out of bed and hit him, but her fists would only bounce off his chest. She remembered how he used to laugh when he picked her up and tossed her whenever she fussed. Tears began to slide down her cheeks—tears for herself, tears for him, tears for what they had lost. She reached to the nightstand, turned on the light, and opened her Bible. She sought some comfort, but all she could think was, "Where was God last night when I needed him?"

I Need You

Sleep eluded Missy, though she was tired all the time. Dark circles began to develop under dull eyes. She told her mother she was fighting a cold or that her stomach was upset—at least that wasn't a lie—and she kept going.

Julie repeatedly asked her what was wrong. "Missy, did you hear anything I've been saying?" Julie fussed. "Your eyes look dull. Where are my friend's sparkly eyes? Something's wrong."

Missy gave her a crooked half-smile. "Worried about Jimmy mostly. I miss my brother. He said he'd never be a drunk like Daddy, and the crowd he's running with is a bad influence."

"I haven't seen that old, black truck around in weeks."

Missy turned her head so Julie couldn't see her eyes, and she said in a bright voice, "I've always been jealous of you all our lives, you know?"

"Me? Whatever for?"

"I wish I could be long and blonde, willowy and graceful, but I'm just Pop's little pony, a sturdy, brown, Indian girl," Missy said, attempting to divert her friend.

"Gosh, you are cute, smart, and you run like the wind. How come no one can ever be satisfied with who they are?"

"Did I tell you Mr. Andrews hired Jimmy at his garage? That's a ray of hope. Mom's happy." Missy stood to exit the bus and waved back when she stepped off.

When Jimmy's truck pulled in later, Missy slammed her textbook. It wasn't doing her any good anyway. She'd been staring at it, waiting for him. She hurried outside, trying to catch him before he took off for parts unknown. He had been avoiding her since that night, as if he couldn't stand to be around her, but he never said a word about it.

"Jimmy, I've got to talk to you." She picked her way down the broken stairs, remembering the pride her Pops had taken in the old farmhouse. He bought the farm with Veteran's benefits after the Korean War, when he brought his bride home. He'd joined the military to gain respect. Her grandmother's father had been a code talker in World War II, but Native Americans still faced a lot of prejudice in Randolph County. Her Pops kept the house trim and tidy, freshly painted, and in good repair. She looked up at the beloved home and felt ashamed. After her grandparents were killed, her own father never kept the place up.

Her Gram was half-Navaho, and the couple lived quietly, mostly in isolation. Her Gram was a respected teacher, once even West Virginia's teacher of the year, and her Pops drove the school bus, ran cattle, and harvested hay on their 120 acres. He picked up odd jobs, plowing and mowing. The farm wouldn't have deteriorated like this under his watch! He painted every two years. Now, the porch swing hung crookedly off a broken chain on the end of the long porch that ran across the front of the house. The once comfortable, five-room house was peeling and in need of repairs, which Alice, their only child, neither had the money nor the physical strength to do.

She shook herself. She'd been emotional ever since the night of her assault. She drew near to Jimmy, who had his head under the hood. "What's up, Missy?" He poked around the engine, avoiding looking at her.

"Look at me, Jimmy!" Missy raised her voice. "You've got to help me. I don't know what to do." Her voice broke.

"Missy, come on! What's the matter now? I got a job. Can't you get off my back?" He shouted at her like this was her fault, and Missy wanted to slap him.

Tears began to stream down her face. With a furtive glance, she looked at the house, checking to see if their mother was in hearing distance. She lowered her tone. "Jimmy, I'm...I'm late on my period—almost a month."

Jimmy's head banged on the hood. He grabbed a rag out of his back pocket and wiped his hands before rubbing his head, giving his sister a blank stare. "What do you mean?"

"I'm late, Jimmy, for my period. You know what that means."

"It's not possible." His voice trailed off.

"Yes, it is. It happened. It's true." Missy cried harder. "What am I going to do?"

Jimmy walked around the truck and pulled her into a clumsy embrace. "Hey, don't cry and get all upset about nothing. I'll pick you up at school tomorrow and take you to the health department. They'll do a pregnancy test, and you'll know you got all upset about nothing. I've heard about things like that happening when girls get scared."

Missy sobbed and fisted her hand in her brother's shirt. "Oh, God, what am I going to do? Jimmy, you don't know what they did to me."

Jimmy patted her awkwardly. "Missy—Miss, I'm sorry. You've got to believe me. I never thought they'd do something like that. I kept trying to get up, but it was like I heard things from a long way off, and my muscles were Jell-O. I'll never let them come back here, ever again. I swear to God, Missy. Jeez, stop crying. Let's go inside and get something to eat. Do you have to work tonight? Come on. I'll fix you something. Where's Mom?"

"When I came outside, she was taking a shower." They figured she'd be drying her hair, pressing her drip-dry uniform, and getting ready for the night shift. They trudged up the stairs, clinging to one another like they used to when they were little children, whenever their Mom's car backed out of the driveway, leaving them with their grandparents yet again.

"When Dad got drunk, Mom would bring us here. I can almost hear Gram's voice, 'Come on, kids. Let's make some cookies.' Remember?" Jimmy asked.

"Yeah, and Pops would ruffle our hair, trying to be cheerful and distracting."

"Maybe I could bake you some cookies," Jimmy suggested. Missy sniffled through her giggles, thinking about Jimmy trying to bake anything.

When they got inside, Jimmy persuaded her to let him call her boss and tell him she was sick. "It's true, Miss. You're sick with worry. We'll get through this. You'll see." Jimmy made the call, and together they made sandwiches. Missy splashed cold water on her face in the old, chipped sink in the tiny kitchen, which was located to the right of the front door. When their mom joined them, they all sat down around the table and ate together. Jimmy told their mother he'd called work for Missy and told them she was sick.

"I'm glad you're staying home tonight. You've looked peaked lately. Take it easy, and go to bed early. I'll see you in the morning." Alice gathered her keys and leaned to kiss her daughter. "Jimmy, I hate to nag, but would stay home tonight? Could you make sure your sister gets some rest?" She picked up her pocketbook and hugged Jimmy's shoulders.

"I'll be right here with her, Mom. Promise. I won't go anywhere. Maybe we can catch something on TV if I can get her head out of the books." "It's no sin to get some rest, Missy. Take a night off. You studied all afternoon."

Missy and Jimmy did just that. They popped popcorn and watched a movie. They even managed a pillow fight. It seemed like old times, and Missy's heart swelled to see her brother back. He hadn't had a drink since he started his job. Maybe everything would be all right. Maybe this nightmare would be over.

The Nightmare Continues

Jimmy pulled in at school the next day, as he promised. He watched his sister as she twisted her hands in her lap while he drove to the health department. Waiting in the truck while she went inside, he tapped on the steering wheel for fifteen minutes, wondering if he could even remember how to pray. He'd given up three years ago, when he and his father struggled and exchanged blows until he gasped, "Get out, and leave us alone. Get out of our lives. We'd be better off without you." He was, what, fifteen? His dad could have taken him down, even drunk, but he stood, shook himself, and staggered out the door. And disappeared.

"I'm sure out of practice," he muttered to himself. "Maybe God doesn't even want to talk to a screw-up like me." He got out of the truck, slammed the door, and started up the steps. Then he turned around, made a fist, and, not knowing what to do with it, slammed it into the side of his truck. He opened the door, climbed in, and sat behind the wheel, cradling his hand. He leaned his head back on the seat. Thirty minutes. *What is taking so long?*

Finally, he saw the door open, and when Missy walked out, looking pale, Jimmy scrambled out of the truck and rushed around to open the passenger door for her. He lifted her into the truck, realizing again how tiny she was and how he used to look after her.

"Well, Miss, what? What did they say?"

"Let's get out of here, Jimmy. Take me home."

"Missy?" Jimmy started the truck, glancing over at her. Silent tears were streaming down her cheeks, her fist was shoved in her mouth, and her shoulders began to shake.

"I knew it. It's positive. I'm...I'm pregnant." Missy rocked herself back and forth. "Oh, God," she moaned over and over. "Oh, God."

Jimmy cursed and hit his bruised fist on the steering wheel. He swore again. "It couldn't be. I mean, this was your first time, wasn't it? Of course it was. I know that. How could it happen the first time?"

"After I hadn't started, I asked my health teacher when a girl could get pregnant, and she said, 'right in the middle of your cycle.' I knew it then; I was in the middle when it happened. Oh, God, what are we going to tell Mom? What am I going to do?"

Jimmy turned hard onto their gravel road. "Pull yourself together, Missy. I'll do something. Don't tell Mom anything until we figure this out."

"What can you do? We have to tell her."

"I'll call those..." Jimmy rattled off a volley of curses. "I'll make them pay—they'll have to pay for it. If every one of them comes up with something, we can get it taken care of."

"What are you saying? What do you mean 'get it taken care of,' Jimmy?"

"Suzanne Conners had it taken care of, and she only missed one day of school. Didn't have to tell her mom or anything. I'll take a day off, and we'll go to Pittsburgh or Cumberland to one of those clinics."

"You mean an *abortion?*"

"Yeah, sure. It'll be all right. You'll see. I'll make them pay for it."

"Jimmy, I don't know. I mean, I don't want to kill a baby."

"Missy, it's not a baby. It's a blob of tissue, and this is a *rape*. Nobody expects you to carry a rape. Even pro-life people say rape is an exception." Jimmy returned to cursing his former buddies for what they had done to his little sister, and he cursed himself for failing to protect her.

"Jimmy, stop it! That isn't going to change anything. I saw a movie of a ten-week baby, with all his fingers and toes, jumping around inside."

"Look, Missy, this is a blob. It's not ten weeks. It's only a couple of weeks, and it's a blob. Use your head. You'll be a senior next year. With your grades, you'll get a scholarship. You won't have to be a dumb grease monkey like me or work in McDonald's all your life."

"I heard a lady at Youth Group say the baby's heart beats at twenty-one days, maybe sooner. I'm over a month late—that's fourteen plus fourteen. Twenty-eight days. This baby has a beating heart."

Jimmy swore again. "A rat's heart beats. That doesn't make it a baby." Jimmy had stopped the truck at the house, but neither of them moved to get out. Missy stopped arguing and began to cry. Jimmy got out and came around to help her out. He put his arm around her and lifted her gently to the ground.

"Okay, okay. Mom might be up. Promise me you won't say anything to her until you think this through." Keeping his arm around her, he walked her up the stairs. "I've got to fix these dumb stairs before someone gets hurt." Missy leaned against him, and he practically carried her into the house. "God knows, I'm sorry, Missy. I'm so sorry. This is all my fault." He put his arms around her, and she clung to him. Hot tears stung his eyes. "I haven't been much help to Mom, but this is a mess. I never meant for anything like this to happen. You've got to believe me, Missy."

"I know you didn't. I'll talk to the pastor on Sunday. We need to be quiet so Mom doesn't hear us."

"He'll mess with your mind. We can take care of this."

Jimmy watched Missy shake her head and walk away from him, heading for her bedroom. She stopped and looked back to where Jimmy stood, dazed, in the middle of the living room. "Can you take me to work?" She lowered her voice to a whisper. "If you take me, I won't have to talk to Mom right now. Julie said she'd bring me home. Please?"

"Yeah, sure, Miss. Whatever."

Alice called out from her room. "Where were you guys? I was getting worried."

Jimmy looked at Missy, holding a finger to his lips. "I wanted to show Missy another truck I'm looking at, you know, after I sell this one and pay you back. But I can't afford to buy anything now." Missy scurried to her room to avoid her mother.

"But you will," Alice said as she came into the living room. "If you keep working the way you are, you'll be able to afford it sooner than you think." She straightened her scrubs. "I'm really proud of you, son!"

Jimmy thought about how his mother wouldn't be proud of him if she knew what he'd done to his sister. "Do you want me to fix a sandwich for you?"

"Where's Missy? We need to leave so I can drop her off and not be late."

"She needs to change. I'll take her."

"If you'll do that, I can pick up a hot meal at the hospital cafeteria. Thanks." Alice walked out of the door, and Jimmy figured she was happy to see her kids getting close again, like old times. She probably figured he only needed to get a job, that's all, and that things were looking up for the first time since Missy and Jimmy's father, Ian, left. *Dear God, if she only knew!* Jimmy blinked back sudden tears. He knew his sister. She'd go through with this pregnancy.

Jimmy learned that Missy asked for the night shift on Sunday so she would have time to talk to her pastor after the morning service. He didn't know how she put one foot in front of the other when she had no hope and no plan. Jimmy couldn't figure out how their pastor could come up with some direction, and he worried about what would become of her.

The Body of Christ

John Potter whistled as he prepared the coffee. His wife, Brenda, was rousing the children. He smiled as he heard one of the boys dashing to the bathroom. Sunday dawned, warm and sunny, but he didn't know it was mocking two teens' despair. The earth was waking after its long, winter sleep. Spring was in the air. New life exploded all around. Nature acted as if she had every right to begin anew, and Pastor Potter was unaware Missy O'Malley had a care in the world.

After service, Jimmy pulled his mother into a conversation while Missy dawdled by the pastor, looking for an opportunity to talk to him.

When the crowd moved, their pastor turned to her. "Hello, Missy. How are you on this beautiful day?" He smiled at one of his finest youth leaders, but he realized he hadn't seen her usual bright smile for several weeks. He reached out and touched her arm. "Is everything okay?"

"May I speak to you somewhere? I mean, not here. I need to talk to you. Please, sir, may I?" she begged.

John Potter took her arm and guided the distraught girl toward his office. Leading her down the hall, he stifled a sigh, longing to be home, with his rambunctious toddlers crawling on his lap for an afternoon romp. He'd spent most of Saturday at the hospital, but his heart reached out to the slight girl beside him. Whatever was bothering her, she seemed upset. John didn't remember ever seeing her dark eyes quite that black. He couldn't even distinguish her pupils, but they were shimmering with tears. Thinking about her brave mother, who picked up the pieces and kept the family together after their father's disappearance, John knew they didn't need anything else to add to their troubles.

Leaving the door slightly ajar, he turned to her. "What's going on? How can I help you?"

Missy's tears flooded. Through gulping sobs, she told him she was pregnant.

Shocked, he blurted, "But, Missy, I didn't even know you had a boyfriend."

Missy threw herself into his arms, pouring out the story. After leading her to a chair beside his desk, he pressed the intercom. When someone answered, he asked if Mrs. Potter could come to the office and if she would ask her sister to take the kids.

Brenda Potter popped her head in and took a quick survey of the scene. She closed the door behind her and drew Missy into her arms while John filled her in. Lowering Missy into the chair, she knelt in front of her. Missy curled herself into a miserable ball. Brenda took the girl into her arms and rocked her back and forth.

"It's going to be okay, sweetie. It's not your fault. Rape is not your fault." After a few minutes, she suggested to John that he go find Alice and ask if Missy could be excused to come to their house. "We need to take her home, John." He nodded and slipped out of the office, leaving the girl to his wife's tender care. Alice was ready to get some sleep, and Jimmy agreed to take her home, taking her arm and all but dragging her out the door.

"We'll get Missy home in time to get to work," John assured her.

The Potters took Missy to their home. The cluttered house looked as if two rowdy toddlers had been hastened to Sunday school, leaving clean-up for later. John flipped the switch, lighting the den, and Brenda took Missy to the couch.

"Are you hungry?" she asked. Missy shook her head without a word, so they sat. They supported her with murmured reassurances, agreeing that the baby was a living person, separate and distinct, with the DNA of a unique individual. Pastor John Potter said many women choose abortion after a rape, but over half do not. Knowing her family situation, he didn't attempt to make plans for her. He spoke in a slow, quiet tone and leaned close to hear her quiet murmurings.

Brenda sat next to Missy on the couch, holding her hand and hugging her often. Surrounded by their love, Missy felt better than she had since her awful night. The feeling of filth that clung to her melted under their assurances that she wasn't dirty or unclean. Brenda took her face between her slender hands, looked straight into her eyes, and repeated, "It's not your fault."

Missy was no longer alone. Someone knew her dark secret.

John rose. "We need to help you tell your mother. She hasn't slept long enough, but she'd want to be here." He gave Missy a little hug before driving to the farmhouse to get Alice. He filled her in on the drive back, giving her time to calm herself and focus her concern on her daughter.

As they drove, Alice asked, "Why, Pastor Potter? Why Missy? She's such a good girl. Why would God allow such a horrible thing to happen to her?"

"If I said I knew, I'd be lying. All I know is that we've got to see her through it, and we will."

Alice walked into the house and drew Missy into her arms, rocking her back and forth. "Oh, my poor, poor baby," she crooned. "We're going to get through this, Missy. We will. God has been with us, and He will not fail or forsake us. Somehow, some way, we'll make it." Then Alice walked her over to a big easy chair and drew her into her lap like a little girl, holding her and weeping with her. Missy's hand clung to her mother's, and their fingers laced together, brown on brown.

Pastor John suggested they contact the police. Two officers came to the house and took a report. They weighed her options, recognizing they had no physical evidence and figuring the boys would stick together—their word against hers. They talked about the agony of going to court in this kind of a case and all the publicity surrounding it. The kindly older officer suggested she get an abortion and put it behind her. The adults thanked them for their kindness and took their cards in case they decided to pursue it.

Alice also supported Missy's concerns for the baby. Brenda volunteered to take her to a doctor far enough from the little town of Beverly and Elkins High to avoid gossip.

"We need to see the baby is taken care of and brought safely into this life," Alice said, "but we must take care of you. You're the one who has to see this thing through."

Missy squared her shoulders. "I feel better because you know and understand. I have lots to think about, and I need time."

The pastor promised that he would arrange rape counseling for her and that the church would pay for it. He would also contact a Christian maternity home and get all the information they had. They arranged to meet again after school on Tuesday.

"I know of a wonderful place in Columbus, Ohio," John added. "It's around eight to nine hours from here, but they stay full. We can see if it would be an option for you." Missy stood. "I've got time to think about my decisions, but I know this—it's not the baby's fault either. She didn't choose to get here this way. Only God can give life, so He must have a plan for her."

The adults exchanged glances, recognizing her wisdom and courage and realizing she had the right stuff to make it through. Alice suggested they both take the night off, but Missy said, "No, I called in the night before, when Jimmy took me to the health department. I can't lose my job, and you can't either. One day at a time begins right now. Let's go."

"We'll drop you off on our way to get the kids," John said. Once again thankful for her sister's willingness to pick up the slack when called upon, Brenda called her. She promised the clamoring kids a special night and ordered a pizza to pick up on the way home. On the way to get their children, John broke into their silence.

"Rats, why is it? This family has had more than they deserve. Where is God, Bren? Where is He for them? That poor little thing. I could take those punks and smash their faces."

"I guess we have to ask God about that, but there is one thing I know. Like Alice said, He will not leave or forsake her. He'll keep her safe in the bearing of this child, and He has a plan for their lives. God must have a wonderful plan—past our knowing."

John sighed. Sometimes being a pastor was more than he bargained for. The baby dedications, baptisms of new believers, responses to altar calls...

those were all good; but the tragedies, the long, drawn-out cancers, sudden untimely deaths, and now this...those were another thing.

Brenda saw tears slipping down her husband's cheeks. She reached over and took his hand. "Father God, we don't understand, but we trust. Please help John to minister to this family. Help Missy to find her way through this awful thing that happened to her. Make meaning and purpose come out of this for as many people as possible, Lord, and we'll give You all the glory, In Jesus's Name. Strengthen him for Your service, Lord. This has been a long weekend, and the kids want their daddy."

"Amen. Thanks, Brenda. Thanks for the millionth time. That's why God gave you to me." He began to drive a little faster, urging his old car toward their children.

* * *

Missy made it through the evening shift. Thankfully, the busy night left no time for talking. She glanced up when headlights swept the glass door right before closing. Jimmy! Missy breathed a sigh of relief. She knew Julie wanted to take her home so she could pry.

She smiled, proud of her brother. Jimmy, cold sober, hair trimmed, clean shirt and jeans—jeans he wore to church that morning—walked in the door, looking good.

"I'm here to pick you up," he announced, reaching across the counter to pull her thick braid. "Gimme a shake?"

Julie looked at him adoringly and murmured, "Hi, Jimmy."

"Hiya, kid. How's school treating you?"

"Good. I made the volleyball team."

"That's great! Your height will be an advantage. Spike those balls, girl." He turned to Missy. "Ready to go?"

"You go on. I'll finish here," Julie said.

Missy walked ahead of Jimmy, who pulled open the door for her and followed her out into the night.

As soon as they were settled into the truck, he took a draw from his shake and said, "Spill. How'd it go? How's Mom? And how're you?"

Missy told him about the possibility of a maternity home in Ohio. "It's so far away. I've never been out of Randolph County except to go to the church camp—and that was less than a week. This will be months! But it's not the baby's fault. She deserves to have a life of her own."

"You keep talking about a girl. What if it's a boy?"

"I think she's a girl."

"Are you gonna keep it? Raise it yourself?"

"I can't go that far yet, but the weight has lifted. Mom knows. Pastor John and Brenda were sweet to me. Did you know he's on the board of the Pregnancy Care ministry in Buckhannon? He said the volunteers would be glad to talk to me. But I realized something important today. God doesn't make mistakes. He wants this baby for some reason, and it's up to me to bring her safely into this world."

Her brother started the car. "I'm not there yet. Those guys should never have done that to you, and you sure didn't do anything to deserve this. I'm the screw-up. I deserve to have something bad happen to me. You've always done everything right, made the right choices, and now your chances for college are flushed."

"I haven't done everything right. I've messed up a lot, but God is here for me, and He'll help me go through this. Gram taught us, 'Yea, though I walk through the Valley of Death, behold, Thou art with me.' Women in this day-and-age don't usually have to face death to have a baby, but He'll be with me. Maybe He chose me to have this baby because He could trust me to do the right thing."

She leaned back as Jimmy nudged the gas. The old truck purred with contentment under his care.

"You're too much. Let's go home," he said. They drove in silence. Every so often, Jimmy shook his head. When they stopped in front of the little farmhouse, he turned to her. "I want you to know that I'm here for you too. I haven't done very well since...well, since Dad took off. I've pretty much been no help at all to you and Mom. In fact, I've broken Mom's heart. But I'll go back to church, and I'll be here for you. If you raise the baby, I'll help. I'll be the best darn uncle. God knows. I promise you." He choked, swallowed hard, and hit his fist on the steering wheel. "You just tell me what to do."

Missy patted his arm. "I don't know. I don't know what I'm going to do. I'll live one day at a time, but I need you, whatever I do. Thanks for coming by tonight. I couldn't face Julie. Thanks for taking Mom to work. Thanks for being my big brother."

After school on Tuesday, Missy saw her mother pull up, and they drove to the church. Missy told her about her conversation with Jimmy, and they rejoiced that he was getting himself together. "God has a plan for all of us in this, Missy. You'll see. Remember '...all things work together...'"

Missy picked up the verse and joined her, "'. . .for the good of those who love the Lord, and are the called according to His purpose.'"

Missy reached over to hug Alice when she unbuckled her seat belt. She had heard her mother weeping alone in her room many times since she discovered what happened, but she was strong and encouraging in Missy's presence. "Gram used to say that verse over and over, and I kept hanging on to it when they died...and afterward, with all the things with your dad. I'm not just saying it; I've lived it. I'm proud of you, honey. I really am."

"Jimmy needs to keep those guys out of my face," Missy fumed. "I could kill them! Then I'd be guilty of murder, and you'd have to visit me in jail."

"He's promised me they'll never darken our doorway again, and the police said you could file a restraining order if you want. Anytime you feel the least bit scared, you let me know. They haven't tried to contact you, have they?"

"No, I haven't seen hide nor hair of them since...since."

Missy felt her mother's soft touch. "Let's hear what the pastor has found out," she said.

John Potter was waiting, and he led them into his quiet study. He learned that the maternity home called Hope House had space for Missy. They had a program to keep her in school, and she wouldn't miss her senior year. She could stay in Columbus to finish her senior year, or she could return home. They figured the baby would be born around Thanksgiving.

"I'd like to finish this school year here, leave sometime this summer, and come back for the spring semester of my senior year. At least, I think so now. I shouldn't start to show until summer. I have some time."

"That sounds wise, Missy. The counselor at the home..." The pastor shuffled some papers around on his desk before continuing, "Beth thought you'd do that. She seems like a nice person. Now, we need to set an appointment with a rape counselor and the folks at the Pregnancy Center. And what has been done about your medical care?"

"Brenda has set her up with an appointment in Weston," Alice told him. "I'm relieved you're thinking about Missy for now. We can worry about the baby later, but I want to take care of *my* baby right now."

They left the Church with lighter hearts and a plan. Missy would finish her school year, go to counseling, and work. When he learned Alice's medical plan wouldn't cover those expenses, Pastor Potter overwhelmed them with an offer to pay for counseling out of church funds. Missy could apply for maternity care as an emancipated minor.

Spring comes in fits and starts in West Virginia—warm a few days, maybe even hot, and then bitterly cold for a week. When it finally burst forth in its beauty, it proclaimed that new life had a perfect right to grow and bloom, with no regard to Missy's mood swings, her mom's tearful, late-night prayers, or Jimmy's seething rage. Some mornings, Missy dragged herself to school and later to work, trying to sort through her feelings. Grief and anger alternated, along with an increasing concerned awareness for the tiny creature growing within her. She didn't throw up too much, thank God, but she was tired.

Jimmy hovered over her, taking her to school and work. He repaired the front steps and tackled the front yard. Best of all, he did well at his job and hadn't touched a drop to drink. With his job, he contributed to the family, and things weren't as tight. In June, he even scraped and painted the house.

Missy would catch her mother humming, and then she'd wonder how that could be, considering all their troubles. On her days off, they'd sometimes splurge with steaks Jimmy cooked on the grill. Missy pulled out of her fatigue by summer but kept putting off her departure. She felt bitter-sweet. She was getting her family back, but she'd have to leave home.

"It's not too far, Miss. We can come see you," Jimmy promised. But Missy knew her mother worked most weekends, and traveling such a distance would cost a lot. Jimmy pulled her braid. "You aren't going to the moon, so relax, will you?"

Missy kept working. They needed the money, but the inevitable time came when her clothes were getting tight and her figure was rounding out. Before her friends began to ask questions, she had to go.

Pastor Potter called the home to make final arrangements, and the day was appointed. Missy's mom got two days off, Jimmy arranged to be off work, and they left after church one Sunday. They arrived late, but the long summer days gave them enough light to explore the old historic section where Missy would be living. Following the directions the pastor had printed, they found the address and marveled at the huge, old house where Missy would be staying before driving back to the highway to find an economy motel.

After checking in, they walked across the parking lot to a nearby restaurant and settled in a booth. With a huge sigh, Missy said, "My last meal with my family."

"Good grief, you make it sound like death row," Jimmy protested. "It won't be long, Miss, and we'll come see you every time we can."

"But you guys will be far away."

"Maybe we should have gone in and met the folks this evening," Alice said.

"I want you guys all to myself tonight."

The bright lights and the hustle and bustle of the swirling city unnerved Missy. She'd never seen such traffic! "I'll never feel at home here. I wish I could be home, walking around the square." Beverly, West Virginia, was a dot on the map, and the "downtown" was hardly a block long. In their small town, the Courthouse dominated the square. Its broad steps were cracked, but the grandeur of the old majesty, built when coal was king, brought pride to everyone in the community. Little shops and a café clung to its edges, surrounding it with the life of the town. The historical marker in front read, "Built in 1808," and folks laughed and said nothing had changed since then. Some of the older folks remembered the great storm that took away the grand old trees that once stood out front. Younger folks couldn't remember, but to their parents and grandparents, the Courthouse looked stripped and naked, and her age showed badly these days.

Dismissing thoughts of home, Missy trudged across the parking lot. Jimmy grabbed her hand and suggested a movie on TV. He got snacks from the vending machine and stretched across one of the double beds. Alice propped herself on the other, and Missy sat in a chair. They laughed out loud at the movie, and after it was over, Jimmy picked up a pillow and threw it at his sister. The free-for-all reduced them to giggles as they both collapsed on the bed.

"Gosh, I'm going to miss you, Sis," Jimmy panted. Missy burst into tears, and Jimmy got frantic, looking at his mother. "What have I done? What did I say? Don't cry, Missy, please."

"It's okay, Jimmy." Missy sniffed. "I've missed you. Now you're back, and I wish I didn't have to go."

Jimmy handed her a box of tissues.

Alice pulled her daughter into her arms. "You don't have to go. If you want to go home, we'll turn around and take you there tomorrow." She drew her daughter's head down onto her shoulder, and they stood, rocking gently.

"This is best, Mom. I know it is, but it's hard."

"It's time to pray," Alice replied. "Heavenly Father, You've been with us throughout this whole time while we've faced the trying of our faith. We don't see the end, but You do. Help us all to have the strength for the months ahead. Help me to do without Missy and to trust her to Your never-failing care and love. Help Jimmy to continue to do well in his job, and open doors of opportunity for him. Most of all, Dear Lord, help Missy. Help her to make friends, to feel Your presence, to know what You would have her to do as she faces the decisions she must make. Take care of this baby. Keep them safe and healthy, Lord. In Jesus' Name." Missy echoed the "amen" and smiled when she heard her brother's voice chime in. Somehow, everything would work out.

They stayed up into the wee hours of the morning, watching TV and talking, not wanting to face the next day, but they were when surprised they slept in. Both Missy and her mother were early risers, and sleeping in was a rare treat for this hard-working family. They slept in one double bed, with plenty of room to spare. Alice nudged Missy and pointed to Jimmy's big frame sprawled over the other bed, arms and legs dangling off the edges.

He cracked open his eyes, hearing them move in and out of the bathroom. They felt warm and close, wrapped in love, despite the strange, sterile room. Alice unpacked the ice chest, and they ate sandwiches and fruit while they took turns in the shower.

Hope House

They checked out and drove over to the Home at their appointed time. The housemother was waiting for them, sitting on the wide front porch in a large, white rocker. She waved as they came up the stone sidewalk.

Rising, she called, "Hello, I've been watching for you." She walked down the broad steps and took Missy's hands in hers. "Welcome, Missy. We're glad to have you. I'm Ginny Randall, the housemother. Please come in." Ginny looked around to include Alice and Jimmy, but she'd taken Missy by the hand. "I'm sure you'll all want to look around. We've been praying for you, and we have everything ready," She smiled warmly at the family, waving them inside the door she held open.

Jimmy stared at the huge door that led into the three-story mansion known as Hope House. "Would you look at the size of that door? When was this place built? You can't even find pieces of lumber that size anymore."

"The house was built in the early part of the twentieth century. It remained in private hands until a family donated it to be a pregnancy care ministry and a maternity home. The office is located right over there, to your right, but it is usually closed in the afternoons. Beth, our caseworker, is a volunteer. She has a Master's Degree in social work, but she has three children of her own, early preschool to elementary, and she's only scheduled to come in three mornings a week. She ends up in and out all the time—she and her precious husband come whenever we need them. You'll meet her tomorrow."

"Go ahead and look around. The family that lived here had a hotline, and a genuine burden for women who were pregnant, frightened, and without hope. Abortion is an easy and convenient choice. We're blessed by their gift. Here, let me unlock the door so you can peek." Ginny pushed another large door open, revealing a small office, with pictures of developing babies covering the walls of the bright, cheerful room. Missy took some pamphlets from the racks about fetal development, which were similar to the ones she'd been given in the Pregnancy Care office in Buckhannon.

On a beautiful, hand-carved mantle, Missy saw a few photos of babies. She walked closer to look at them. Seeing her, Ginny said, "Those are some of 'our' babies. Their mothers lived at Hope House and gave them life. Some were placed for adoption, and some of the girls chose to keep them, but all are alive today because their mothers chose life." Ginny turned to Missy. "But Pastor Potter told us you never considered an abortion. Good for you! What a brave young lady you are."

"I'm a Christian. I can't remember when I didn't pray. I can't say the thought didn't cross my mind, but I couldn't do that to a baby. A woman from a pregnancy ministry nearby spoke at our youth meeting. She showed us fetal models, like those you have on the table, and showed us a video of a sonogram. We could hear the heart beating and see the baby moving around. I figure that giving life is God's business, and my job is to protect what He's given."

Missy watched Jimmy drop his head and fidget with his hands. She remembered how he urged her to "get rid" of her problem. She thought she heard him whisper, "Make this work out for Missy, please, please, God. If You will hear me, take care of her, sir. You know she did the right thing." She took his hand and squeezed, and she felt a peace settle over them—God had been waiting for Jimmy, and He was right there the moment he turned to Him.

Ginny pulled the heavy door shut and walked them through a large, comfortable living room. An oversized sectional wrapped around the room, facing a big TV. "The girls share the use of the only TV. Sometimes it requires a lot of negotiation and compromise, but having TVs in their rooms would bring many negatives and more supervision. We have a large selection of movies, and movie night is a fun time."

"Where is everyone?" Alice asked. "I thought you had six residents?"

"In the summer, some girls have jobs. Others are in summer school, but a few are too far along for outside activities. Come on. I'll introduce you around and show you to your room. You are going to share with Cathy. She's due in October."

Ginny Randall's warmth seemed to fill the air around them, and they found themselves trailing along, heartened by her comfortable presence. Jimmy got Missy's suitcases out of the trunk and carried them up the wide stairs.

"Wow, this is a big, old house," Missy said. "I saw the pictures, but I didn't realize. It's so pretty."

Missy, Jimmy, and Alice walked behind Ginny up the grand staircase in the foyer. They heard a cheerful voice.

"Hi, Missy. I'm Cathy. Is Miss Ginny giving you the lay of the land? I was doing dishes. Have you seen the room yet? I'm glad you're here."

Missy turned and smiled at the vivacious brunette, who almost bounced up the stairs, despite her enlarged belly, to lead the way. "Hi, Cathy. It's nice to meet you. This is my Mom and my brother, Jimmy."

"Let's go put your stuff away. I'm sorry I'm not much help. My doctor said no more heavy lifting. I'm due in eight weeks."

"I'll get it, Cathy...if they let guys go upstairs," Jimmy said, carrying one suitcase in each hand.

"Thanks for asking," Ginny said, "but this time of day, it's fine."

Alice carried the small makeup case and trailed behind the chattering young folks, thankful Cathy was outgoing. She bit her lip, blinking back tears. *Why, God? Why does my precious daughter suffer for the sins of others? All she's ever done is give. She carried the load when I was in school, picking up the housework, even while she had a part-time job and made good grades. It isn't fair, God. She deserves better than this. Where is her reward?*

Alice stood motionless on the spacious landing in the middle of the stairs until Ginny glanced back and saw her. The housemother let the younger trio go past as they continued moving upstairs to the hall. Catching a glimpse of

Alice's pain, Ginny's heart went out to Missy's mother, and she hung back, allowing Cathy to show Missy into their room.

Alice stood frozen. Ginny waited for her, then came back down the stairs and took the broken-hearted mother's arm. "It's got to be hard for you. Pastor Potter told me what a pillar Missy's been for the family."

"Sometimes I don't understand. I prayed and prayed for their father, and he up and left one night. This precious child picked up the pieces and never once complained. I'm sure you heard...this was not her fault. She's such a good girl." Alice choked. Tears began to spill over.

"While you girls settle in," Ginny called to the chattering teens, "I'm going to show Alice my quarters. We'll be back in a bit." Alice felt Ginny take her by the arm and walk her farther down the hall. "Down here at the end of the hall is my room. I have a little reading area in the master suite, and I even have a teapot and a microwave. Would you care for a cup of tea?"

"Here I am, falling apart, and Missy needs you. Whatever am I doing? God, help me."

Once they stepped into the room, Alice fell into Ginny's open arms as the tears spilled over, running down her cheeks without any control. Her shoulders shook, and Ginny rubbed her back. "Cathy is the best thing for Missy right now," the housemother said. "Let's give you a breather. I understand you've been working awfully hard to keep your family together. You're made of strong stuff, and you've given that to Missy. By the grace of God, she'll come through this stronger and better, although she already seems pretty fine right now."

Alice took the tissue Ginny offered and blew her nose. "I can't understand. It's so unfair! She's such a good girl."

"They say that sometimes bad things happen to good people." Ginny stood back and regarded Missy's mother. "Life isn't fair. But this one thing we know—God's in control. Like Joseph said, what other people meant for evil will bring much good. Because of her courage, a new life will join us, and God knows that little one and has a plan for him too." She moved over to the little sitting area, plugging in her electric teapot and reaching into the cabinet to select some tea bags.

Alice managed a smile. "Missy's sure it's a girl, but I don't know what she's going to do. She makes good grades, and she always planned to go to college, but now...and I don't know what to tell her."

"You don't have to tell her anything. This is a choice she'll have to make, and we promise to be with her every step of the way. One thing we've learned around here is that life isn't over after the baby arrives. Girls do get their lives together and go on, stronger than they were before. We'll help her work through her choices: single parenting or adoption. She'll continue school here, and we'll make sure her credits transfer. If she needs a home-bound teacher, she'll have it. The most important thing you can say and do, you already have. She knows you love her, you'll support her, and you'll stand behind whatever decision she makes." Ginny's quiet assurance as she arranged the teacups had a calming effect on Alice.

"I will, but bringing a baby back to our small town would be hard. She'll face questions, and what can she say when people ask who the father is? And what if those evil boys try to interfere in the baby's life? But this is my grand-child, so how can I part with that? And, God knows, we're barely making it as it is. It's confusing." She took the offered cup of tea. "Thank you."

"Let's sit here a minute and say a little prayer. Would you like that?"

"I would." Alice bowed her head. "Forgive me, Lord, for I've been car-rying my cares instead of casting them on You, and You do a much better a job of handling them. You know and love Missy even better than I do, and You've reminded us that all things work together for good to those who love You. I don't see how good can come out of this heartbreak, and I want to take all this pain from her, but she's Yours, Lord, and I'll trust You. Help me to trust You. God, please help Ginny and the others to help Missy."

"Father," Ginny added, "I agree with my sister, and I ask You to comfort her mother's heart. Thank You for our volunteers, who love these girls with Your love. We look to You because You do all things well. Make the coming months a time of growth for Missy. Strengthen her and comfort her as she lives apart from her family for this time. May their bonds grow during this separation, and bless Jimmy and Alice as well. In Jesus' Name."

Both women had barely said amen when the young people's voices called through the door. "Mom, where are you? Come see my room and what Cathy made for me."

Putting the teacups on the coffee table, the women stood and looked out the door. Missy stuck her head out of a doorway farther down the hall. "Come see. Isn't this nice?"

The room Missy and Cathy shared was warm and comfortable. Twin beds hugged the side walls, and in the middle of the back wall, a wide window framed with cheerful, yellow curtains allowed the eastern sunlight to flood into the room. The matching bedspreads gave the room a cozy feel. Two desks faced the wall at the foot of each bed, with shelves above them for books and knick-knacks.

"Look, Mom. See what Cathy made me?" Missy shoved a soft, little, stuffed kitty into Alice's hands. "Isn't that cute? She made it, and she said she could teach me how to make them too."

"Why, Cathy, how thoughtful. What a nice thing to do. Thank you, honey."

Cathy beamed. "Mrs. O'Malley, I'm learning that if you do things for others, you don't feel sorry for yourself, and I want Missy to feel as good as she can. I was pretty bummed when I first came, and I wasn't too pleasant to be around."

Ginny laughed and put her arm around Cathy. "You've come a long way. I'll say that!"

"I told you, Missy. I still have some rough edges, but Jesus has given me a new heart and a new life. He brought me here to come to know Him. You're lucky to have been brought up in a Christian home!"

A silence fell. Alice and Jimmy struggled with bitter thoughts about the 'luck' of the innocent victim they loved, but Missy seemed unaware.

"Cathy, I thank God every day for His love. I couldn't live through this without Him. He'll bring me through, and He'll show me the reason someday. And you've made me feel better. I feel welcome and at home, so thank you. But the only bad thing about having a Christian Mom is that she's so wonderful, I don't know how I'll make it without her. It's going to be hard." Tears sprung to her eyes. "I don't think I can let you go, Mom."

Alice gathered her into her arms, and they rocked silently, their tears mingling.

Jimmy shuffled from one foot to another, giving them awkward pats. "Guys, this isn't making it any easier."

Cathy handed Alice and Missy some tissues. "We buy these by the boxcar around here."

They smiled, wiped their tears, and pulled apart. "Jimmy's right. We probably should get on our way."

"Can't you stay a little longer?" Missy pleaded.

"I have to go to work tomorrow night. I should get home and try to sleep. I'm pulling a long weekend to make up for the time we spent coming over."

Alice was grateful when Ginny put an arm around Missy. "Your orientation begins this afternoon, Missy. You'll meet the other girls, learn your way, and I'll give you the chore list. Tomorrow, we need to set up a doctor's appointment for you, and maybe we'll have time to take you over to the school for pre-enrollment. I've spoken to the counselor, and she'll show you around, if you like, and set up your class schedule."

"Where are the other girls?" Alice asked.

"Candy and Myra are doing their chores in the basement. They're waiting for the GED class to start back. We have two in summer school—that's Laura and Michelle. With Cathy and Missy, we're at capacity."

"Sounds like a lot of females in once place to me," Jimmy commented, and they all laughed. "Here, Missy, let me lift that suitcase up on your closet shelf." Missy had already arranged her things in her half of the large dresser that ran between the beds under the window.

They headed downstairs, Missy trailing along, looking like her feet felt too heavy to lift one after another. Ginny saw Cathy take her hand and squeeze, and Missy held her new friend's hand as if it were a life preserver.

"I guess this is it." Jimmy pulled his sister into a quick hug. "But we'll be back, Missy. We'll come to see you as soon as we can."

The newest resident couldn't trust herself to speak. With her mother's schedule, Jimmy's new job, and money being tight, they wouldn't be able to come, but the teen took a deep breath and tried to smile. "That's all right. You better write to me, now, you hear?"

Alice, too, couldn't trust herself to linger. Missy's mother drew her into a quick embrace. "You'll be fine, sweetie. I feel much better after meeting Ginny and Cathy. You girls will have a great time together."

"We'll take good care of her; I promise," Ginny said.

"You got that right," Cathy added.

"Would you like a few minutes to yourselves?" Ginny offered.

"No, thank you. We'd better get on the road," Alice replied.

"Okay, kid, take care of yourself now, and let your old brother know if you need anything, you hear?"

"I don't think I can let you go," Missy said to her brother as she threw herself into his arms. "Who's going to look after me?" She held him so tightly, he could hardly breathe, and her tiny body clung to him. He let her cling, swallowed hard, and patted her back.

"We'll be back, kiddo. We're only a few hours away, and if you need me, I'll be here. I promise."

"You'll take care of Mom, won't you?"

"You bet!" he responded.

Missy let him go and stepped back. "Go on now. Mom, take care. I love you."

"I love you too, sweetie. We'll call you when we get home."

Ginny put her arm around Missy as Jimmy and Alice walked to the car. They waved as it pulled off and then turned to go inside. Cathy stood by the door, watching a family like she had never known, feeling a mixed sense of envy and longing.

"Miss Ginny, will I live through this?" Missy asked.

"One day at a time, honey, one day at a time. His grace is sufficient for each day, and we'll handle it one day at a time." Far too wise to give any easy answers, the older woman added, "It won't be easy, but a lot of us here are committed to helping you."

"Come on, Missy," Cathy said. "Tell me more about that handsome brother of yours. Hair to die for, and those curls are a sin on a guy! And those green eyes sparkle like some kind of emerald!"

"O'Malley...sounds right off the boat from the old country...and thoroughly Irish, devilish good looks to go with it," Ginny said.

Missy's heart leapt with love. "The Irish is from my dad's side. They both have always been too good-looking for their own good, and they both have the curse of the drink too. My earliest memories are seeing his red curls descending off the school bus. The first thing he would ask every day was, 'Do you need your big brother?' And I knew he was asking about Dad—if he was having good, bad, or worse day. Jimmy always looked after me. He was so much bigger, and he wasn't embarrassed to pick me up for a hug. I'd climb back on my tricycle and plow through the rocks on our driveway. Sometimes he'd hop on the back and push me." She dashed the back of her hand against her cheek.

"Let's go meet Candy and Myra. Maybe they'd like some help with the laundry." Cathy tugged on Missy's arm and led her downstairs.

* * *

While the girls turned to seek out the others, Jimmy drove out of town without a word, still pondering in his heart. Occasionally, Alice sighed, and several times she reached into her pocketbook for another tissue.

After a few miles, Jimmy said, "She's going to be fine, Mom—she really is. She's tough, like you, and they seem like such nice people at the home, don't you think?"

"Yes, they do, Jimmy, and she'll be fine. Maybe it's me I'm worried about...I don't know what *I'm* going to do without her."

"I'll do better. I'll try to help you. I'm not Missy, and I'm sure you don't want me to cook for you, but I promise I won't be a butt like I've been. I've been such a creep, and all this is my fault."

"Jimmy, you've changed. I see that. This has been hard for you too, but God will see all of us through."

"Mom, I've asked God's forgiveness, but can you ever forgive me? Can Missy?"

"I'm your mother! Of course I forgive you. I see you reaching out to God, and He'll be there for all of us, and Missy knows too."

"I felt him there, in the office. I prayed for Missy, and I felt Him."

"I'm glad, Jimmy. God is in that place. He sure shines out of Ginny Randall."

The silence enveloping them was warm and comfortable, and Alice leaned her head back and nodded off.

Jimmy glanced over and smiled. *We're going to make it,* and he wondered why he'd ever gotten angry at this gentle creature. He shook his head. She was a brave woman, his mom was, and a new respect swept over him as he headed home. Although massive choices remained before her, Missy would be fine, and this would all be over in a few months.

Meeting the Girls

Missy's first day at Hope House was exhausting. She found a mix of girls at the maternity home, and learning to like some of them wasn't going to be easy. Her first challenge was in the basement. Cathy was a saint. Jesus had touched her in a profound way, but the next two residents Missy met were a piece of work, and after meeting them, she questioned her decision to come. She was terrified of one of them, a girl named Myra. She was a punk gal, straight off the streets, and she looked like she would beat up anyone to get her kicks.

"Hey, Myra, Candy, this is the new girl we've been expecting," Cathy said to the two girls as they entered the laundry room. Missy looked around the basement room, which had paneling covering the framed-in walls. The rest of the basement looked creepy and dark, with concrete walls. In a room off to the side, she noticed a huge boxy furnace.

"The girl we've been waiting for. First she's coming; then she isn't; then it's later. You finally made up your mind—beginning to show, huh?" said a short, dark-haired girl with black, punk hair and several piercings.

"Welcome to the workhouse, whatever your name is," added a too-blonde teen with dark roots. The girls laughed. They were sitting around a long table, with several laundry baskets in front of them. Missy and Cathy sat in the two remaining chairs.

"Her name is Missy, for your information, and you couldn't forget—we've been praying for her for weeks," Cathy retorted.

"Yeah, right, whatever," the bleach blonde girl responded. "Hey, Miss."

Missy reached into the clothes basket and began folding towels. Only Jimmy had ever called her "Miss," and the familiar name caught her by surprise. She gasped.

The girl that Cathy had called Candy took a hard look at the newcomer. "You okay? Myra and me...we ain't the most 'sensitive' gals to be around." She patted Missy's hand, but Myra scoffed with a short, bitter laugh. "You don't have to do this," the blonde said. "It's our day to do laundry."

"Candy's from Mississippi, Missy," Cathy said, adding, "Myra's from Jersey."

Myra interrupted, "Yeah, the little southern lady is being corrupted by the eeevil, northern, Yankee witch!" The girls laughed again.

"I don't mind helping," Missy said. "Since my dad left, my mom's been trying to do it alone, and my brother and I have to pitch in. Mom went back to school, but she's a nurse now and has a good job at the hospital. I'm really proud of her."

"Who's heard of 'Dad' anyway?" Myra asked. "From what I hear, I'm better off without the sperm donor who dropped me into Mom eighteen years ago. Frankly, I never met the turd."

Candy wouldn't be outdone, adding her story. "The only 'dad' I know is my mom's boyfriend, who got me pregnant last May. She'd rather have him than me, so here I am. I'm glad to get away from him and the bitch mother who wouldn't believe me. It's been going on since I was 13, would you believe that? Creep."

Missy tried to conceal her horror, realizing again she had much to be thankful for. The culture shock slammed her, and tears welled up in her eyes, although she tried to wipe them.

Candy noticed and dropped the clothes she was folding. "Aw, here you are on your first day, and we're dumping all this crap on you. Gosh, are you scared. Miss? Sounds like your mom is nice."

Missy wondered how many tears she could cry in one afternoon. Her head started to ache. "No one except my brother has ever called me 'Miss' before," she explained, "and it was hard when they left. I love them so much."

Candy took Missy in her arms and patted her on the back. "That's okay. We stick together around here. We'll help you get used to the place. It ain't that bad, really. Food's good."

"Speak for yourself, you dumb blonde. I ain't sticking up for no sissy-Missy. Life's tough—get used to it, kid. And gimme those towels before you get me in a bunch of trouble—or is that what you're trying to do?" Myra snatched the towels out of Missy's hands and glared at Cathy. "Did you set her up to this, righteous Cathy?"

Cathy jumped to her feet. "Shut up, Myra. You're such a bitch. Of course not! She's trying to be helpful. I can't believe how mean you are!"

Candy peeped at Myra and dropped her arms.

Missy whispered to Candy, "I'm sorry. I didn't mean to cause any trouble, really."

Cathy took her by the arm, dragging her toward the stairs. "Come on, Missy. Let's let these two..." she stopped and checked herself before continuing, "...girls finish their chores."

They went up the stairs that opened into the kitchen and found Miss Ginny fixing a snack. "You met Myra and Candy. Are they about done? I have iced tea and some oatmeal cookies for the four of you. Laura and Michelle should be here soon. This is a late day for them. They had some extra tutoring after school."

"Miss Ginny, you wouldn't believe how mean they were to Missy."

Missy interrupted. "They were okay. I need to get to know them, that's all. I hope I didn't start off on their bad side by making any mistakes."

"Missy, you can't let those girls push you around. If you show any weakness, Myra will be on you like white on rice."

Miss Ginny shut the refrigerator door with her hip as she brought out trays of ice and set them on the table. At that point, Myra and Candy came up the stairs with several baskets of laundry.

"Tattling on us already, Miss Righteous one?" Myra taunted. "I wasn't the one cussing."

Missy looked from the girls to Cathy and then to Miss Ginny. *What have I gotten myself into?* Cathy was smoldering, and Myra began to circle, like she was ready to jump into a fight.

"Now, girls, you know the rules—no name calling, Myra. And Cathy, we let each girl work out her own relationships. I'm pleased to see you finished the laundry so nicely, Myra and Candy, thank you. Leave those baskets right on the counter for now while we have a little snack."

Cathy took a deep breath, unclenching her fingers. She glanced at Missy with a shamed face and sat down at the cozy table. "Come on, Myra. Let's call it a day. I'm sorry. Missy has enough to face without us fighting on her first day. Missy, tell us about your handsome hunk of a brother. You should've seen him! He is cu-ute, with nice red hair, not the orange red but a gorgeous deep red. What a sin on a guy, curls and all!"

Missy was relieved to get on neutral territory and glad she could brag on Jimmy, since he'd been doing well all summer. Sure, he was still a drop-out, but he was talking about going to vocational school this fall, and he was fixing up the house and repairing any car that came his way at the garage. He had even gotten the old clunker Mom bought him running reliably.

Suddenly the back door banged open, and two teenagers came noisily into the kitchen. "Hey, Miss G., we both did good on our pre-tests!" Laura leaned over and gave the smiling housemother a peck on the cheek. Though she was lively, she was quite big, Missy thought, trying to remember if Cathy told her she wasn't due until October. She looked bigger than Cathy, who said she was also due in October. Miss was relieved when the two normal looking girls burst in the door. Laura and Michelle looked like average teen-agers. Laura was the pretty, preppy cheerleader type, and Michelle was a plain girl, with thick glasses, but her clothes betrayed she was wealthy and used to the best.

Michelle gave a shy smile and handed over her report slip.

"Oh, honey, this is excellent!" Ginny exclaimed, looking at the slips one by one. She reached over, took the timid girl in her arms, and hugged her. "Good job, girls!"

In the corner of her eye, Missy saw Myra silently mimic Ginny, and Candy smothered a laugh. "Missy, this is Laura and Michelle. I told you they're in summer school. They have tests this week and then a break until the next session begins, but we're planning for Laura and Cathy to have home-bound teachers for the fall classes."

"I don't know how long I'll be going with this little interruption coming in October." Laura pointed to her bulging baby. "I really should get off my feet. My ankles are swollen."

"They are, Miss G. Look at them," Michelle echoed nervously.

"Oh, Laura, let's put you on the couch in the living room. I'll bring your snack in there."

With a snide look, Myra commented, "Don't you love it when the rules have exceptions?"

"Now, Myra," Ginny responded, "I did the same for you. Don't you remember when you were nauseous and I brought you crackers and peppermint tea out to the living room couch?"

"Yeah, sure." Myra shrugged.

Missy automatically picked up the plate of cookies Ginny had set out for Laura and followed her out to the living room. The housemother set the iced tea down on the coffee table and settled two pillows under Laura's head. "What we need to do is elevate your feet. Goodness me, let's get these sneakers off!"

Cathy came down the stairs as quickly as her bulky body could manage, holding out several pillows. "Here, don't you need these? I remember what we did for Brenda when her feet swelled."

"You're absolutely right, and you saved me a trip upstairs. Thank you!"

Cathy beamed at the praise, but then her face clouded. "I'm sorry I tattled, Miss Ginny. I try hard, but sometimes I mess up. I called Myra a bad name downstairs, and that messes up my witness. You told me to ignore her, and I try, but she gets to me sometimes. She was mean to Missy; she was!"

Ginny smiled. "We have an Advocate with the Father. Why don't you go to Jesus with this, and of course, you'll have to ask for Myra's forgiveness."

"Crap, she should ask me...Yes, Ma'am." Cathy looked helplessly at Missy. "Excuse me, guys, I'm going to go to my—our—room for a sec." She moved slowly upstairs.

"Gosh, Miss G, you were kind of tough on Cathy. You know what a... mean person Myra can be. Couldn't you cut her some slack?"

"Maybe you're right, Laura, but God must have convicted, or she wouldn't have confessed to me, and now only He can restore her to Himself."

"Sometimes you guys are a little too heavy for me. I'm a Christian and all, and I asked for God's forgiveness for getting myself pregnant, but fighting with Myra is a fact of life."

"If we could show her the kind of love she's never experienced in her life, maybe she wouldn't be hard to get along with."

Laura rolled her eyes and looked over at Missy. "Hey, Missy, we've been praying for you. Looks like you walked into something."

"Hi, Laura, what grade are you in?"

"I was supposed to be a senior this year, but I fell apart pretty bad when this happened to me, and my grades sort of tanked last semester. I mean, when I knew about the baby. I thought I'd have an abortion, but my boyfriend threw a fit. He thought it was a baby when we first started to get scared. He told me I couldn't kill his kid. I was mad at him. I had a girlfriend who had an abortion, and she was going to get everything all set up. I even got the medical card, and then the dumb guy threatened to go to my folks! What a traitor! But by the time we told my folks, I realized it was a baby. They didn't want anything to do with it, of course, and Dad thought abortion was the best plan, but Sam, my boyfriend, was firm about it. They came up with this place pretty fast, let me tell you." She laughed, rubbing her tummy. "I'm glad now, of course. It's obviously a baby now, and he'll make his parents happy."

"Aren't you? I mean..."

Seeing Missy's confusion, Ginny said, "Laura plans to place her baby with an adoptive family, Missy, and we'll consider your choices in time."

"Pastor Potter and I talked about adoption. I don't know. I mean, I don't know how I could give up my baby. I might be feeling her. Is it too early to be feeling her?"

"You girls are both going to the doctor next week. You can ask her. And you might be going sooner, Laura, if we don't get that swelling down. No more walking from the bus stop. I'll be picking you up at school the rest of the week."

"I'm going to place him. Sam and I talked about it. I told him I'd carry this baby for nine months, and I'll give it life, but I'm going to college. I've ruined my senior year, missed cheerleading, and screwed up my chances for a scholarship, but I'm not giving up my *whole* life!"

Laura turned to Missy. "I've met the family, and I like them. Some of these couples on the waiting list have tried everything, all kinds of expensive treatments, and they can't have a baby. This little guy will have a great home with parents who are ready for a kid. They'll be happy; I'll be happy—it may be tough, but it's better. I'm a kid myself. I want to join a sorority, and I'm not ready for a baby."

"I'll have to come to that point, but I'll think about it later. You're very brave, and I'm glad you gave your baby life. We had a woman come to our youth group who talked about her abortion, and it haunted her for years. I guess it still does, although she found healing in Jesus."

"I hope I can be brave when the time comes to shove this kid out of me. But I think God sent you here to help me through this. Miss G., can I watch TV now? *Gilmore Girls* is coming on, and you know I love that show. You wanna sit and watch with me, Missy?"

"No thanks. I'll go upstairs and see if it's okay with Cathy if I finish unpacking. We watched TV last night in the motel, but I'm not a big TV watcher. Never had time for it, really. I mean, it's okay if you like your show..."

"Gosh, Missy, it's okay if you don't like TV. Don't freak out! What happened? Did Myra threaten to beat you up? She does that all the time. Ignore her, and try to stay out of her way." She clicked on the remote, took another bite of cookie, and settled down to watch. Michelle came in from the kitchen, looking like she was about to cry. "Here, 'Chelle, sit by me," Laura said, patting the couch. "Don't let them make you feel bad. Have some of my cookies."

Ginny assured the girls she would bring more and headed into the kitchen. Missy took a deep breath and wondered what those two said to Michelle to upset her. She went upstairs and knocked gently on the door, calling, "Hey, Cathy, can I come in?"

"Yeah, come on." Missy found Cathy sitting by her desk. "Do you know the place where it says you do what you don't want to do?"

"You mean Romans 8?" Missy said. "If I can find my Bible. Oh, here it is, on the nightstand." She read the passage out loud, and then the girls flipped through the pages of their Bibles and compared notes. They didn't realize it was time for dinner until Ginny tapped quietly and stuck her head in the door.

"Missy, I'm sorry to ask you to do chores on your very first day, but it's Michelle and Laura's turn to set the table and help with dinner. Would you mind terribly to help her out? I want Laura to stay off her feet. Michelle's in the dining room, and she'll show you what to do."

"Oh, sure, Miss Ginny, I'll be glad to—it will feel more like home."

"Looks like you girls were having a good time studying God's Word."

Cathy said, "Miss G, Missy's really nice. She knows her Bible like the back of her hand." She turned to Missy, "But you aren't stuck up. You don't talk down to me. You explain things to me. God sent you here to help me learn how to be a Christian." She pulled Missy into a side hug.

"Maybe she was sent here to help us all. She does seem to be a solid blessing, doesn't she? Did you get it all together, Cathy?"

"Oh, yes, Ma'am. Me and Missy prayed, and I felt God come right down here in this room and forgive me. Again. He's patient with us, isn't He, Miss Ginny?"

"Amen. Why don't you wash your face and come down? We'll eat in fifteen minutes."

Missy was pouring the boiling water off the pasta when Ginny came into the kitchen, and the girls had set the table.

"I hope I didn't do anything wrong, but it was done, and I didn't want it to get soggy," Missy told her.

"No, that's a big help, thank you. The table looks nice. Did Michelle show you where everything was?"

Coming into the kitchen, Michelle overheard Ginny. "Of course I did, Miss Ginny. Did you think I'd be mean to her too?"

"Sweetheart, you don't have it in you to be mean to a flea," Ginny replied, smiling at Michelle. The smile lighting the teen's plain face made her look almost pretty, Missy thought. They put the sauce and noodles in serving bowls and carried the steaming platters to the dining room. "Everyone, come down for dinner," Ginny called. Hungry girls in various stages of pregnancy poured eagerly into the room.

Because of the tension in the air, Ginny didn't call on anyone to say grace. Instead, she bowed her head and blessed the food herself. Missy heard quiet 'amen's' from Cathy, Laura, and Michelle, and she heard grunts from Candy and Myra. She looked around at the dark paneling in the elegant old room. The whole farmhouse could fit in this dining room, but that was an exaggeration—maybe the living room plus the dining room, though. Then she wondered if the chair railing around the room was a plate rack, like the molding in her grandmother's kitchen where they put Gram's good plates. If they put some things on the little shelf, it would brighten the place. She'd have to investigate it later. She could hardly eat in such grand surroundings. She had noticed the dining room off to her left when they were standing in the foyer, but as she gazed around, she thought that in its day, this house must have been the home of some truly rich people.

Glancing around the table, she saw that the girls were busy eating their spaghetti, and she realized the smell was making her hungry too. Missy's eyes widened when she put the first spoonful in her mouth. "This is really good, Miss Ginny!" she exclaimed.

"Try this garlic bread, Missy," Candy said, passing a basket down the long table. "It's to die for. I eat better in this place than I ever ate!"

Cathy agreed, handing the bread to Missy. Myra grunted as she shoved in another mouthful. "This beats the school cafeteria. First really homemade cooking I ever ate."

"I'm always so hungry, I could eat anything. But this is good, Miss G; you've outdone yourself making a welcome dinner for Missy," Laura said.

Michelle looked up. "We always have good food, Laura." The girls quickly agreed.

"I'd rather cook than do the accounts," Ginny said. "This is the fun and easy part of my job."

"I like to cook," Missy agreed, "but my spaghetti doesn't taste like this. I'd love to learn your recipe!"

Myra muttered, "Suck up," under her breath and glared at Missy.

"Pardon me, Myra, what did you say?" asked Ginny from the other end of the table.

"Nothing," came the reply.

Cathy, who heard the jab, covered quickly, "Oh, she wanted the tea." And she reached for the pitcher, passing it over to Myra.

Myra took it, pouring what she could into the half-full glass in front of her. "Thanks," she said to Cathy.

Missy Learns the Ropes and Gives One

The next morning, Missy went into Ginny's room to talk. The house-mother reviewed the girls' simple chores: clean their rooms, two to do laundry, two to help with meals and setting the table, and two to clean up after meals. A volunteer came in twice a week to do the major cleaning, but every girl was supposed to wipe down the sink and the shower or tub after she used it.

I'll have a third of the work I had at home, plus no job. I should do well in school this semester.

"Pardon me?" Missy realized she hadn't heard what Ginny had said.

"Penny for your thoughts, child. You were miles away."

"Back home, actually." And Missy shared her thoughts with Ginny.

"Physical work is the easiest part of living in a community like this, Missy. You've already had a glimpse of how tough living together can be. Plus, you'll be facing big decisions and a lot of physical changes in your body, and we have our weekly sessions with the group facilitator and your meetings with the caseworker." She explained that the group therapist helped them get along together and process some of their thinking about their lives.

"You've already seen the caseworker. Beth's a volunteer. She has a Master's degree, but she's chosen to be a stay-at-home mom. She comes three mornings a week—sometimes more—but she needs to pick up her daughter at preschool at one. Her other children are in school. The group leader is wonderful! You'll like John. He's a small man with a great, big heart. He comes on Thursday nights."

"What happens if I have a test or something the day after a 'group night?' I really have to do well if I'm going to go back to school for spring semester and graduate on time."

"We rarely make exceptions. Group night is important for all of us because it helps us get through the tough times of living with different people from various walks of life, who are all facing tremendous decisions and challenges. You'll like it; you'll see. And John doesn't waste our time. He's very prompt. You'll find yourself planning so you won't miss. We try to select roommates who will help one another. Cathy's a new Christian and needs a mature Christian to help her. Her delivery is in two months, and she doesn't need any challenging roomies. Although, I'm afraid we've put too much on Candy, poor dear. She doesn't have the strength to be independent. It seemed logical to place the two girls going to GED together and to place the two girls in school, Laura and Michelle, together so they could get up early and have quiet times to study."

"Miss Ginny," Missy questioned. "When did they all get here?"

"Hmm, let's see. Myra came in after Michelle, who came in June."

"June!" exclaimed Missy, "I thought she wasn't due until next March."

"She came immediately after her parents discovered she was pregnant. She'll talk to you about that, I'm sure. Then Candy came in June. Laura was here—she came in April. Cathy probably told you she's been here since March."

"But I have heard of some girls who were here and left, and you told Pastor Potter I could come anytime. Where would you have put me?"

"We were juggling. We even thought of having you stay with a family from one of the churches, but you kept delaying, and it worked out, didn't it? God knew, and He brought you right on time. Right on time for Cathy and Laura." Leaning forward, Ginny patted Missy's hand. "Now, let's go downstairs and see if Beth has some time for you this morning."

When they arrived downstairs, however, the little office door off the living room was shut. Candy glanced up from her studies, her papers spread all over the dining room table. "I'm trying to get ready for when classes start again. Looking for Beth? She's in there with Cathy. What do you think it will be today...keep the baby or place her?" Candy grinned. "She changes her mind every week."

"She told me last night. It isn't an easy choice for any of us. I'm glad I have time to think it through. When are you due, Candy?"

"They estimate in December, and you?"

"In November."

"You know for sure?"

"Yeah, it was...only one time."

"Oh. You would know for sure. Miss G., I can't get this math. It's too hard. It makes me mad. Myra is smart, and she don't care, and I work and work and can't get it."

"Let me see, Candy. Maybe I can help," Missy offered.

"That would be wonderful. I have some bills to pay, and math isn't my favorite thing. It's all I can do to pay the bills!"

Missy liked Candy, who was far behind on her language skills, and they sat together throughout the morning while Missy explained case and gender to her new friend. Candy had grown up in a very rural area, where the dialect of her community trained her in improper verb tense and gender agreement. Missy, who loved to write and made excellent grades in language arts, found herself enjoying teaching her skills. Missy was from a rural town too, and grammar was poor in her community, but her teacher, otherwise known as her grandmother, ruthlessly corrected her. Her Gram had moved to the farm after meeting Missy's grandfather when he was in the military and stationed in Northern Virginia. Native-American, like her husband, her Gram was determined to act and sound like the well-educated woman she was. The kids in school teased Missy about her manner of speaking, and they called her grandmother a "flat-land foreigner," but everyone loved her. What was not to love? She was kind, and, despite being well educated in eastern schools, she never looked down on anyone. She pitched in at church, worked their small farm, and learned to can and quilt with the best of them. Missy sighed, knowing she'd always miss her grandmother. Her grandmother planted dreams in Missy. Her Gram grieved that her own daughter had married young, but the handsome O'Malley boy had swept Missy's mother off her feet, promising more romance and adventure than life on the farm offered. Suddenly Missy realized Jimmy was born in February. She counted back—her mom had to get married, she thought with a start, and a lot of things in their life made more sense to her.

Around noon, Ginny peeked into the dining room and smiled at Missy, who was pointing out something to Candy. Candy's straight blonde hair, with its horrible dark roots, straggled down beside her pretty face. Candy had a broad, open face—it was pleasant but guarded. Of course it would be, with so much hidden pain. Cathy came out of the office and went into the dining room, where the two girls were studying together on one end of the long table. She followed Ginny into the kitchen and asked if she could help with the lunch.

"It's Missy's turn, and you like to teach us to do our share, but she can explain stuff to Candy. Michelle has tried for months, and you know how smart she is! Missy is a good teacher, and Candy needs help. I'll be glad to do it, if that's okay."

"Cathy, I see evidence of your new life in Christ. Taking on someone else's chores is a sacrifice, and I appreciate it. Until you came to Christ, you never would've seen that, much less taken on someone else's assignment," Ginny praised. They busied themselves with preparing lunch.

Missy pulled the next stack of books toward her, relieved to see it was easy, household finance. She'd balanced a checkbook ever since her first job. She showed Candy how to fill in the check register and balance out at the end of the month. They worked a few problems together, and then Candy could do it on her own. "You're getting it, Candy. You'll be helping Miss Ginny with the bills before long."

Candy looked up happily. "You made it simple, Missy. I've been staring and staring at this for a week. I couldn't do it."

"Sure you could have. You let Myra get you upset this morning. Cathy tells me you have to stand up to Myra."

"If I could stand up to anybody, I wouldn't be pregnant now, would I?"

"I don't know how anybody got here except Cathy. She told me last night, and I felt so bad for her. I can't imagine." Missy shuddered.

"Yeah, Cathy had it bad. I was never hungry or used by lots of men... only the one I was supposed to call 'Dad.' He was mom's boyfriend, and he's the only dad I remember, but he started using me like that when I was about 12 or 13. I was scared to tell Mom. She loved him like crazy. I went to the health department to get birth control, but last year I ran out. Before I could get some more, it happened. It wasn't every night; it was only when Mom worked night shifts and he got drunk. Anyway, when I told Mom I was pregnant and that Lester was the father, she wouldn't believe me—said I was lying. She slapped me, hard, and told me I was a slut, and she asked what kind of a girl would steal her mother's man." Tears began to trickle down Candy's cheeks, and Missy was choking up while listening to her. "She slapped me, Missy, right there in front of him, with him acting all smug. I went to the school counselor—she knew me. I hadn't been doing well in school since all this started, but I never told her what was going on. She was cool and called in social services, and I ended up here. I've got some time to think about it, like you, but I don't know how I could give it up. I know I'd be a better mom than my mom was. I'd love it, and I would never love anyone more than my baby."

"I don't know how I could give up my baby either, but I have to think about a lot more lives than my own."

"What do you mean?"

"I have to think about my mom. She worked hard to get us off welfare. She took an LPN course at the vocational school, and now she has a job at the hospital. She's a nurse. And then my brother—he took it hard when Dad left, blamed himself, I think, because they had a huge fight. I love my daddy, but it was the best thing that ever happened to us because he had a drinking problem. Jimmy was bad off for a while. He dropped out of school and drank a lot. But now he's holding down a job and doing fine. I need to think about them. We have a small house. What if the baby cried all night and kept them up, causing them to not be good workers? Or what if they had to take time off from their new jobs and got fired? I live in a small town, and nobody knows. I was...raped, you know. My church would believe me and stand by me, but what would people think? I mean, what would they think about the youth group and some girl having a baby? But, most of all,

I must hear from God. I'll have to seek His answers for my life and for this baby's life."

"Gosh, Missy, I didn't know. I was far along when it all came down, but I didn't you know you were early? Why didn't you get an abortion?"

"I heard a lady from the Pregnancy Center at youth group. She told us the baby's heart beats at 18 or 21 days, and her DNA is her own. She's uniquely created by God. I couldn't kill her."

"They talk like that around here, like you can talk to God about any-thing. And I've learned to say grace and all, and when we go to church, something seems to be pulling me, but I don't know Him like that."

"It's easier than you think. I asked Jesus to come into my heart when I was young. I was so little that I don't even remember. Then I got kind of mad at God, I guess, when Daddy was drinking bad and threatening us—well, he was mostly threatening Jimmy. One night, he came in roaring drunk and hit Mom. I'd never seen him hit her, but he threw her against the wall. Jimmy jumped him and started hitting him over and over. Jimmy's a big guy. He was on the football squad when he dropped out of school, but he was no match for our dad. That's where he gets his size, but Dad's older and more filled out. Of course, Dad was drunk, plain mean drunk." Candy nodded in sympathy. "But one summer at youth camp, after Daddy had left that past spring and Jimmy was acting so badly, I gave it up. I asked Jesus to be Lord of my life, to take control. I was tired of trying to do things my way, tired of being angry, and I surrendered it all to God. I can't say it's been a piece of cake since then. I mean, I went through hell the night...you know, the night...and when I realized I was late for my period. And telling Mom. It was awful. But she was wonderful, like always, and she was right there for me. Oh, Candy, I'm sorry, that was mean. I'm sorry."

"Hey, Missy, you're luckier than I am. Guess I drew the short straw." Candy gave a bitter laugh and shook her head. "But you're right, I mean, about how it's a baby and all. I wouldn't give anything for this kid now. He's mine. And I'm glad you have a cool mom. That's great. I know I can be a better mom than my mom. I want to be like your mom. Do you think God would help even me? I mean, I didn't run around or anything, but you're sweet, and I'm not sweet, let me tell you. I hate my mom and the creep she lives with. I hate him. I do, and that's the honest truth, Missy. Do you think God would help me?"

"Oh, Candy, I know He would."

"How can you say that after what I did to you yesterday? Me and Myra was mean to you. I felt bad. I don't even want to do stuff like that!"

"You were sweet to me. You gave me a hug, and I needed that. Do you want to find Miss Ginny and pray right now?"

Beth walked quietly up to them. "Missy, I didn't mean to eavesdrop, but you're having a conversation we've all prayed for! Miss Ginny would rather pray with Candy than do bills or fix lunch. What do you think, Candy? We don't want to rush you into this life-changing step to receive Christ."

Cathy came in from the kitchen with things to set on the table and caught the last of the conversation. "Man, Candy, it's cool to trust God. I'm glad I asked Jesus to come into my heart. I still make a lot of mistakes, like calling Myra a bad name yesterday. I had to ask her to forgive me last night, but God is real. Yesterday, when Missy and I prayed, I could feel His forgiveness, like liquid love. It was cool."

"Everyone has a different experience and different feelings," Beth explained, "but one thing we can count on is His word, and the Bible says if we believe Jesus died for our sins and rose from the dead, we can be born a new creation, and all things will become new. You can count on that, Candy." Beth put her arms around Candy and hugged her. "This can be the beginning of a new life for you. All the guilt and all the shame can be washed away in a moment."

Candy looked around the circle. "I'd like that. Let's go in the kitchen and find Miss G."

"I can join you here," Ginny said from the doorway. She had a huge smile on her face. She pulled up a chair and took Candy by the hand. "Do you want me to lead you in a prayer?"

Beth and the girls repeated the prayer with Candy, and when they finished, Myra came inside, threw her sweater on a chair, and grumbled, "You girls are going to have to pick up all that stuff. I have to set the table."

Missy assured her they would, and they removed the offending textbooks from the table. "We'll get this, Candy. You go on in the kitchen and help Miss Ginny. Sorry, Myra, we'll get it. We're finished anyway."

Candy came out of the kitchen, sniffing a bit, and looked up at the clock. "Gosh, it's only a little past noon! I usually hate this math stuff, but I'm already ahead on my homework today. The teacher ain't gonna get trouble from me when I come back next Monday. Boy, will she be surprised. Thanks, Missy, I'm glad you're here, and I hope you stay."

Missy looked surprised. "You mean some girls don't stay? What do they do? Where do they go?"

Myra snorted and let out an oath. "If I had anywhere to go, I'd blow this place. Nothing here but chores and preaching, working and sleeping. It's the dullest place. If we do go anywhere, it's to church. Come on, Candy," she shouted. "You got to help me today."

"I'll be right there in a sec." Candy called in from the kitchen.

"She's lazy," Myra muttered under her breath. "She always leaves me with all the work."

"I can help, Myra," Cathy said quickly. "I don't have anything else to do. Let me take some stuff up to my room." She hurried up the stairs and returned quickly, counting out the silverware and going back and forth to the table, working alongside Myra without a word.

Blessed are the peacemakers, and, God, help me to be one. Missy was frightened by Myra's tough exterior, and she wanted to steer as clear of her as she could. Suddenly she realized she was supposed to help in the kitchen. She went looking for Ginny and found Cathy working in her place. "I'm sorry! My first day with chores, and I'm not doing my share. I'll do this."

"You're doing what none of us has been able to do— getting Candy to understand grammar and personal finance. Gosh, she made me crazy! You go, girl."

Candy grinned. "I do believe I understand it, Miss G."

I believe I've got the best roommate in the place. Missy saw Cathy carry out the platters of sandwiches. *Laura is so...cheerleaderish...and Michelle is so serious and quiet, not fun at all. And Candy, well, Candy's sweet, but she isn't much to talk to. She's probably never read a whole book in her life. Myra...she scares me. She is tough*. Shaking those thoughts out of her head, Missy began arranging veggies on the tray.

Carrying several bowls of chips out, Ginny called out: "Lunch is ready."

The girls rushed to their chairs and hurried through grace, reaching for the sandwiches in the middle of the table as they said, "Amen."

Cathy's Story

Missy wrote home every day. She hated being away from her mom and brother, but she was glad her mother didn't have to take care of her, and, as much as she missed Jimmy, she was glad his anxious face wasn't staring at her. His hovering was a sign of his love, but she realized he felt guilty every time he looked at her. Early the next morning, she got up to dash off a quick note.

Things settled down that night. Missy helped Michelle study. She was very bright but lacked self-confidence. She rattled off all the chemistry definitions Missy called out to her, and when Missy studied her, she realized her new friend wasn't that plain, and a plan began to form in Missy's head, although she didn't have the skills to pull it off. Later that night, she talked to Cathy in their room.

"Cathy, do you know anything about makeup? You do a good job on yourself, but do you know how to do makeup on anybody else, like what color they are and stuff?"

"I know all about that stuff. Are you thinking what I have been thinking? I saw you helping Michelle—do you think she can be pretty? She can be not as— plain—and, well, you know."

"When she came in and showed Miss Ginny her grade, she smiled and looked almost pretty for a minute. But I don't know what to do to bring that out."

"More smiles would help, poor thing."

"What's her story, Cathy?"

"Miss Ginny wants every girl to share her own story, and she doesn't want us to gossip. But let's say that her fancy daddy was busy with his rich career, and her fancy mommy was busy with him. Nobody noticed mousey Michelle, and some stupid jerk told her he loved her, then dumped her when she got pregnant. Mommy and Daddy couldn't talk her into an abortion, so they got rid of her as fast as they could."

For the second time in that eventful evening, Missy thanked God for her loving mother and wonderful brother, thinking that one bad night was better than a lifetime of rejection and pain. Having a drunk for a dad wasn't so much fun, but, with the exception of Jimmy's brief months of acting out, life had been good since he'd been gone. Her mom had always been a saint, and certainly being a Christian had made life much easier.

"Has she found Jesus since she's been here?" Missy asked

"She's definitely asking questions. She's Catholic, and she's been serious about going to confession. We drop her off on our way to church. The rest of us go to the main church that sponsors the home. I'm too new at this myself to be much help. Maybe God brought you here for her, Missy—although I already told Miss G that He brought you here for me!"

"I'm thankful for you too, Cathy. I don't know how I would have made it through this without you. I've never been away from home before."

"You're kidding me? Never been away from home?"

"I've been to youth camps with my church and all, and I planned to go on a mission trip this summer, but..."

"Missy, you sure are one lucky girl. My folks never wanted me at home. I spent time at boarding school while they did their thing. Me and Michelle, poor little rich kids, I guess. Only, she was better at it than I was. She stayed at her fancy boarding school, studied hard, and now plans to go to college. I finally dropped out and ran away."

"You're kidding! Wasn't that scary?"

"Yeah, but I never was much good at school. I did good turning tricks..." Seeing the puzzled look on Missy's face, she explained, "I was a prostitute."

"Gosh, how old are you? You couldn't have been very old. I thought you had to be...like, old to do that."

Cathy laughed. "Nope, at fifteen, I wasn't the youngest girl on the streets. But our pimp didn't like it when we were stupid and got pregnant. I made it okay for a couple of years. I was careful. But, one night, this guy beat me up and raped me. I was in the hospital a while before getting discharged to a homeless shelter, and when we discovered I was pregnant, they got me here. I had my sixteenth birthday there. They were cool. It was my first experience with the love of God, and it blew my mind. They didn't condemn me or anything. After I get my GED and Junior arrives, I'll enroll in the community college."

"What about your folks; do they know where you are?"

"Yeah, the shelter contacted them to get their permission to put me here. I don't know if they were glad to hear from me. They hadn't heard from me for almost two years. They didn't want me to come home, of course, especially pregnant, and I sure didn't want to go there. That was never home to me—I felt more at home at the homeless shelter than I'd ever felt in my life. Funny, huh? But my dad sent a signed permission form for me to come here. I hear they're separated now. When I ran away from school, they realized they'd messed up, and it all fell apart. Beth's trying to help me forgive them. I guess my mom was kind of cowed by my dad and never stood up for me or for herself, so I feel sorry for her. Miss Ginny...wow...I wish I had a mom like her. My dad doesn't visit or anything, but he sends Hope House money."

"What are you going to do, I mean, about the baby?"

"I have to decide soon, and I don't know, Missy. I don't think I know how to be a mom like Ginny—she has five adult children. They come by every so often. They even bring stuff for us girls. Miss Ginny's grandkids adore her. They crawl all over her from the minute they get here until they leave! One of Miss Ginny's kids has her church do baby showers for us a couple of times a year—she lives in Cleveland. Another goes to our church—you'll meet her tomorrow. She's a teacher. Anyway, I don't want to be like my mom, and she won't—maybe she can't—help me. I'd have to do this alone, and I need more education to support a kid. What do you think I should do, Missy?"

"Golly, I don't even know what I'm going to do. We have to each decide for ourselves. That's what my pastor told me. My mom, my brother, and my

Church would help, but I don't know if it's fair to ask them. I don't know what to do. Don't they help us here at the Home to make a decision?"

"Oh, they do. I talk with Beth, and I have worked through all the books. But one week I think I'll keep him and the next week I think I'll place him—you know, with a family that longs for a child."

"You know it's a boy?"

"That's what the ultrasound says."

They fell quiet. Cathy reached over and turned off the light. The room wasn't dark. With the streetlights filtering through the shades, Missy wondered if she'd ever learn to go to sleep in the bright city.

Missy returned to the question at hand. "Got any ideas about Michelle?"

"Candy's going to beauty school after her baby comes. She isn't due till December or January. The next class starts at the end of January, so we're all praying the timing will work out. She likes to do hair, and she's good—she fixed Laura's hair, and Laura's hard to please. She cut Myra's hair—exactly the way she asked her to, believe it or not—and Myra didn't kill her! If she's that good, she should do something with her own. Those dark roots are awful! Oh, I'm sorry, that was mean. I shouldn't have said that."

Missy giggled. "Maybe we shouldn't say it, but it's the truth!"

Cathy told her that Candy didn't have two nickels to rub together. "She couldn't buy hair color if it was on sale at the Dollar Store. She's not a bad sort...if you get her away from Myra. Let's ask her."

With that happy plot in mind, they settled into their pillows. "Missy?" a little voice piped in the dark. "Do you mind if we pray together, I mean, about all these things—what to do about our babies, and helping Michelle fix herself up, and maybe even reaching Myra?" Their quiet voices joined together, and Ginny heard them as she walked by their room on her way down the hall. The house fell silent as each girl turned to her own thoughts. Missy thought it was almost like spending the night with Julie, but Julie never asked her to pray. She found herself drifting off comfortably, unaware a quiet voice down the hall was agreeing with another voice miles away in West Virginia, beseeching the Father on behalf of this precious girl. One voice belonged to someone who was quickly learning to love, and the other belonged to someone who had loved Missy all her life.

Early the next morning, Cathy was up and heading for the shower while Missy began writing her letter to send home. "Dear Mom," she started. "It's not too bad here, really. Some of the girls are sweet. You met Cathy—I love her. And Laura is a pretty girl. She and Michelle are in summer school, trying to catch up with schoolwork they have missed. Laura's grades suffered because of her situation—she tried to hide it and wore big clothes. Her grades went down, so she is repeating some classes to bring her average up. My timing is good. I'll be enrolled in school here this fall, finish the semester, and after the baby is born, I (we?) will be home in time for Christmas, I hope. I miss you guys awfully bad, but it's better that I'm here. We'll have group meetings some evenings to talk about our babies, nutrition, and what we plan to do after—stuff we all share."

Cathy came into the room, trying to hold her robe around her bulging belly. "The bathroom is all yours, and you'd better get in there before Laura. She uses up all the hot water and takes forever with her shampoo. If we didn't have mirrors in our bedrooms, no one else would ever get ready!"

Missy hurried to the hall bathroom, but Laura was there first.

"Do you mind awfully, Missy? I have to be ready for school in an hour, and Miss Ginny makes sure we all eat breakfast."

"No prob. I was writing a letter home anyway."

"Must be nice. My folks wouldn't have time to read it if I did write home, so why bother? But I do write to Sam all the time. He is a good boyfriend. He writes me too, which is really something for a guy, huh?"

Ginny watched the exchange as she walked down the hall. "That was sweet, Missy. Why don't you come help me with breakfast? Since you don't have any deadlines, you can come in your jammies. It's Laura and Michelle's week to help with meals, but they're in such a rush to get out in the mornings that I try to be flexible. Besides, breakfast is simple."

When they got down to the dining room, Michelle was dressed and ready in a perfectly matched orange sweater and designer jeans. She was setting the table and humming a little tune. She smiled shyly at Missy when she walked in. "I see Laura conned you out of the shower."

"Maybe we'll have to make a chart for that, I mean, around everybody's schedules and all. What about Myra and Candy?"

"Didn't you see the other bathroom at the end of the hall? They actually have a tub!" Smiling at the two girls working side by side, Ginny went into the kitchen, and soon they smelled bacon.

Missy went into the kitchen and saw the eggs sitting beside a bowl. "Scrambled eggs, Miss G?" she asked. When Ginny nodded, Missy began breaking them into the bowl and scrambling them. "Do you want to season them?"

"You go ahead. You look like you know what you're doing."

"I got up every morning to cook for Mom when she got off work. Oh, dear, she'll never eat now, and she'll lose weight. She never takes care of herself." Once again, Missy felt tears welling up.

"She's at it again!" Myra exclaimed, walking into the room, dressed all in black. Her dark purple punk hair was filled with gel, and it stuck straight out in all directions from her head. "You are such a crybaby! I told you that you're gonna to have to get over it. Life sucks."

Candy, hanging behind Myra, looked at Missy sadly.

Michelle put her arms around the newcomer and said. "You go ahead and cry, honey. We're all jealous because we don't have families like yours. Cathy told me how sweet your mother is."

Myra glared at her. "They rushed out of here in a big hurry. I didn't meet them. I bet they couldn't wait to dump her, just like the rest of us were dumped."

Ginny spoke up firmly. "Myra, that's enough! Please, have a little patience while Missy settles in. Thank you, Michelle, that's sweet of you. Now let me watch these eggs before they scorch."

Michelle walked over to the toaster, popped in more slices of bread, and began buttering the toasted ones.

"Where is Lazy Laura today? Already conned the new girl into her work?" At a glance from Ginny, Myra fell silent, shrugging her shoulders. "Whatever." She walked into the dining room and sat at the table while Candy and Missy helped Michelle carry out the juice glasses.

Laura and Cathy came downstairs. "Yummy! Smells wonderful. Thanks, Missy, you covered for me again," Laura said.

"I'm starving. This baby eats like a trucker!" Cathy complained, walking in behind her.

Candy laughed. "I'm glad I have an excuse to eat like a pig, and I really do like the food. I ain't never eaten this good."

After breakfast, the summer school girls got their books together and started out the door, but Ginny picked up her pocketbook and went out with them. "No school bus the rest of the week; I'm driving you."

"All right," they chorused happily, heading out the door.

Missy said, "I don't know the routine, but if they do dishes this week, it looks like we'll have to catch that."

"Not me," said Myra. "I do laundry this week, and we got it all done yesterday."

"I'll help you, Missy," Candy offered, ignoring Myra's glare.

"Cathy and I are supposed to clean up," Missy said, "so, Candy, you don't have to, but I'd love to have your help."

The girls gathered up dishes and carried them into the kitchen. Missy already felt comfortable in the warm, sunny kitchen. Big windows over the sink looked out into a small, fenced back yard. She stood on tiptoe and looked. She saw a birdfeeder and a white birdbath surrounded by cheerful marigolds and a curved bench.

Cathy noticed her looking. "It's pretty out there. The Catholic Daughters planted the garden and donated a nice picnic bench so we can eat outside. See the bench? It's a Memorial to the Unborn—the Knights of Columbus donated it."

Loud music came from the living room, where Myra was plopped on the couch, idly channel-surfing.

"Gosh, she knows we're not supposed to watch MTV," Candy said. "It's like she wants to get in trouble, you know? What is she, stupid? Don't answer that."

"Be glad you're in here with me, Candy. I'll vouch for you. Besides, I have an idea that Cathy and I want to run by you. We were wondering last night if we could possible do something to help Michelle, you know, to look better. You're good with that. What you did with Laura's hair was great—awesome—what do you think?"

"I don't know if I could do a make-over. Her folks would probably send her some money to go to a beauty shop if we encouraged her—they're always throwing money at her. Her clothes are gorgeous! She's a fall, with brown hair and...what color are her eyes? Behind those thick glasses, it's hard to tell."

"They're dark. Maybe they're brown. She could get contacts!"

The girls were giggling when Ginny came in through the back door and hung her coat on the hook. She smiled at them, headed straight through the dining room, crossed the living room, and clicked off the loud TV.

"No TV for a week, Myra. You know the rules, and you must be trustworthy when I'm out of the house."

"Oh, what the..." Myra swore.

Ginny calmly said, "Make that two weeks."

Myra threw the pillow across the room and stomped up the stairs.

"What goes here?" asked Beth, who had opened the front door with a key.

"It's Myra again. I took the girls to school because Laura's feet were terribly swollen last night, and I didn't want her walking and riding the bus. They finish up on Friday. I have appointments at the doctor for her, Cathy, and Missy next Monday, but I may have to take her in earlier if this keeps up."

"It was hot yesterday, and I'll bet she's been drinking pop. We'll keep an eye on her."

"I came in, and there sat Myra, big as life, watching MTV as cool as you please. I told her no TV for a week, and then she swore, threw the pillows across the room, and stomped upstairs. Beth, I can't reach that child. I'm losing her."

"I'll go talk to her." Beth headed up the stairs.

Candy looked through the kitchen door and whispered to Missy, "There's Beth. She hardly got in the door today. I'm glad I'm not in trouble."

"Missy," Ginny said as she walked back into the kitchen, "do you want to plan the next few days, make our appointments?"

"Go ahead, Missy. I'll finish up here, Miss Ginny," Candy said. "We can finish talking about our plan later."

"Plan? What plan?" Ginny asked.

"Oh, never mind," the girls chorused. Ginny looked at them and shook her head, smiling.

"You girls did a good job on this kitchen. Candy, are you ready to go back to Adult Education on Monday? I get Laura and Michelle out of summer school, and GED classes start back for you and Myra. No rest for me! I'll be getting Missy's schedule worked out, and Cathy needs to talk to Beth after she comes downstairs."

"Missy and I haven't straightened our room. We'll quickly do that." Missy looked at Candy, knowing she wouldn't dare walk into her room with Myra on a tear.

Ginny caught the eye contact between them. "Candy, don't worry about your room chores now. Are your books in there? Do you need me to get them for you?"

"No, Ma'am. I set them on the bookcase yesterday afternoon. I'll get started on those math problems. I don't get it! It's too hard."

"Maybe after I'm finished, I can help you," Missy offered.

Settling in and Running Out

Ginny thought Candy's prayer time was the big excitement for the week. The teen said she experienced a "lighter load than she had been toting," and most of the girls were excited for her. She looked forward to going to church. She said it was confusing before, but she thought she 'got' it now. Ginny worried about Myra, who kept getting more and more difficult and truculent, not wanting to do her chores, mouthing off, and refusing to work on preparation for her GED. She never talked to Missy except to call her names for turning Candy against her. But Candy didn't turn on Myra. She got sweeter and sweeter to everybody, and she became more excited about Michelle's make-over, which they scheduled for the next Saturday. Michelle and Laura finished school for the summer, and Michelle's dad sent her enough money to schedule an appointment for both Michelle and Candy at a real beauty shop.

Ginny dropped the girls off. Candy was excited about joining Michelle at a beauty salon—she'd never been to a hair stylist. Only once did her mother take her to a barber. After leaving them, Ginny drove the big van to the mall, the rest of the girls with her. The girls were giggly, as teenage girls can be. It was a fun day!

But it fell apart. Myra kept wandering off at the mall, and they found her in the smoking section of the food court. Beth's family had joined the group at the mall, so they told Ginny they'd bring the five other girls home later so Ginny could take Myra back to Hope House. Beth's husband went to move their car seats into the House van, and Ginny took Myra back to the House in their smaller van.

Despite Beth's attempts to cheer them, a pall hung over the group, as if something foreboding was about to happen. Beth had the credit card, and she urged the girls to look at back-to-school sales. Michelle and Cathy had everything money could buy, and Laura's folks sent her enough as well. Jimmy sent Missy a money order, which she cashed at the mall bank. The girls decided to sit for a makeover at one of the beauty counters, but they waited for Michelle and Candy to join them.

Some of the girls didn't need too much, but Candy needed it all. She had no contact from family. The Court had given Hope House custody until she was eighteen, which would be a few months before the baby was due.

The girls were enthusiastic about dressing "the new Candy" and found clothes reflecting a Christian appearance. "No more tight blouses to show off your boobs, Candy," Cathy said. Candy was humble, asking about each item she picked up, and the harshness of her former appearance melted when she dressed in clothes that fit her appropriately. Missy hugged her when she came out of the dressing room with a pair of jeans and a maternity top, but Candy protested that she looked...pregnant!

"You look positively adorable. Look at me!" Laura said. "We'll have to turn sidewise to hug each other soon."

Wanting to give Ginny ample time for Myra, Beth suggested they go to the ice cream shop, which doubled as a reward for her own kids. Her husband, Tom, was frayed after running after the boys, who had been on every ride in the mall. Laura, worried about her weight, chose a small yogurt cone. Cathy said that since she was about to lose a lot of weight, she'd indulge, so she chose a banana split.

Missy looked at her. "You're going to have to lose *all* that weight too," she reminded her, so Cathy made Missy share it. The mood lightened as the girls gathered around a couple of tables scooted together and played with Beth and Tom's kids. Candy and Michelle looked pretty after their appointments. Candy told Missy she felt like they were like family and that for the first time in her life she had sisters. Missy agreed, even though she missed her mom and Jimmy a lot, and she missed Julie too. But because the Hope House girls were at a point of vulnerability in their lives, they opened their souls to one another.

"This is more fun than hanging with Myra," Candy said. "I knew I was doing things that were...wrong, you know. We would sneak around and smoke—not that I wouldn't like a cigarette—is smoking a sin, Beth?"

"Smoking doesn't keep you out of heaven, if that's what you're asking, but it's not healthy. Babies born to women who smoke have smaller birth weights. Remember how Missy was telling you your body is the temple of the Holy Spirit and that you want it to look pretty so people will see Jesus in you? Because our bodies belong to God, He wants us to use them for Him. We want to eat healthy, dress appropriately, and not put things into them to make us ill. God wants healthy children who can be His hands and feet on the earth."

The girls entered in a lively discussion about their food, companions, clothing choices, and everything it means to be a Christian. "Gosh," Laura finally said. "There's a whole lot more to this being a Christian thing than I ever thought. I was sorry I got pregnant, but I had never heard about saving sex for marriage, until I got here."

Missy leaned toward Laura. "When you get back, what will Sam say about it? Do you think you can keep the choices you've made here? It's going to be tough. You guys seem to really love each other."

"We do, Missy, but I've been writing him about what we've learned. And what if we don't get married? I always thought we'd get married, but I don't want to go to WVU, and he has a scholarship there. It's going to be hard."

Cathy piped in. "Didn't you say all the kids in your youth group were having sex too? Sounds to me like you need to find a new church!"

"I don't know how Mom and Dad would like that. They're big leaders in the church. Dad is on the vestry, and Mom's on the altar guild. They haven't said much about my 'Christian experience,' except to say they hope I'm happy and don't get fanatic."

Beth listened to their conversation and added, "We can't let you go back home without some spiritual support, Laura. I'll do some research about Christian groups in your area, and maybe we can find a good Fellowship of

Christian Athletes or Youth Alive for you. Let's not forget to do that, because Cathy's right. You'll need some support. Being a Christian is swimming upstream in today's culture."

The toddler had nodded off in Tom's arms, and the boys had finished their ice cream. Their adventure was coming to an end.

* * *

At Hope House, the talk hadn't gone well, and Ginny let Myra stomp off to her room. Often she prayed sitting in her chair, but after the door slammed, she dropped to her knees. "Father God, I place Myra in Your loving hands. I don't know what to do anymore. Do I tighten up? Let go? Forgive and forget? But then I must think of the example for the other girls. We follow the same rules, and You gave us the Ten Commandments, not the ten suggestions. But, God, she's hurting so, and You died for her. You love her more than I do, and You'll be with her. Please draw her to Yourself. May she find the comfort in Your arms. God, I fear for her and her baby if she goes back out on the streets." Tears slipped down Ginny's cheeks. Soon the girls would be back, and she couldn't let them see her like this, and, despite Myra's attitude, she needed to eat lunch. She rose and crossed over to her vanity to powder her nose, wondering if she was too old for this job.

"Myra," Ginny called, "let's fix some lunch. The others won't be back until later."

"All your little pets get to go out, but here I am, grounded again. It's not fair!"

"You may have whatever you want for lunch. Pizza? A hamburger?"

"It all tastes like crap to me. I'm sick of homemade food!"

"Why don't we call in some pizza? We can order it from the place down the road, or Domino's, or even Pizza Hut."

"Domino's is okay, I guess," Myra muttered.

"I'll call it in right now. What toppings do you want?" Ginny hoped they could sit together and have a pleasant chat, but when the pizza arrived, Myra grabbed it and headed off to her room. Ginny sighed and thought she'd call her daughter and have a chat to lift her spirits, but she wasn't home.

Having an unheard-of moment to herself, Ginny put her concerns for Myra aside and picked up a book. If Ginny had a hobby, it was reading. She didn't relax over knitting, as some women did. She was a good cook, but her real pleasure was reading, and she was engrossed in her book when the girls tiptoed in.

"Surprise!" they all cried. Ginny looked up and couldn't believe the butterflies her two girls had become. She was eager to see Michelle and Candy, delighted that Michelle included Candy in her mother's largesse.

"Oh, girls, you look—you look absolutely beautiful! Come here; let me see what they've done to you. Michelle, the color of your shirt is fabulous on you, and the cut makes you look bright and happy. Look how the cut frames her face—what a pretty shape your face has. I never noticed before. And, Candy, look at you! That color...is that your natural color? It's perfect."

Candy was babbling with excitement. "Oh, man, I'm glad to get rid of those God-awful roots. I ain't never had my hair cut in a real beauty shop before. Mom took me to a barber once, but mostly my Grandma cut it. You should have seen that place, Miss G. It was a swanky joint. Look at my nails. They even did my toenails."

"And that's a nice color, subdued and attractive, like your makeup. It's subtle and gentle, like your new sweet spirit. You glow, and I'm proud of you!"

"My makeup was like a neon light, but Michelle done got me all this expensive stuff that I'll never be able to afford, ever again."

Laura laughed. "You're such a beautiful advertisement—when you finish beauty school, you'll work in a fancy shop like that one and make all kinds of money!" The girls chorused their agreement, and Candy laughed with them.

"I hope I make a decent living. I don't want to live on welfare—maybe someday I'll even have a real house and not a trailer. I'll have to start off, you know, work a while until I can afford something. Maybe. But if I have a kid, it'll be tough, twice as tough."

Missy hugged her. "If God leads you to keep this baby, Candy, He'll provide. I know He will. Don't be afraid. We'll help you trust Him."

"See, Miss Ginny, didn't I tell you?" Cathy exclaimed, "Missy always knows what to say—it's like the Lord gives her the words. I needed to hear that too, Missy. I can't give my baby up. I can't. He's all I've got, but I don't know how I'll feed him or put clothes on his back, and I don't want him in a homeless shelter like I was. Or worse, on the streets. I can't drag him around on the streets."

The girls gathered around her, looking to Ginny for an answer.

"Cathy," Ginny said, taking a deep breath, "we have to take one day at a time. 'Sufficient unto the day is the evil thereof,' the Master says. Let's don't jump ahead too far."

"My baby's due in six weeks," Cathy said, "and I'm out of here. No roof over my head; no plan in sight. It would be better for him if I gave him up, but I can't. I swear, I can't. God knows I can't. Even if I know it would be best for him, he's mine, and he's all I've got." The girls looked around at each other, their excitement crushed with the weight of their friend's sorrow. Ginny took Cathy in her arms, rocking her back and forth like the wounded child she was.

"I know," Michelle exclaimed. "Let's pray! I don't know how to do that very well, but I see it working around here all the time."

Beth, who stood inside the door of Ginny's room, said, "Good idea. Let's pray. I've got to get out of here and relieve my poor husband, who has three kids in the van on this lovely Saturday. Come on. Gather around. We'll pray for Cathy and ask God to give her wisdom and provide for her and her son."

After they prayed, Candy suggested they show Ginny their new look, and she went with Michelle to the room she shared with Laura. Missy and Cathy went up to their room to put their purchases away, promising a fashion show in Ginny's room in a few minutes.

"I absolutely have to go, or Tom will kill me," Beth said. "But I talked to John about next week's group meeting. I suggested he focus on reconciliation. I've taken the liberty of calling Cathy's mother. She's broken-hearted and terribly sorry about the mistakes she made with Cathy. She's been writing to her and wanting to come visit, but all she gets are polite responses."

"Maybe God is opening doors. We've got a lot to pray about, and Cathy's right...we're running out of time for her."

"Obviously, we never just kick anyone out without a plan. She'll have the full six weeks after the birth. She wants to enroll at the community college, and she has the grades for it, but we have to find day care for the baby."

"She's going to keep him?"

"I don't think it would be healthy for her to give her baby up. She's experienced a lot of rejection in her own life, and she'd feel guilty. She'd feel like she rejected him. She needs this baby—she's right...the baby is all she has, at least right now. I wanted to let you know what's in the works. Maybe if you have a chance to talk with her, and if God opens the conversation, you can put in a good word for her mother. The woman really wants to come see her."

"Regardless of what happens with this beginning, we have to find forgiveness in our hearts. Unforgiveness is such a hurtful thing, and Cathy's awfully bitter. Thanks for telling me this. I'll keep my ears open. May God give us opportunities to speak into her life."

"Thanks. I'd love to stay and see the show, but I've got to go. See you at church tomorrow."

Ginny waved her off. "Go—go to that handsome husband of yours, and give him a hug for me. I had to ground Myra, and in her state, now we can't trust her here alone."

"I couldn't make an inch of progress with her the other day. I fear she's hardening her heart," Beth replied.

Ginny agreed. "She doesn't seem ready to let love in. I fear for the baby. And for his mom."

"Let it go, Ginny. Trust the Lord; it's His job. All we can do is love."

"God, help me to love well," Ginny replied. "And, God, help me to get to the beauty shop myself. These girls make me realize how awful my own my hair is!"

"I'll be here all three mornings next week. Why don't you schedule an appointment for yourself?"

"On Monday, I take Laura, Cathy, and Missy to the doctor, and I take Missy over to the high school to register for fall semester. But maybe I could get an appointment for Wednesday or Friday—but I sure can't afford that swanky shop Michelle's dad paid for!"

"Guilt money pays for a lot, but it doesn't pay for love. You have tons of love, Ginny."

"I do, and I wouldn't trade what I do for the all the tea in China," Ginny replied, remembering her doubts from earlier in the morning. "And this job gives me good food and this beautiful home to stay in. I'm blessed. What else could give a poor widow all this?"

"We thank God for sending you to us."

"Get out of here. You've stayed too long. Go to your family."

"I will. Bye—and I love you, Ginny!"

"Love you back."

Ginny walked over to the long windows on the driveway side of the house. She pulled the floor length drapes aside and watched Tom playing hide-and-go-seek with the two older boys, holding the little girl in his arms. She smiled, realizing the children were in plain sight, wanting their daddy to find them. She saw Beth walk up to him and take the baby so he could chase the boys around the side yard. *How blessed we are to have a godly example of a loving family for these girls to see.* After piling the laughing boys into the van, they backed out and pulled off, and Ginny let the rose-colored drapes fall into place. Her eyes swept across the spacious bedroom. Although her burgundies had matched well, her little suite of furniture would have been swallowed up in here if some volunteers hadn't built in a little kitchenette with a microwave and an electric teapot on her little counter. The Board also provided her with a handsome desk, where she managed the accounts, and added a love-seat and coffee table to give her a personal space. She sat on the comfortable easy chair, and soon the room was filled by five girls, eager to show off their new clothes.

"All ready, Miss G?" the girls chorused. "Here she is: Miss America," they sang as Candy showed off her first new outfit.

"Yeah, Miss Pregnant America." Candy giggled, and laughter filled the room.

The big, heavy mommies-to-be sat on the love seat while Michelle and Missy sat on the floor. Shoe boxes were opened, packages were sorted out, and every once in a while, the girls would run to their rooms to put on a blouse or a pair of jeans.

"You girls are certainly ready for school—except...did you buy pencils and paper, notebooks and backpacks?"

Quiet fell over the room as the girls looked at one another, and then great laughter erupted, and Missy said, "We didn't think of that minor detail."

Ginny joined the laughter. "We'll have to make a stop at Walmart on the way home from church. Now, let's make a list of who needs what. You summer school girls should be all set, and, Candy, you'll be taking your first GED test Monday, so we can wait to see what is the next step for you." Michelle needed new pencils, and Missy was ashamed she'd spent all her money when she realized she still needed a backpack, a notebook, pencils, pens, and paper. Ginny assured her they had money in the budget to provide for the girls.

"When I get some money from Mom, Miss Ginny, I'll pay you back," Missy promised. "Jimmy's working well now, and he's more than replacing the little bit I made at McDonald's. I'll pay you back."

"It's fine, Missy. We can keep your receipts if you like, but for now, let's get it done. And get all this trash out of my room and put it away," she ordered with pretend sternness and a smile. "Are you hungry? We ordered enough pizza for everyone!"

The girls scrambled up and scattered, but Candy lingered. "Miss G," she paused, "I know we shouldn't say nothing bad about anyone, but I really don't want to go to my room. Myra is...she ain't fun to be around right now."

"I'm sure, honey. We have a roll-away—let's see if Cathy and Missy would mind if you bunked in with them until Myra cools off." While Cathy and Missy rolled the cot into their room, the others went downstairs to warm the pizza for supper.

What a Mighty God

Cathy and Missy didn't know what Ginny and Beth had discussed, but the girls prayed extra hard for God to make a way where there was no way for her, and Missy explained to her friend that God is a way-maker. Cathy went to sleep excited about taking Missy to church with Miss Ginny and the girls.

They got up early, knowing they had to teach Michelle and Candy how to use their makeup. Michelle told Candy to go use Missy's mirror. "I'm as nervous as a cat putting on all this fancy stuff. I've never worn it before," Michelle said. Laura assured her she could teach her. The one thing she did well was applying cosmetics!

"You got that right," Cathy teased, and all the girls laughed.

Laura stuck out her tongue as she linked arms with Michelle and drug her to their room.

Cathy and Missy turned their attention to Candy, who said, "Thanks for letting me bunk in here. I'm glad I didn't have to go to my room. It's cold as ice in there. Myra acts like she hates me. Ever since I prayed, she's been nasty. The night I slept in there, I had dreams of her coming over and slapping me silly in my bed."

Cathy murmured her sympathy. Myra had been difficult for all of them, and they were walking on eggshells around her. "It's tough, Candy. She used to lead you around and made you do uncomfortable stuff, and she can't do that anymore, because now you have Jesus."

"She does drugs—I never did. I worried about the baby."

"Good for you!" Cathy told her.

"It's spiritual warfare. The enemy doesn't like you giving your heart to Jesus, and he's trying to get you to turn back," Missy said.

Cathy pointed to the assorted lipstick, eye shadow, and foundation. "Let's get you fixed up, girl."

Cathy noticed that Missy looked nervous and tried to reassure her. "Everyone is going to love you. It's a loving church—they love everybody, and look how quickly we all came to love you."

"You two walk beside me, and I'll make it." Missy urged them toward the stairs. "Candy, you are perfect, adorable—your hair, your makeup. You're gorgeous! Come on."

Candy stopped in the hall and stared. "Look at Michelle. You are drop-dead good looking, girl!"

Michelle touched her hair. "Do you like it?" All the girls exclaimed that it was fantastic, and they hurried down the steps and out the back door, piling into the back of the van.

Myra was already in the shotgun seat, ignoring the others as much as possible. They dropped off Michelle at the Catholic Church and went on to theirs.

The sermon focused on forgiveness. "Didn't Jesus teach that we are forgiven in the same way we forgive our debtors?" the pastor challenged. He led the congregation in a recitation of the Lord's Prayer. "Are you experiencing God's forgiveness? Do you question if you're forgiven?" Then he read the story of the steward, who had his large debt canceled and threw his fellow servant in jail for a much less sum. "King David made many mistakes in his life, bad ones. He took a forbidden census, which cost 70,000 lives. He committed adultery and murder, but God called him a man after His own heart because he had a repentant heart. He humbled himself, cried out for forgiveness, and showed mercy to others. He took Mephibosheth into his own palace and dined him at his table, even after his grandfather, Saul, tried to kill him for years."

I'm forgiven, and I hate my mother and father. They made mistakes, and they hurt me—they never let me come home on vacations. I felt lonely at boarding school. I wanted to go home, like the other girls. Even if I was at home, they were out, doing this or that, but they made sure I was clothed and fed, and they gave me anything I wanted. And I took off, ran away, and dropped out with no word. I hated them—that's sin. God forgave me and welcomed me home, like the Prodigal. Cathy whispered, "God, You are the source of love, and they don't know you. Father forgive them, for they didn't know what they were doing to me." Tears began to slip down Cathy's cheeks, and she got up to move toward the altar.

Myra crossed her arms and kicked her legs, muttering, "Sucker."

Candy took Cathy's hand and walked with her. "I've got a lot of forgiving to do too."

Laura, Missy, and Ginny bowed their heads. Beth met them in the aisle, and a small man with glasses met them at the front.

"Who's the guy?" Missy whispered.

"He's the group leader. We'll start our meetings again this Thursday night," Laura told her.

Together, the social worker and the group therapist prayed with Cathy and Candy, and after service, the pastor came to the girls, who were standing with Ginny, and asked who the new face was, reaching out his hand toward Missy.

After they'd been introduced, Ginny told him she'd enjoyed standing next to Missy, because she sang beautifully, and the minister asked her if she'd been in a choir in her church at home. She said they didn't have a weekly choir, but she'd been in special productions.

"One of our choir members lives near Hope House. If you're interested, I'm sure she'd stop by and bring you to practice. Why don't you get settled, and we'll talk about it next week?"

Cathy saw her roommate respond to the pastor, a gentle man. Missy had told her about the love she felt from Pastor Potter at home, and Missy had said she felt the same love from Ginny and Beth—the love of Christ, who gave His life for her. Cathy hoped her friend felt comfortable and at home, even while missing her loved ones. In a way, she thought, Missy was home. They were all home in the family of God.

A lady in the church had pressed a luscious-looking cake in their hands as they walked out, and Candy held it in her lap, teasing about drooling on it all the way home. Miss Ginny had a terrific casserole in the oven. When they walked in and smelled it, the girls hurried to set the table and dig in. After the meal, the girls drifted off. Laura wrote Sam, and Missy scribbled a note to Jimmy. Others watched TV, and Michelle and Ginny read books.

The Midwife

On Monday, Cathy, Laura, and Missy went to the doctor. Missy liked the warm, comfortable woman, and her heart rose in joy when she saw her little one moving around in the ultrasound. *See, I was right—she's there, a little person in her own right, moving and growing. God, help me to care for her, and help me to do the right thing for this precious life.*

"Didn't I hear that you think the baby is a girl?" When Missy agreed, the midwife said, "You're right, and it looks like your date is right on."

Missy told her about the night the baby was conceived, and the wise woman said nothing; instead, she merely took her in her arms and held her as she wept. "I thought I'd shed all the tears I had, but every time I think about it..." Missy shuddered, and the midwife tightened her embrace.

"You're an amazing person. I can tell you love this little one. Have you made a plan for her yet?"

"I haven't crossed that bridge. I want to keep her. I do love her, but I want what's best for her, my mom, and my brother."

"What's best for you, Missy?"

"I don't know, but God will lead me and provide for me. He'll show me what to do. Every baby is His gift, and He has a plan for my baby."

"You're right. We'll leave things in His hands. You're healthy, and the baby's healthy, and we'll pray for a good outcome for both of you."

"Thank you," Missy said as she reached for her clothes. The midwife handed her some tissues, hugged her briefly again, and slipped out the door.

In the car, Ginny announced that it looked like Laura's baby would arrive before Cathy's.

"I thought you weren't due until October," Cathy cried. "You bum. You'll be unpregnant before me. I can't believe this! It's unfair."

"How could you not know when the baby's due? Don't you know the night you and Sam made a mistake?" Missy questioned.

"Sam and I had been 'making mistakes' for a year, Missy. I was on the pill—all you have to do is go to the health department for them—but I forgot to take it sometimes." Laura responded.

"But I thought you were a Christian, and you went to church."

"I told you that most of the kids in that youth group were doing it." Laura replied. "We didn't get taught the way you were. It was no big deal. We'd go to parties and split off into the bedrooms."

"Babies come when they will. The good news is that you're all healthy," Ginny reassured them.

"I wish my baby would slow down and give me more time," Cathy said, "but then I wish he'd get out of there. He's really crowding me!"

"I know what you mean," Laura agreed as she climbed out of the van.

"We'll be back after lunch, girls. Missy's going to register for classes. Beth said she'd stay until I got back."

"That's all right, Miss G; we'll keep a lid on things," Laura assured her.

Missy was amazed at what the school in this city had to offer: Interior Decorating! She loved it. After looking at her grades and her SAT scores, Mrs. Lovelace suggested she take her English and math classes at the community college in order to get a leg up on her credits.

"Will that be a problem, Mrs. Randall? Can transportation be arranged?"

Ginny paused only a moment before agreeing.

"All right—what do you think, Missy?"

"Can I do that? With the baby and all, maybe it isn't such a good idea. Maybe I won't be able to study like I should."

"Looking at your IQ scores, it shouldn't be a problem. If you are homebound for any time, we'll get a teacher to come to Hope House for you."

"If you think I can do it, I'll try."

"The college grades will count for your high school graduation. Let's see how many you need to graduate in time. Will you be with us the whole year?"

"No, Ma'am. My baby's due in November, and I hope to be home for Christmas. I want to graduate with my class at home."

"We'll have to arrange for early testing so you can complete your courses. You're interested in Interior Decorating? It's not easy. You'll have some projects to complete."

"But it sounds like fun!" Missy and the counselor bent over the schedule.

"If we get you in morning classes at the college, you can come back here for Interior Decorating and sewing—that's an easy one. Do you sew?"

"Some, but not very well. I've never made anything to wear, but I've repaired hems and stuff."

"When you finish Mrs. Cook's class, you'll be making clothes, and if you're interested in Interior Decorating, you may be custom-making drapes one day."

Missy bounced out of school. "I can't wait! I need to get back and write my mom about this." She grabbed a sandwich and went upstairs to write home. Soon she was back downstairs, looking for a stamp, but she found the place in an uproar.

"Hold on!" Ginny's voice rose above the din. "Who saw her last, and when? Maybe she's rebelling against being grounded and will be back later."

"Miss G," Candy said, "all her stuff's gone—the clothes the Home provided for her. Doesn't that belong here? But she wouldn't take it if she was coming back, would she?"

"We need to think about the baby and hope she comes back," Ginny said.

Candy looked around. "God, forgive me, but I hope she doesn't—it's been living hell around here lately."

"Miss G, you wouldn't be wanting her back if you had heard her cussing you last night. We should've told you, but we aren't supposed to tattle, and I was afraid to say anything," Laura said.

"Honey, we don't tattle, but we need to report serious things. Now, who saw her last?"

"I saw her right after we got back. She asked where you were and when you were getting back, and then I went into the office to talk to Beth," Cathy said.

"Candy and I were in my room, giving Michelle some makeup tips," Laura explained. "We're on the opposite end of the hall. Maybe she snuck out then. We didn't think anything was wrong until Cathy came up—we figured she'd gone into the office with Beth, but then she walked out and asked where Myra was."

"We ran upstairs. I thought something was wrong, so we went to my room and saw she'd taken all her stuff." Candy looked miserable. "Gosh, maybe we made her run away? I'm such a bad Christian, being glad to get rid of her."

Beth put her arm around Candy. "Myra has been pulling away from all of us lately. She's jealous of your friendship with Missy and your new-found life in Christ, and she's unwilling to make changes in her own life." She looked significantly at Ginny. "Everyone has offered her love, and she doesn't appear to be ready to receive it right now. Let's call the police and report her missing. Then I'll call my sister to pick up Lizzie at kindergarten so she won't be standing on the street corner."

Soon two officers stopped by, talked about the missing girl, took a picture of her, and assured them they'd be on the lookout for her. After they left, the girls, Ginny, and Beth formed a circle and prayed for Myra.

God Moved Mightily

Missy's head spun as they geared up for school. GED classes started Wednesday, and Candy, Cathy, and Michelle would start their next session. Michelle and Cathy both decided to enroll in the community college, so they were shooting for a GED. Laura would be homebound. Missy was eager to begin the following Monday, but the miracle started on the weekend. Thursday night at their group meeting, John turned the discussion to the sermon from Sunday, asking the girls what they thought about it.

Candy asked if she had to forgive her abusive step-father, and John explained that forgiving didn't mean she had to have a relationship with him. She simply needed to let it go in order to avoid being bitter.

"Turn him over to God, Candy. Let Him deal with the man. Can you do that?"

The girls gathered around and prayed, and then Missy said her pastor helped her to forgive the boys who raped her.

John let out a breath. "You girls are my heroes. You face horrible circumstances and overcome them. I see a lot of courage in this room." His gentle encouragement brought smiles through their tears.

"I forgive Sam. We were in it together, and he's standing with me," Laura said.

"I have to forgive myself—I was stupid," Michelle added.

Cathy let out a sigh. "I need to deal with my hard heart. I prayed at the altar about my parents—my mom didn't do anything that bad...nothing like Candy faced. I got mad at my father and ran away. My mom's been wanting to visit, and Beth wants to set it up for this weekend. Candy, if you'll bunk with Missy, I'll stay in your room with my mom. God, help me."

Once again, the girls formed a circle to pray.

Cathy's mother arrived Friday. She looked timid and reached tentatively to hug her daughter. Beth brought them into her office. Laura and Missy quietly prayed, avoiding the office and hoping for the best.

"She seems nice," Laura offered quietly, "but what? Beat down?"

"Maybe they can help each other," Missy said.

The girls looked up when Beth's sister came in to drop off her daughter. Beth heard the piping voice calling for her mommy, and she came out of her office to gather her daughter into a hug.

"I regret that I didn't care for my baby like that," Cathy's mother said, coming out behind her. "Now we're adult strangers. You are...fortunate."

"Blessed," Beth corrected. "I have a wonderful, supportive, loving husband. It makes all the difference."

Cathy took her mother's hand. "You're right, Beth. Mom's not so bad after all. We can get through it together, Mom."

"You're wise for your age. You've learned things in your short life that I'm still learning."

"You don't want to know the stuff I've learned, Mom. I've made mistakes I don't want anyone to make."

"You're remarkable. I don't understand how you can be where you are in your life, in your thinking."

"God's moved mightily in Cathy's life, Audrey. I knew you'd be proud of her. If you want to take her out to dinner for some private time, I'll tell Ginny."

"Can she stay another night?" Cathy asked. "I want to take her to church Sunday."

"I'm sure it's not a problem. I'll pass it on to Ginny as well. Have a good time, ladies." Beth, who was still carrying her daughter, went into the kitchen to consult with Ginny before leaving.

At around three-thirty, the bus dropped off the three adult education girls. Michelle felt confident that she'd done well on her GED placement test and that she'd be able to enroll in the community college with Cathy.

"But you guys should have seen this guy in our class looking at Candy! Man, his tongue was hanging out."

Candy picked up a pillow and hit Michelle with it. "Cut it out, 'Chelle. Joe's nice to everyone."

"Sure, Candy...But he has the hots for you!"

"Michelle, he knows the Hope House girls are pregnant."

"I still say he likes you."

"Tell us more about this guy. Who is he? How old? What does he look like?" Laura demanded.

"You guys, stop," Candy protested. "He lives with his mom and has a night job. He's going to GED because he wants to go to the electrician program at the trade school."

Michelle raised her eyebrows. "You learned this...how?"

Candy blushed. "We eat lunch together. He's a nice guy. Lots of the people in the class look down at us, but he never has."

"Hmm, sounds very interesting," Laura teased.

"Leave her alone, you two. It's not like we all don't need friends," Missy said. "Cathy's mom was here today. She seems...nice. Sad. Timid. They're going out to dinner, but I think it's a good start, don't you, Laura?"

Candy shot Missy a grateful look, glad to have the topic turned away.

"You'll get to meet her—I think she's staying another night." Laura told them.

"I prayed for God to make a way where there was no way. I hope it works out," Missy said.

Ginny came into the living room, wiping her hands on a dish towel. "You're all set, Michelle. The test scores are wonderful, and you are enrolled, starting Monday. You and Cathy start together, and Missy will be over there in the mornings."

Michelle started to cry when the girls hugged her.

"I told you!" Missy exclaimed. "I knew you could do it. You're really smart, 'Chelle. Where did you ever get that 'I'm-so-stupid' thing anyway?"

She shrugged. "It was pretty stupid to get pregnant."

"Join the club, girlfriend." Laura laughed.

"The GED teacher had no doubts, Michelle," Ginny said. "She pre-enrolled you before you took the test. She said you were the brightest young lady who'd ever gone through the program—and in record time."

"We need to celebrate," Missy enthused. "Popcorn and movie night! Our last weekend to party. School starts Monday. Why do they start school on Monday and then give us Labor Day off? That's dumb."

"First, we need to eat supper—cheesesteak hoagies tonight, girls. Missy, would you get that phone, please?"

"Jimmy! What in the world?"

Ginny winked at the girls. "Come help me set the tables, and let them have some privacy." The girls grinned when they heard Missy squeal.

"You know what this is about, don't you, Miss G?" Laura asked.

"I do. But I'll let her tell you."

"He's coming to see her, I bet," Candy guessed.

Ginny didn't say a word, but her eyes were twinkling.

Julie Learns

Julie had been haunting Jimmy ever since Missy left, demanding to know what was going on. She didn't swallow the story of some distant relative in Ohio, otherwise known as Miss Ginny, who suddenly needed Missy so much that she had to leave school the first semester of her senior year. Julie knew her friend was in trouble. She'd seen her red eyes, watched her moodiness. Something was wrong, and she wanted to know what. She marched into Andrew's Garage Friday evening, demanding that Jimmy tell her what was going on.

He put his wrench down, serious and troubled at the confrontation, but he saw Missy's friend's eyes swimming with tears. "Please, please, Jimmy. I miss her so much, and she hasn't written a word. Do you hear from her?"

"All the time. Mom gets a letter one day, and I get one the next. She's fine."

"I have to talk to her."

"Wait till I get away from here. About fifteen minutes. Can you wait for me at Hardee's?"

"If no one from McDonald's sees me. All the girls and customers are asking me about her. Everyone loves Missy."

"I know. I'll be there in a jiffy, okay?"

On her drive to Hardee's, the only thing Julie could imagine was that somehow Jimmy and Missy's dad had reappeared and that Missy was nursing Ian as he lay dying. Missy would do it; she would talk about forgiving him and leading him to Christ. Surely Jimmy wouldn't leave her alone with him.

Julie was knotting up a napkin and crying by the time Jimmy pushed open the door.

He walked quickly over to the table and sat beside her, putting his arm around her shoulder. "It's okay, Julie, really. She's fine. I got a letter from her yesterday."

"Where is she? She and I talked every day, and I don't even have an address. What can I do? Something's got to be wrong. I'd do anything for her. You know that, Jimmy."

"The most important thing you can do is guard her secret."

"Since I don't even know her secret, how can I spill it? You know me better than that—I hid you two in the tree house when we were kids...whenever your dad was on a rampage."

"Yeah, I know, but she's never been...this way before, and she's kind of... sensitive."

"Missy is not sensitive—except that she's sensitive of everyone else's feelings. Why hasn't she written me? I'm her best friend, forever. I won't tell anyone else in the whole wide world."

Jimmy chuckled. Julie sounded like the little girl who came to play with them on Gram and Pop's farm. She lived at the next farm over, and they were together constantly. She was right—she and Missy were inseparable. He put his hand over hers. "I know, but I have to ask her for permission before I tell you. I'll call her tonight."

"I was supposed to close at McDonald's, but I got off early to come by the shop. I'll come home with you, and we'll call her right now."

When Miss G told her to answer the phone, Missy grabbed it. She told Jimmy she was fine. "I'm going to love school. They've set up the neatest program for me. But why are you calling? Is everything okay? Is Mom...?"

Julie was blinking back tears while she listened to the conversation. "Mom's fine, Miss. It's Julie. She came by the shop today, asking questions. She doesn't believe our story. You guys have been close. You haven't called or written, and she's pretty upset."

Missy collapsed on the telephone chair. "I didn't know what to say. I'm not a good liar. I knew this wouldn't work. Now the whole dumb town will know."

Julie couldn't hear Missy, but Jimmy said, "Come on; be fair. It's not the whole town. It's your best friend. She loves you, and she's worried sick."

"You're right. I've never kept anything from Julie before. She could tell when Daddy was drinking just by looking at me, and she never said a word. She'd touch my hand—how many times did she hide us, do you reckon?"

"Trust her, Miss. I trust her."

"What can I tell her?"

"The truth. It's not your fault. I told her I couldn't say anything till I talked to you." Jimmy looked over the phone at Julie and crossed his fingers.

"I miss her. I'd feel better talking to her, even if I don't know what to say."

"I'll fill her in on the details. Would you like to talk to her now?"
"You bum! Is she there? Give her the phone right now!"

Julie Burns became the only one outside the family who knew Missy's secret. After Missy assured her that she was well, that she'd be home, probably by Christmas, and that she was enrolled in school in Ohio, Missy left the rest of the storytelling to her brother. They chatted about school, friends, and classes, and then they said good-bye.

Jimmy took Julie by the hand and led her to the couch, where he gave her the horrible details of the night when he couldn't lift a finger as his no-good former buddies raped Missy.

"How did she do it? How did she keep working and going to school? I knew it was something awful, but I never dreamed..." Julie put her head in her hands and wept for her friend. Jimmy's arm circled her shoulders. "Let's go see her, Jimmy. Can we? Next weekend is Labor Day. Could we go?"

"I'll call the Home and see, Jules. Why don't you write her a letter? I'll give you the address."

"Why didn't she have an abortion?"

"I suggested it, but she wouldn't hear of it. She said God is the Author of life, and she believes He must have a plan for this baby. She said maybe God chose her to carry this baby because He could trust her. She never blamed the baby."

Julie looked down at her hands, which were twisted around a tissue in her lap. "She's got more faith than I do. Maybe I should visit your church sometime."

"We'll pick you up Sunday," Jimmy promised. The next day, he called Hope House and talked to Ginny, who called Beth, and they both decided a visit with Jimmy and Julie would be helpful to Missy. They called him back and arranged for them to come the next Friday.

Baby Moses

"Missy," came the soft whisper at the door. The bathroom light from the hall spilled a sliver of light across the carpet. Looking up, Missy saw Laura standing at the door. She slid out of bed and looked at Cathy, who was fast asleep.

"What's the matter? Are you okay?"

"Something's happening. Come see."

Missy followed her into the bathroom and looked at a pair of pajama slacks on the floor.

"That's definitely blood. Did you put on a pad? How do you feel?"

"Crampy, I guess. Not too bad." She moved, and water gushed down her legs.

"Your water broke. I'm getting Miss Ginny. Stay right here."

Laura got pale. "I'm not going anywhere!" She doubled over, moaning. Missy hesitated, afraid to leave her. "You'd better get her—go!" Laura clutched her belly.

In a minute, Missy was back, reaching for her friend. "She's coming. She's calling to ask Beth to come over and stay at the house so she can take you to the hospital. Let me get a cool cloth for your forehead. Would you be more comfortable on the floor?" Missy eased Laura down.

Ginny came in, brisk, efficient, and gentle. "Here, sweetie, let's get you downstairs. Missy, take this stack of flannel sheets to the van. We'll get her in there so we can leave as soon as Beth arrives."

Laura groaned and rocked over her belly.

Ginny looked at her watch. "We'll let this contraction pass before we lift her up and help her dress." It eased, and Ginny murmured, "Heave ho, up you go," as she and Missy helped her.

"Oh, Miss Ginny, I messed up the bath mat."

"Silly girl, that's the least of our worries." Between the two of them, they got Laura up off the floor and wrapped her in a bathrobe, but they were barely downstairs when another contraction hit. Ginny looked at her watch again. "Five minutes. Come on, Beth."

Missy watched Ginny's face, but the older woman remained calm, and they slowly progressed to the door.

When they arrived at the van, Missy arranged the sheets on the seat while Laura leaned on the door. "I thought you were 'a bit crampy,' Laura,'" Missy teased.

Laura tried to laugh. "That was then. This is now."

Missy reclined the seat, and together, she and Ginny lifted Laura inside. Beth turned in the driveway.

Getting out of the car, still in her pajamas, Beth said, "I had a feeling I should hurry. Go, guys."

Missy was closing the door when Laura's eyes got wide and she grabbed her friend's hand. "You're coming with me, Missy, aren't you? Please, Beth, can she come?"

Beth looked at Missy with a question. "We can't take time for you to change clothes."

"I'm in sweats. I'll be all right. Should I?"

Beth nodded to Missy. "If you want. Ginny, I'll call the midwife."

The sun was lighting the eastern sky as they pulled into the hospital. The midwife who worked with the Hope House girls was waiting and settled Laura in the room while Missy and Ginny waited in the hall.

"She's going to go fast, but she's fine. I knew at her last visit that we'd missed the date, but this baby is even earlier than I thought."

Missy crept in and found Laura on her side, with one knee pulled up. "How're you doing, hon?" Missy whispered, and Laura reached out her hand.

"Where's Miss Ginny?"

"Right here, sweet thing. I'm right here."

Laura moaned again and began to cry.

"Remember what we practiced, Laura. Breathe now. Missy, she seems to be having back labor, so you could rub her back, right here, like this. Ginny, come around here where she can see you. You're doing fine. The good Lord knows what He's doing. Women give birth every day."

A nurse rolled in a tray of instruments and stationed them against the wall.

"If you could get a chair for my other pregnant girl, it would be a help," Ginny said.

The nurse looked up in alarm, but she grinned when she realized she didn't have two girls who were delivering.

Ginny saw Missy quietly praying, and Laura relaxed, so she slipped out into the hall to talk to the midwife. Missy began to sing.

When the midwife returned, she scrubbed her hands, watching Missy. "You're doing a good job. Do you think you'll be a doctor or a nurse?"

"My mom's a nurse, but I don't think so."

Laura groaned, and the midwife put a hand on her belly. "That's a good one. They're getting closer now. This boy is getting ready to meet his mommy. Can you roll over and let me look?"

Missy stood, but Laura grabbed her hand. Noticing how the other teenager imparted calmness, the midwife told her to stay beside the bed.

Laura looked around. "Where's Ginny?" she demanded.

"She went to call Beth, Laura. She'll be right back. This baby is on his way, and we need to get his parents here." She gently rubbed around the opening of the birth canal. "This soothing ointment relaxes the muscles, allowing them to open more easily," she said, trying to educate both girls.

"I want this to be over!"

Ginny scurried in the room and put her hand on Laura's forehead. "We can't hurry nature, honey. Missy, can we roll her a bit?" They turned her on her side, and the midwife made circular motions, indicating that Missy should begin to massage Laura's back with gentle circles.

Laura labored steadily while her mother and Sam drove from Morgantown, West Virginia, and the baby's parents made their way to the hospital.

When the midwife did another check, Ginny asked, "How's she doing?"

"Not too good!" Laura snapped. Missy looked from one woman to the other as they smiled knowingly and nodded. It wasn't long before a wail announced that Laura's son had made his way into the world. Missy watched, awed, as they placed the baby on his mother. Laura smiled and whispered, "Hey, baby."

Looking up, Missy saw Beth in the doorway. She held out her hand. "Let's go get breakfast, Missy." Missy hesitated, and Beth urged her forward with a soft command, "Come on."

They went down to the cafeteria, and while Missy ate, Beth told her about the adoptive parents Laura had chosen. "Ginny has done this lots more times than you have. She's the grown-up here. It's not your job." Missy nodded. "You're a wonderful friend. Laura appreciates it, and she's blessed to have you. Shall we go back?"

"Thanks for breakfast. I do feel better."

"Amazing what a little OJ and protein will do for a body." Beth laughed. "Who has your kids?"

"It's Saturday. Tom's home with them. He's a better mother than I am."

When they got back to the floor, an imperious woman marched up to confront Beth. "The baby is with her! Why did you allow that child to see the baby? What is the meaning of this? We had all this planned. She's giving the baby up."

"Yes, she is, Mrs. Martin. This is the way we choose to do things. If she never sees the baby or knows he's fine, she might fantasize, thinking he has something wrong with him and that no one would want him. Believe me. It's better this way." She looked beyond Laura's mother. "Hi, Sam."

Shuffling his feet, he mumbled a response and asked, "Is Laura doing okay?"

"She's fine," Beth assured him.

"You must be Missy," Mrs. Martin said, waving her arm toward the door. "Go on in. She keeps asking for you. I'm not going in there. I'm in the way." Seeing Beth moving away, Laura's mother demanded to know where she was going.

I hope Laura isn't hearing this. I guess it's her way of dealing with the situation, but right now I could kill her. After catching Sam's eye and giving him a brief smile, Missy went into Laura's room, but she heard Beth explain she was arranging for the adoptive parents to have a room with the baby. "We'll put the baby in the nursery until his parents arrive, and we'll move Laura off this floor so she won't hear the babies and see the visiting relatives." Beth turned and abruptly walked to the nurses' station, saying over her shoulder, "They're on the way. They'll stay in the room with the baby. He's still in Laura's room if you want to see him."

Laura was still holding him in the crook of her arm when Missy came in. "Look, isn't he precious? He has all his fingers and toes."

"He's perfect, Laura. Beautiful. You did well. I'm really proud of you."

"He's small, only five pounds and nine ounces, but he can go home."

Beth came into the room. "His folks have arrived, Laura. You're the boss here. What would you like to do?"

Laura brushed his fuzzy head with her lips, and tears streamed down her face. "I'm ready. Could you bring them in here? Wait."

"Whatever you want, honey."

Laura reached for Missy's hand. "Pray for me."

"Lord, we thank You that this baby is safely with us and that Laura is fine. Thank You for her grand and generous heart, which allowed her to give this baby life and a home. Give her the faith You gave Your servant Jochobed as she placed her baby in the ark of safety and trusted him to Your care. Bless his parents, and help them to train him up in the way he should go. In Jesus' Name. Amen"

Going out the door with Beth, the nurse whispered, "Who's Jochobed?"

"Moses's mother." Seeing the parents, Beth took the mother by the hand. "She's ready. Tearful, of course, but she wants you to come in."

When they stepped into the room, the parents looked hungrily at the baby but asked, "Are you all right, Laura?"

"I am. I know what I want to do. I'm telling him goodbye."

"You take all the time you want," the father said, with tears glistening in his eyes.

"Come here." Laura patted the bed. "I want you to have him. Hold out your arms." Laura lifted the baby and placed him in his mother's arms. "Raise my son for me, and I will bless you forever."

His mother cradled him in her arms and looked at Laura. "We will bless you forever. We'll pray for you and teach him to pray for you."

Beth touched the new father's arm. "We have a room for you." She leaned down to kiss Laura, whispering, "Good job, honey."

The nurse placed the baby in a rolling bassinet. The parents dropped a kiss on Laura's cheek and followed the baby down the hall.

The midwife administered a sedative, and when she told Laura they were moving her, she was already drifting.

Missy watched them roll her friend onto the elevator. Ginny walked to the room with the new parents, and Beth spoke to Laura's mother, who was sitting in the lobby.

"Ginny will go back to Hope House. She's been here all night. Laura's been given a mild sedative, so she'll rest most of the day."

"What am I supposed to do?"

"We thought you'd want to be with your daughter," Beth said. "Do you need me to get you some magazines?"

"No, I have my work," she snapped, picking up a briefcase and storming after the gurney. Sam lingered to talk to Missy. Beth patted his arm. "Your son's parents said if you wanted to see him, you could. They're in room 332." She pointed.

Sam looked conflicted. "Is he good?"

"He's perfect, Sam. He'll be fine. Laura needs you more," Missy said.

"Thanks for being her friend. She talks a lot about you. I think this is for the best. We're too young to be parents. Laura wants to go to college, and I do too."

"You've done a brave and good thing. His parents will love him, and they're ready to be parents." Missy impulsively hugged him. "You guys did great."

"I hope."

"I know. I'm going back to Hope House. Your son kept me up all night—but he was worth it. He's beautiful, Sam."

"Maybe I'll get a peek at him later."

Jules and Gracie

Missy was trying to read her Bible. She knew that Hope House was hours from home and that even if they left at noon, it would be a while before Jimmy and Julie arrived, but she still couldn't sleep. She finally threw back her covers and left without waking Cathy.

Ginny found her in the kitchen, baking breakfast rolls from scratch. She'd had to buy yeast for Missy's baking. "Yum, it smells good in here. Fresh baked bread, coffee—have I died and gone to heaven?"

"If anyone deserves to go to heaven, Miss Ginny, it's you." Missy threw her arms around the housemother. "I love you! I can't wait for you to meet Julie."

"I'm looking forward to it. What are you reading?" Ginny noticed Missy's open Bible.

"I'm reading about Jochobed putting her baby in the ark. I've been going over that ever since Laura was in the hospital. What faith!"

Ginny laughed. "Did you hear the nurse ask Beth who Jochebed was? What made you think of her?" Ginny poured her coffee and sat beside Missy.

"I don't know—she popped into my head. Holy Spirit, I guess. I was thinking about reading that story to Laura this morning. Would it make her sad, do you think? I don't want her to be sad. She did a noble thing."

"She did, but being sad is a stage she's got to go through. She'll grieve for her baby, but grief is good if you work through it. That's why Beth encourages the girls to hold their babies."

"Laura's mom said she was mean and had no mercy."

"Humph, she should talk! We've seen plenty of girls, and it's better. Maybe it's harder at the time, but they get through their grief better."

Missy stood to check her rolls. "One day at a time, I keep saying to myself. If God wants me to put this little girl in a home, He'll give me the courage to do it. I want what's best for her." Missy held the hot pan in the oven mitt. "Can I name her, Ginny?"

Ginny looked over her cup, appraising Missy. "Put that down before you burn yourself. No one's ever asked me that before. Girls have called their babies little names, like junior or such, but you mean, actually give her a name?" Missy set the pan down and nodded. "Most of the time, only the girls planning to keep their babies give them a name. Do you want to keep your baby?"

"Yes, I do, but I don't think I will. Because of the circumstances...the rape and all...it would be better to place her with a family who won't have that history with her, who will love her for who she is—not that I don't love her!"

Ginny had learned to listen, and she remained silent, but when Missy asked her if she believed she could love her baby, a rape baby, Ginny replied, "I know you love your baby, Missy, and she knows it too. You've given your baby a wonderful gift, a Mother's love. I admire you for overcoming all that and still loving her."

"I'm telling Beth I want to see some of those family profiles. I want to start praying for Gracie's family right now."

"You're calling her Gracie?"

"She's taught my heart to sing when I thought it would never sing again, you know? She makes it all worthwhile."

Ginny walked to the coffeepot for a refill, turning her face from Missy so she wouldn't see her tears. "It's a wonderful way to look at it, but you can't name someone else's child for them."

"I know. It's my little name for her. They can name her whatever. Maybe they'll name her after a mother or grandmother—I'd love to have a baby and name her Alice."

"She'd be well-named. Your mother is a fine woman."

"Do you think these are done?" Missy showed Ginny the toothpick she'd pulled out of the bread.

"Definitely," Ginny said, "but I'm not waiting on these lazy girls to get up before I have one." The two of them sat together, swapping farm stories. Finally, Ginny rose. "I'm going to get my shower before everyone starts. It's been quite a week." Ginny was mentally juggling beds. She set her cup in the sink. Myra's departure had given them the flexibility to put Cathy and her mother in a bedroom, and this weekend, Julie and Missy would stay there while Candy bunked with Cathy. Next weekend, Audrey was returning. Beth had been working with her and talking to a lawyer in Pittsburgh about her situation.

Candy bounced into Missy's bedroom. "I get to sleep with Cathy this weekend." She stripped the beds and put clean sheets on in two rooms. Candy was a worker. Missy was singing—the girls loved to hear her sing.

Laura was about to come downstairs for breakfast, but she was currently still in her room, trying to get dressed and fussing because nothing fit and Missy's guests were coming. Michelle was laughing at her.

"You aren't going to shrink in a day! Give it some time. You're going to rupture yourself—do you plan to start aerobics tomorrow?"

Ginny stuck her head in the door. "If you do too much, we'll keep you up here next week."

"I'll be good," Laura promised. "Please let me go downstairs, please."

"Missy's got hot rolls, but these girls have got to go to school, so wait to take a shower."

"Yes, Ma'am."

"The homebound teacher is coming today for Cathy. Would you like to work with her too?"

"Sure. It'll give me something to do."

Missy thought a day had never gone so slowly. She kept sneaking a look at the clock on the wall, watching the hands that never moved. She climbed into the bus, looking for Candy, who walked over from the GED class to ride home. She saw her waving to a cute guy, who grinned at her—the infamous Joe!

Candy dropped down in the seat beside her, and Missy bumped shoulders. "Why didn't you tell me he's so cute, girl?"

Candy blushed. "He's a nice guy. How's Laura doing?"

"She's weepy, but Miss Ginny says it's normal. She's grieving for the baby. She still thinks she did the right thing."

Missy saw Candy's hand drop to her belly, and she rubbed her own as they sat in silence.

They'd been home about fifteen minutes when Ginny brought some sandwiches into the living room, where they were sitting with Laura and watching a movie. They all felt relief, giggling together without Myra's harsh words. Ginny looked out the window.

"Missy, does Jimmy have a truck? That's got to be his red hair."

"They can't be here this early. Oh, they are—they are!" Missy flung open the heavy door and flew down the steps.

Jimmy swung her up, laughing. "You've gotten a bit heavier since I last lifted you, Sis."

"Jimmy," Julie said reproachfully. "Missy, look at you. You look—"

"Pregnant," Missy finished for her. The girls hugged.

"That isn't what I was going to say. You look wonderful! You glow. I thought you'd be all sad."

"Sometimes I get sad, but not when you guys are here! Come on in. I want to introduce you to everybody. Get Julie's bag, Jimmy."

"Yes, Ma'am." Jimmy winked at Julie and lifted her bag out of the truck, following them up the steps in two strides.

"Get in here," Missy urged. "We're only going to do this once. Jimmy, you remember Miss Ginny and Cathy?" He grinned and nodded. "Julie, this is Michelle, Candy, and Laura. Everyone, this is my big brother." She put her arm around him.

"Hi, Jimmy," they all chorused.

"Julie is my forever friend. Candy's giving us her room this weekend, Julie. Come on, Jimmy." Missy waved him upstairs. "I'll show you where it is." She led them upstairs and down the hall to the far end.

When the West Virginians came back downstairs, the girls paused the movie and talked to them. Michelle told them about the community college, where she had started, adding proudly that Missy began there every morning. "And Candy's got herself a boyfriend in her GED class." Candy blushed furiously and threw a pillow at her. They learned that Laura and Cathy had a homebound teacher, and they filled them in on the details of Myra.

Miss Ginny announced dinner would be served as soon as Candy and Cathy set the table. "Jimmy is taking Missy out to dinner." She talked to him about nearby restaurants, and they left.

"Man, Julie isn't Missy's friend. She's Jimmy's girlfriend. Did you see the way he looked at her?" Cathy put her hand on her heart and sighed. "What I'd give to have a handsome guy like that look at me that way. I thought I had a chance, but she's a nice girl, not a..." Cathy's words drifted off, and she blinked.

Candy put her arm around her. "Let's go set the table."

While they were driving, Missy told them about Laura's baby, thankful she'd told Jimmy on the phone so he could clue Julie in.

"Gosh, Missy, could you do that?" Julie asked. "Have you made any decisions?"

"It's been hard on her, and she cries, but you should see how happy those parents are!" Missy described the scene in the hospital. "I never realized how wonderful adoption could be." She described her conversation with Ginny that morning. "What do you think, Jimmy? What do you think Mom would say?"

"She says it's a choice you have to make. The volunteers at the Pregnancy Center have pounded it into her head. I went over once, but she's been several times—last week, as a matter of fact."

"I've talked to your mom about it, and Jimmy's right. She made us promise to leave you alone and stand behind your decision. She'll be fine, Missy. She worries about you. She'd be sad if you made a decision for anyone else."

"The folks at the Center are terrific. I'm glad she's going down there. God has some amazing folks in His family. I've never realized how many people serve Him in so many ways." She told them about the ladies who came to clean for them and the elderly, retired man who kept up the yard at Hope House. "Of course, you know about Miss Ginny and Beth—she's the social worker here. And we have a group therapist. The folks at church are wonderful, always giving us casseroles and desserts. One lady in the choir picks me up for rehearsal."

Julie shuddered when Missy told her about Myra and laughed at her descriptions of some of the fun times they'd had, including the day at the mall. Julie filled her friend in on all the news from home, but Missy thought the most exciting news was before her eyes—she saw Jimmy put his arm around Julie, and when she looked at him, Missy knew her best friend's crush on Jimmy was turning into something else.

"Here's what I want to know. When did Julie become 'Jules,' Jimmy? What's going on between you two?"

Julie ducked her head, and Jimmy said, "She's been pestering me to death about you and hanging around all the time. She grew on me." He pulled her closer.

"All I needed to do was leave, and you finally saw each other?"

"Guess so," Jimmy replied.

Missy was happy the two people she loved most in the world were falling in love, but the next week Cathy teased about losing her chance with Missy's hunky brother. Jimmy was taken, but Candy was quiet. She didn't talk much about Joe, but she wasn't interested in Jimmy. She looked forward to going to class, however, and any time Missy could spare from her own studies, she helped her.

One afternoon Joe followed them into the house. They introduced him to Ginny, who said nothing after she welcomed him but smiled as she put another plate of cookies on the table.

"I told Joe that Missy was gonna help me with grammar, and he might as well listen in. He was brought up in the country, like me."

"Where are you from, Joe?"

"Kentucky, Ma'am," he drawled. He rose, put his dishes in the sink, and gathered his books together.

Missy pointed to the dining room table. "We'll work in there." And they did. She went through the parts of speech and noun and verb agreement.

"Okay, I'm getting this, but isn't swimming a verb?" Joe asked.

"Yes. It's an action word—verbs are action and being words, remember?"

"But if you say, 'swimming is my favorite sport,' it's the subject of the sentence, and you say you need a noun as subject."

Missy laughed. "Smart guy! A verb ending in 'ing' can be a gerund. It's a verb used as a noun."

Joe groaned. "I thought I was getting this. Will that be on the test?"

"Maybe, but you spotted it right away, and you knew it was the subject of the sentence."

Joe stood. "I need to fix supper for my mom before I leave for work. Thanks, Missy, you helped me out a lot. Thanks for inviting me, Candy. Mrs. Randall, where's the bus stop?"

"Beth will be leaving soon, Joe. She'll be glad to drop you off."

Hearing her name, Beth came in, pulling on her coat as she walked. When Joe told her where he lived, she assured him it wasn't too far out of her way, and they walked out together.

Ginny turned to the kitchen. "Fried chicken tonight, girls."

"Smells yum, Miss G," they answered, and they cleared off the table. That night they talked about what a nice young man Joe seemed to be and about Cathy's mother, who was returning on Friday for another weekend—which meant Candy would be sleeping in with Missy.

"Maybe you'll talk in your sleep and tell me more about Joe," Missy teased. "What is it they say? If you put someone's hand in warm water and ask them questions when they're asleep, they'll tell all?"

"No, you nut," Laura said, "they'll pee the bed." The girls giggled. "Come on, 'Chelle, let's help."

Missy observed Cathy when her mother came the next weekend. With Beth and John's help, they learned about one another, and communication brought forgiveness. During one session, Missy sat on the couch outside the counseling room, praying for her friend. Cathy came out in tears, angry with her father and desperate about how to tell her mother she had been a prostitute. Audrey was confused about "all the religion" at Hope House, but she acknowledged her daughter was much gentler. She had pressed to be with Cathy when the baby came, and she was sad that she wanted Missy and Ginny. Beth explained the special bonds the girls shared with one another as they went through their struggles, and Audrey reluctantly accepted Cathy's choice. With Beth's help, Audrey secured an attorney, who obtained support for her, enabling her to move to Columbus and rent an apartment big enough for the three of them: herself, Cathy, and the baby. She planned to get an associate degree in medical billing at the community college so she would be more employable. It was rocky at times, but when Stanley was born, Audrey's evident delight and devotion to her grandson brought them closer, and when her time at Hope House was over, Cathy moved into her mother's apartment willingly. She came back for group meetings and continued to go to the church, and Audrey attended with her. Cathy's joy overflowed one Sunday when her mother responded to the altar call.

With continued support, Cathy and her mother's relationship developed. Audrey learned to trust her daughter's love, and Cathy realized she had rejected her mother as much as she thought her mother rejected her. They both sought one another's forgiveness and learned to give each other the space they needed as two adults living together.

Missy was glad to see Cathy often, but she also enjoyed her new roommate—Candy. A new girl, Jill, came to Hope House. Jill was friendly and funny, and they awaited yet another new resident. Laura moved out as well, but instead of returning home, she moved in with Cathy and her mom. The girls planned a shower for Candy, who agreed to marry Joe when she turned eighteen on the second of November. John worked with them to make decisions. Joe was 24 and in the electrician program at the vocational school. He lived with his mother, who had been sexually abused herself and loved Candy like a daughter. Candy wanted to wait to marry after the baby was born. Joe supported her decision to keep and raise the child, but he insisted they marry before the birth so his name would be on the birth certificate. Promising her and John that he would not approach her intimately until after the birth, when they were mutually ready, Joe convinced her, and they were married at Hope House.

After the wedding, Missy was worn out. She had decorated and baked, and when the couple went home, she collapsed.

"I was afraid you'd have that baby before you could pull this off, Missy."

"I prayed hard about that. I adore Candy and Joe, and I think they'll make it. She's blessed..." Missy's voice quavered. "To have a father for her baby. Joe will be a good father."

"His mother is a love too," Ginny added. "She'll be a mother to Candy. She's more than ready to help with the baby."

"Candy felt worthless. She said she didn't deserve Joe's love. His mom's acceptance and understanding helped her a lot."

"John's counseling is helping them break the cycles of abuse," Ginny said. "I do believe we've had miracles this season at Hope House, and you've been a large part of it. Your godly wisdom, your prayers, your love for all of us. I wonder whether God brought you here for us to help you or for you to be a part of our lives."

Missy stepped into Ginny's arms. "It's my turn. I need you more than I can tell you."

"And we'll be here for you, sweetie."

"I know, and I'm sure about my choice. I love Gracie's parents. They're perfect for my girl. But it'll be hard." Ginny held her while she wept.

Missy continued going to school. She loved her program, enjoyed the choirs at church and school, and didn't want to be homebound. Beth worked with her guidance counselor at Elkins High and even found out about an interior decorating degree at WVU. Missy set her sights, recognizing she'd have a life after Gracie.

Gracie

Right before Thanksgiving break, Ginny heard someone moving around downstairs in the middle of the night, and Missy was on the phone. "Mom, you need to come. Can Jimmy come?"

Ginny was by her side when she hung up. "Were you going to wake me, young lady?

"I was, but it's early, like two o'clock or something. I feel bad, not too bad, no blood or anything, but I feel yucky, and it's a long drive for them."

"They told us at the office the other day that it'd be anytime now. Do you want a cup of tea?"

"I want my mommy."

Ginny leaned Missy's head against her breast. "She's on her way, honey. She'll be here. For all you've been through, you've been blessed to have your sweet mother."

Missy rubbed her belly. "You wait, Gracie. Wait until your Uncle Jimmy gets here." By the time the other girls came downstairs, Missy was lying on her side on the couch.

Michelle crept in and knelt beside her. "Can I do anything? I'll tell the Prof today and get your assignments. Pretty good timing—we're off Wednesday for Thanksgiving break."

"Thanks, 'Chelle," Missy mumbled.

"You sound like Laura. Didn't God work things out well for her to be able to live with Cathy and her mom and not have to go back to her mean old mother? I'll call them, Missy. They'll be excited and praying for you too. Hang in there."

"Go to school, Michelle. I don't want you to get in trouble."

Michelle leaned over and placed a soft kiss on Missy's brow. "I love you, Missy O'Malley."

"Love you too."

Shortly after the girls left for school, Beth arrived. She came over to check on Missy, and she helped her to the bathroom. When Missy sat, the floods came, and Beth called for Ginny.

"We're not waiting, Missy. Your mom is on the way. They can find you at the hospital. I'm calling the midwife. Let's load her up, Beth. I put the sheets in the van earlier." Ginny realized how miserable Missy was when she offered no protest.

At the hospital, because she was pre-admitted, they took her directly to the birthing room. Missy never complained and smiled at the nurse, who recognized her.

"You're pretty familiar with the routine, Missy. Are you ready for your turn?"

"Do I have a choice?" Missy joked.

"I'd say not," the nurse replied.

"I'm glad she's here today. I like her," Missy told Ginny.

The midwife entered the room, scrubbed up, and examined her. She told them it'd be a few hours yet, but Missy was moving along.

Ginny and Beth moved into the hallway as the midwife was talking to Missy.

"She wants to wait for her mother to get here," Ginny said.

"Babies don't wait," Beth reminded her, "but she's got a while yet. I'll go call the adoptive parents and stay at the Home until things start to pop around here."

"How long is their trip? I thought they lived in Richmond."

"They do, but after her appointment the day before yesterday, they came over. I heard from them last night. They're at the Hampton."

"I love all my girls, but Missy is going to tear my heart out."

"She'll take it hard—she loves deeply."

"And she loves her baby."

"God will see her through. Call me, and keep me posted."

When the housemother went into the room, she found Missy lying on her side, not quite asleep but peacefully resting.

"Would you read to me?" came the quiet voice from the bed.

Seeing Missy's Bible beside her, Ginny picked it up. She read her some well-marked Psalms and turned to the story of baby Moses. "Would you like me to read about Jochobed, or would it be too painful?"

Missy smiled at the memory they shared. "Please read it."

Ginny spooned ice chips into her mouth, and she remained meek and uncomplaining as the time passed. The midwife and the nurses were in and out.

Where's Mom? Surely they are here by now. I hope nothing's wrong. God, bring them here safely—and soon! Missy saw an aide quietly roll the instrument tray into the room.

The door cracked, and Alice stuck her head inside. "Is she doing okay?"

"Mom?"

"I'm here, precious. We had awful traffic and road construction. We came straight to the hospital. I figured you'd be here by now."

"Is Jimmy here?"

"He's parking the car. He'll be right in."

Missy closed her eyes. Another contraction was rolling over her, and Ginny signaled Alice to come by her side. "She's never complained, but they rolled the cart in, and I knew it wouldn't be long."

Alice pushed Missy's dark hair off her brow, a mother's soothing gesture. "I like your haircut."

"Daddy won't recognize me without the braid."

"All you have to do is sing, honey."

Jimmy entered the room, looking pale and anxious, but he relaxed when he saw that his sister was still and quiet. "Looks like we made in in plenty of time." Missy closed her eyes, and her hand dropped to her belly.

The midwife came in and ordered everyone to wash. "I'm glad you made it. I thought she'd hold onto the baby until midnight if you didn't get here." She patted Missy's knee. "Let's get you in position. Are you ready to do this?"

Missy nodded, and the nurse dropped the end of the bed into the birthing position, telling Jimmy to move to the head of the bed and hold his sister's hand. Missy grabbed his hand and held on with a fierce grip.

"You are ready, girl. Let's push with the next contraction."

And Missy pushed. Jimmy had seen linebackers that didn't push as hard. Sweat popped out on her brow, and Alice gently wiped it.

"Good one," the midwife encouraged. "Another with your next one."

Jimmy looked across the bed, and Missy thought she heard him whisper, "I'm glad I'm not a woman!" But she focused on her labor and her mother's gentle whispered words of encouragement.

When the triumphant wail of a newborn pierced the air, Jimmy saw Missy's radiant face and thought he'd never experienced anything this beautiful. Missy reached for her little girl, and the midwife laid her on Missy's tummy before she turned to deliver the afterbirth.

"Hi, Gracie," Missy whispered, her eyes bright with tears.

Alice almost reached to care for her granddaughter—she was a maternity nurse, after all, and it was instinctive. "You did a fine job, sweetie. She's beautiful."

"No stitches. Very good job." Knowing her patient, the midwife pulled down the covering sheet. "Let's do a little skin to skin, Mom."

The baby looked for Missy and relaxed when she was laid on her mommy's warm tummy. The end of the bed was pulled into position, and Alice elevated the head. Missy brought the baby to her breast.

"Would it be all right...could I...could I nurse her, just this once?"

The midwife slowly exhaled. "It will make it harder for you."

"I know, but it's better—the colostrum will clean her out, and nursing helps my womb."

"True, but I'm thinking about your heart, Missy."

"It's already broken," Missy whispered.

Looking at the midwife, who nodded, the nurse helped Missy settle the babe to her breast. Gracie rooted and took hold, drawing deeply from her mother. With tears streaming down her face, Missy smiled and stroked her baby's cheek.

Jimmy turned abruptly and looked out the window, his chest heaving as he tried to gulp in air.

When Gracie had nursed on both sides and was tired, the nurse took her and wrapped her in a pink blanket. "What's next?" she asked.

Beth had slipped in and watched. She went over to the bed. "Your call, Missy."

Missy took a deep breath. "I'm ready. Can I hold her once more?"

"Of course." Beth signaled to the nurse, who brought the baby to her mother.

Missy reached up for the pink bundle and cradled her in her arms. She leaned over to place a soft kiss on her cheek and whispered, "Goodbye, Gracie. Mommy loves you." She looked up at Beth. "I can't do it. I wanted to be brave, like Laura, but I can't. Would you take her to Lee and tell her I love her?"

"I will."

The nurse stepped forward and put the baby in the bassinette. As they left the room, Missy began to recite the Twenty-Third Psalm, and Alice quietly joined her. Jimmy turned his back on the room once again, his fists in his pockets as he stared out the window.

"Mom, go to Lee. You'll love her. They are precious. I want you to know I've done the right thing. I'm sure."

At Missy's urging, Alice left and caught up with Beth as she got to the door.

"Forgive me, Alice," Beth said. "I bet you'd like to stop by the nursery and rock her, wouldn't you?"

"Could I?"

"Of course."

Alice rocked Gracie, holding her first grandchild. Beth heard her singing a lullaby and wondered if it was Gaelic.

"I should get back to Missy, but she wanted me to meet her parents."

"Come on then." They walked into the room together.

Lee stood there. Her hands were trembling, and her husband eased her down into a chair. She saw Alice and said, "You're her mother. She looks exactly like you."

"She's a little brown Indian girl, like me, but I think this one's got her grandfather's Irish side. I believe you've got a redhead. Her eyes could be sea blue or as green as emeralds. She'll be beautiful."

Gracie rested quietly in Lee's arms. "She is beautiful," her daddy said.

"Missy wanted me to thank you. I need to get back—she's having a tough time, but she knows she's done the right thing. She doesn't have a single doubt. She trusts you."

Lee nodded without a word, and her husband knelt beside the rocker. He caressed the baby's fair cheek, looked up, and softly said, "Tell her thank you."

Alice nodded. She walked into the hall, shoving her fist into her mouth. Missy's nurse was waiting for her, and she drew her into an embrace, walking her down the hall. "I have to get myself together for Missy."

"You need to get this out too. We've loved Missy around here. She helped two of her Hope House friends deliver. She's a wonderful person, and now we know where she got it." The nurse pulled Alice into an office and let her cry. She rinsed a cloth in cold water and handed it to her.

"Thanks." Alice stood and straightened her shoulders. She rested the cloth on her eyes a moment and handed it back. "For everything," she added.

"They're moving her to another floor now."

Alice quickened her step to follow.

* * *

Beth left the new parents to get acquainted and returned to Missy's room to help gather up her belongings. Hearing her enter, Jimmy swung around from where he stood by the window.

"Are you sure she wants to do this? She sobbed and sobbed until they gave her a shot. Is this really the best thing?"

Beth reminded him they had worked on the decision for months. Missy had met the adoptive parents, corresponded with them, talked to them on the phone, and thought through her options.

"Maybe she likes them—Missy is tenderhearted. Maybe she doesn't want to disappoint them. You saw her. She loves that baby. It's too hard on her."

Beth placed her hand on Jimmy's arm and looked up at him. "Too hard for Missy, Jimmy, or too hard for you?"

Jimmy began to weep. "I can't stand to see her suffer."

Beth knew about the night of the rape, and she could only imagine the guilt this brother felt. "It is hard. It does hurt—maybe it always will—but we need you and Alice to be brave for her."

"I'm sorry. You know what you're doing." He swiped his nose on his sweater sleeve.

"It's all right. My husband says it takes a real man to cry. The next few weeks will be tough going, but you will get through this—and it would help you to see those parents. She has given them an incredible gift, and they're grateful."

Missy was never alone. Alice and Jimmy never left the hospital, and when she returned to Hope House the next day, Missy sent Jimmy back to the hospital, instructing him to buy the biggest bouquet he could find and take it to the adoptive couple. He did like his niece's parents. They were warm, loving, and very grateful.

"Her hair looks red, and I hope she has your curls," Lee said. "Isn't she beautiful?" Jimmy couldn't speak, but he saw why Missy loved them, and he did feel better. Alice stopped by the next day and met the new parents. She kissed her granddaughter good-bye one last time.

Missy's family remained in Columbus the full waiting period, three days, until she signed the surrender papers giving up her claim to her daughter. They saw the Hope House girls gather around, including Candy, Laura, and Cathy. Laura had placed her baby, but Cathy's son was home with his grandmother. The girls who had given birth told them how Missy had helped them, and Candy complained because she'd be gone before she delivered.

"We'll be there for you, girl, and Joe will be right by your side. But we'll call Missy to sing to you—her singing carried me through," Cathy said. "She has such a beautiful voice! Do you sing, Mrs. O'Malley?"

"That comes from her father. She sang to the sun when she was in her crib."

"You call me, and I'll sing to you, Candy," Missy promised

Alice and Jimmy felt better about leaving Missy after watching her friends supporting her, and on the drive home, they talked about how close those girls had gotten over the months. They were silent much of the drive, however, remembering the amazing courage of the one they loved.

Michelle brought home Missy's final exams in English and math, and the sewing teacher at school wanted to give her an A without any additional work, but the music teacher enlisted her help with gowns for the Christmas program. Missy needed to keep busy, so she worked on the sewing machine they delivered to her at Hope House. Her CAD teacher waved a portfolio at Ginny, exclaiming, "Look at all the work the child has churned out! I'd give her a higher grade if I had one." Missy had added a music course, dropping business finance, when the church discovered her voice.

Missy wanted to go home, but she wanted to sing in the Christmas program. Ginny called the doctor, and he brought her in four weeks after she gave birth. He told Beth that Missy had an easy birth and that they let those girls get up and walk out after a surgical abortion. He told her to follow up with the doctor who'd seen her at home, and he released her, telling her she could go home for Christmas.

Beth called her mother, and Jimmy drove all night to be there for the school production. He stayed with Beth and her husband and got in a little nap before it started. He put on a dress shirt and new jeans, and he rode with them in their van.

Missy had a solo in the finale, and Jimmy was amazed. He loved to hear his sister sing, but her voice was richer, truer, more trained. The audience made no move to leave—they were spellbound. The choir director shoved Missy back on stage, handing her a mic.

"What should I sing? We didn't rehearse anything."

"Sing anything, a Capella. You can do it. Go!"

A single spot focused on Missy as she stood, looking down. Nodding, she looked up as if she heard something. Surely, firmly, she sang:

Jesus, keep me near the cross,
There a precious fountain,
Free to all, a healing stream,
Flows from Calvary's mountain.

In the Cross, in the Cross,
Be my glory ever,
Till my raptured soul shall find
Rest beyond the river.

Near the cross, a trembling soul,
Love and mercy found me;
There the Bright and Morning Star
Shed its beams around me.

Near the cross, O Lamb of God,
Bring its scenes before me;
Help me walk from day to day,
With its shadows o'er me.

Near the cross I'll watch and wait,
Hoping, trusting ever,
Till I reach the golden strand,
Just beyond the river.

No one moved. The auditorium was silent. Missy bowed from the waist, and the place erupted. One clap, another, until a firestorm swept the place.

Tom leaned over to Beth and whispered, "You can't keep the Holy Spirit out of schools when He lives and moves so powerfully in someone." She reached for his hand, and their fingers intertwined.

Missy smiled brightly. "Let's do Christmas carols, everyone!" And the crowd joined her. When the house lights came up, Christmas break began. Back at Hope House, former and current residents, volunteers, and church members crowded in for Missy's farewell party. It was late, and Tom and Missy both insisted Jimmy go back for a nap before starting home.

The next morning, Missy's suitcases stood by the door. She hugged all her friends and clung to Miss Ginny. "Give Beth, Tom, and her kids hugs for me. I love you all." Jimmy lifted her into the truck, and she waved out the window, knowing she would always carry Hope House in her heart.

To keep from crying, Missy turned to her brother and asked how Julie was. "Jules is good, Missy. She said she'd come stay the weekend if you wanted. She never misses church now."

"Maybe I shouldn't warn you, but she's expecting jewelry for Christmas."

He reached into his pocket and pulled out a small box. "Maybe something like this?"

Missy opened the velvet case and saw the tiny, sparkling diamond. "It's beautiful, Jimmy! She'll love it."

"It's not what she deserves, but I'm only a small-town grease monkey. We thought we'd get married after graduation."

Helping Jimmy

Jimmy couldn't handle the crying bouts Missy couldn't conceal. He urged their mom to call Hope House, and Beth suggested her physician might prescribe something, but Missy refused. Alice tried to explain a woman's hormones to Jimmy, but he withdrew and began drinking. He didn't party, and he went to work, but every night he sat down with a six pack and drank until he was asleep. He was morose, jumpy, and silent.

Jimmy adored Julie, and he knew she loved her ring, so he was stunned when she gave it back to him.

"I've seen your father, Jimmy, and I can't live like your mom did. How can you do this to Missy and your mom? Haven't they been through enough? Mr. Andrews will fire you if you keep it up. Because it'll get worse, you know?" Then she turned her back and slammed the door behind her as she walked out.

He heard his sister on the phone one night. The traitor.

"You did the right thing, Julie," she said. "Hang tough. I learned about co-dependency at Hope House." But he didn't know she and their mother were talking to the counselor and planning a confrontation.

Friday night, Jimmy came in from work, his usual six-pack in his hands. He looked around and saw a room full of people. "What's going on? You ganging up on me?"

His boss, Mr. Andrews, put a hand on his shoulder. "We want to help, son."

"We all love you, Jimmy," Missy said. "We can't bear to see you destroy yourself."

Jimmy exploded in fury. "It's Dad's fault. If he hadn't run off, none of this would've happened. Missy wouldn't have lost her baby. I hate him! You never threw him out all those years—are you throwing me out, Mom?"

Pastor Potter calmly replied, "No one's throwing you out. We're throwing you a lifeline. I have a place lined up where you can get some help. Your mom's giving you until next Friday to make up your mind."

"I can quit anytime," Jimmy vowed. "Watch me."

"Next Friday, same time," Mr. Andrews said. "I'll hold your job if you go to rehab, but if you continue drinking, I have no choice but to fire you."

By ten the same evening, Jimmy was popping his first beer, and over the weekend, he sat in the chair, staring into space. On Sunday, he shaved with a shaky hand and went to church. At the altar, he asked his pastor to take him to Rehabilitation.

He was not allowed to call anyone for two weeks, but the first call he made was to Julie. "I'm gonna do this; I promise. Don't give up on me, babe. I'm doing it for us—for you and me and for Mom and Missy. I'm sorry. I'll work hard. I don't want to be my father."

"I love you, Jimmy, but..."

"I know. I must prove myself, and I will. How's school?"

Julie had started nursing school and loved it.

Jimmy stayed at Center for twelve weeks. When he came home, he was lean and bright. The pastor dropped him off at the house, and Julie was there. He swung her around, then caught Missy by the waist and did the same to her. He drove by the shop Saturday to thank Mr. Andrews, who shook his hand and said he'd see him bright and early on Monday. He took Julie with him to visit various programs, and anytime the folks from the recovery program were in the area, he gave his testimony. Under their auspices, he started a weekly program in Elkins.

During Christmas break, a sober Jimmy and a radiant Julie stood before their pastor to exchange their vows. Jimmy sang a song called "Forever Begins this Day," which he wrote for his beloved. The maid of honor never lost track of her responsibilities, but she looked at the cross and whispered,

"Thank you, Father. You gave me Gracie, and You taught me how to help Jimmy. Keep him on the journey he's begun, with a fine help-mate beside him."

Jimmy kissed Julie tenderly, and they walked down the aisle and into a beautiful falling snow. The reception was in the fellowship hall, and they left for their honeymoon.

Over a cup of tea at home, Alice and Missy reflected on the lovely ceremony, how beautiful Julie looked, how handsome Jimmy was, and how happy they were. "If I'd known how to help your dad," Alice said, "maybe he'd be here with us."

"I thanked God for Gracie and all I learned at Hope House. I miss her, but I'm glad I made that choice. I'm content, and I was able go to Morgantown for school—what are you going to do when Jimmy and I are both gone, Mom?"

"It'll be a change."

PART TWO

Sixteen Years Later

Getting On With Life

On a Tuesday in late May, Missy heard her door chimes. She looked at the grandfather clock in her showroom. *Who could that be? I didn't have any appointments. Why didn't I pull the shades and lock the door?*

A tall guy in his mid-thirties turned at the sound of her boots clicking on the hardwood floor. He held out his hand. "Hello, I'm Tim Raines, with Hefner Construction. We're working on the new subdivision between here and Belington. Have you heard about it?" He smiled and held out a card.

"I did hear something. What can I do for you, Mr. Raines? I'm Missy O'Malley."

"You're the Missy of Missy's Interiors?" He sounded surprised.

"The same. How can I help you?"

He fumbled around in his pocket and brought out one of her brochures. "I thought, with your reputation—I read this. You graduated from WVU with a degree in Interior Decorating. You worked at JCPenney in the Meadowbrook Mall, at Lowe's in Buckhannon, and the one here in Elkins. I thought—I was expecting someone older."

She laughed, a merry, musical sound. "Sorry to disappoint you. I had those jobs right out of college, and I kept trying to get closer to home. I'm a mountain girl. I felt stifled in those jobs, not as creative as I wanted to be, so I wrote up a business plan, took out a gargantuan loan, and opened this shop several years ago."

He looked around. "Nice place. Tasteful. Small."

"I buy what I need for my current projects by keeping friendly relation-ships with local crafters. I do a lot of special orders, and I store some things at my brother's place. If you'd prefer someone more mature...?"

"No, I'm not disappointed. Delighted, in fact. Nice to meet you." Tim stuck out his hand, which swallowed her tiny one. His eyes were bright blue, the color of the summer skies, and his eyes crinkled nicely at the corners. When he wasn't smiling, his skin was paler along his laugh lines.

Missy looked down in confusion and extricated her hand. "Nice to meet you."

"I...uh...as I said, I'm working with this new development, and several people told me you were the best around. We're looking for someone to furnish our model house, at least a room or two. Make it inviting to lure in prospective buyers." He fished around for one of their fliers and handed it to her.

"I'm usually closed on Tuesday afternoons to do book work, look around for furniture and such, so I have some time. Let me pull this shade, and we can discuss what you want. It's a warm day for May," she said, looking over her shoulder. "Would you like some lemonade?"

"That sounds lovely. Yes, please. May I help?"

"I'll just be a minute." She went to the back, returning with two tall, slender glasses on a flowered tray, which she set on the table in front of the couch. She patted it and asked him to sit. Kicking off her ankle boots, she tucked her feet under her.

"Mmm, good. Homemade lemonade." Tim looked around the shop. "I saw some photos in your album. It looks like you're doing well."

"I've poured my heart into this business, and it's taking off, paying the bills and already a big chunk on the loan. It's 12-14 hour days, building a reputation and a clientele. As you noticed, I don't keep a lot of inventory, and I'd need money down and a budget for my work."

"I'm sure that wouldn't be a problem." Tim outlined the details of what his company had in mind, and he suggested, if she had time, that they ride out to the development.

She laughed. "I have time. This is my job, Mr. Raines, trolling up clients. We could stop by the hotel on the way out of town, and you could see one of my projects. I did their re-model last fall." She stood. "My blue Liberty is in the back."

He pointed to his double cab, over-sized truck in front of the store.

"I'll pull out of the driveway and follow you," she suggested.

"Let me follow you to the hotel, and then I'll lead."

"Good enough." She locked up and pulled out onto the street. Pulling into the parking lot, she hopped out of her Jeep and waved to him to follow her into the lobby.

"Hey, Missy. How's my favorite girl?" A balding man behind the desk smiled at her.

She leaned over the counter and gave him a peck on the cheek. "I need you to help me sell a job, Guy. Another one—don't charge me commission!" She introduced the manager to Tim before walking him around the lobby, pointing out the artifacts and local crafts scattered around the warm room. A bright Native American motif carpet circled in front of a stone fireplace.

"Missy here, she did more than we asked. She talked me into this tile—promised it would be better than carpet, easier to clean up—and she was right. We paid more for tile, but we've already saved by not having to replace carpet all the time. You can't find a better bang for your buck than Missy O'Malley. She pinches pennies until they squeal."

"See why I brought you? This man has sold three or four jobs for me."

"Everybody who comes in here can't believe it's the same place. It looks much bigger with the big open window. I'm glad we kept the fireplace."

"It's the centerpiece of the room, Guy—the character of the place. I matched everything around it. Seen enough, Mr. Raines? We can head south now—lead the way." Tim looked impressed, so she looked back at Guy and gave him a thumbs-up. When she turned back, Tim was patiently holding the door for her. "Oops, sorry!"

He chuckled. "I like it. I was amazed by the way you made a functional space warm and inviting—and Appalachian."

"I told you, I'm a mountain maid. I love to work with local crafters. Did you notice the quilt on the west wall? A hometown quilting group. Guy hands out their cards, and many of the visitors stop by the crafters co-op and buy."

"It matched the drapes."

"I twisted one of the lady's arms to sew it for me, using the material from the quilt."

When they pulled into the development, Missy was disappointed. Three ordinary houses were repeated one after the other, row upon row. She thought this guy could be more creative than that. Not her cup of tea. She pulled on the handle of the jeep and hopped out before Tim could get to her vehicle, and she followed him to the door. As he pushed it open, she noticed the ring on his finger. *Darn. But you can't expect a hunk like that to be unattached. I'll get a job out of this anyway.*

She walked into the living area, looked at the beige walls and carpet, and tried not to shudder.

As if he read her thoughts, Tim shrugged. "It's a middle-class subdivision. Not like your beautiful work, I'm afraid, but we pop them out. At least they're solid and not factory built."

Missy walked over to the fireplace, rubbing her hand along its smooth surface. "This is a nice touch—I like the craftsmanship of the molding here."

"It's a fellow by the name of Ken—what is his last name?"

"Perini, Ken Perini. I should have known."

"He's the foreman on this site. Great guy. He added this on his own... asked me if he could deviate from the plans and showed me this. When I explained our financial constraints, he said he wouldn't charge more."

"Ken goes to my church. He helped my brother build his house. You should see his place. It's a log cabin built mostly from scrap material left over from various job sites. His dad does strictly handcrafting, and Ken works in the shop with him, but he says he has to make a living."

"What do you think? I mean, about the job? Could you do anything with it?" Tim swept his arm around the room.

"This living area and what else?"

"Maybe one bedroom. Do you want to see?" He walked her around the one-story home.

The rest of the house was what she expected of a cookie cutter subdivision. "It's almost a bungalow, isn't it?" She looked around. "Furnish two rooms, window dressings...You said I could have some start-up money? I'll refund it and take the stuff out if you don't like it."

"Sure. Why don't you get us a proposal together?"

"I might need a ball park figure. This isn't my usual job. It's rather...It's well-constructed, but..."

"But?"

"It's rather...uh...plain. Could we throw some color on the walls? You do want curtains of some sort? Or just furnishings?"

Tim grinned. "Tactful. Yeah, we could do curtains and mid-grade furniture. No pricey antiques, but not trailer park stuff either."

"I don't do trailer stuff, Mr. Raines."

Tim looked chagrined. "A little levity. I didn't mean to offend."

"I didn't mean to sound offended, sorry. I need work, and I'll do whatever you want." Missy began pacing off the room, fishing in her pocket for a note pad.

"I'll send you dimensions." He looked on her card. "Is this your email?"

"Yes, and that would be a big help. Thanks." Missy walked over to the door. "If we could pull up a tad of carpet here," She pointed, "and lay a little bit of tile... Or I could go with a nice grade of faux tile. I'll tell you what, I'll get alternative prices and include them both in the proposal, but think about it. You're going to ruin the carpet in a couple of snow seasons, which pushes the cost off onto the buyers, but it's not quite fair, is it?"

"I agree. I'll take the proposal to my boss and argue your point. I can get these dimensions to you tonight. I often work out of my home in the evenings."

"Me too. I can pick it up at home, but I need to finish two local jobs this week and drive up to Thomas next Tuesday. It'll probably be next Thursday—but I could pull some over-time and get back to you sooner if you have a deadline."

"I didn't expect to walk in off the street and hire you cold. I hear you are quite a busy lady."

"I'm a one-man operation, but I could have some preliminaries by the first of the week." Missy headed out the door he held open for her. Tim glanced back, looking for something. "My pocketbook is in the car—small town living at its best." She smiled and held out her hand. "If you award it to me, I'll do a good job for you. Thanks for the opportunity."

"I have no doubt. I look forward to working with you." Tim walked her to her car and held the door. "I'll be talking to you." He shut the door, stepped back, and gave her a small wave.

The next Tuesday, Tim was in her shop at noon. "I'm sorry...I misunderstood. I thought we agreed on Thursday. I don't have anything ready for you, only the notes I sent last week."

"You're right. Thursday. Sorry to barge in, but I was on my way to Canaan Valley, and I thought I might take a chance. If you're free for lunch, we can talk shop."

Missy was thoughtful. The guy had a wedding ring, but it would be a working man's lunch. She agreed. She grabbed a file folder and her sweater and locked the door. "We can walk down to the sandwich shop down the street, Mr. Raines."

"Please, call me Tim." They walked the couple of blocks, chatting about the changing West Virginia weather, which had turned chilly again. After they ordered, Tim pulled out a sheaf of papers with his firm logo. "I have some budgets for you, depending on how much you want to do."

Missy's eyes widened as she looked them over. This was an interior decorator's dream, a showcase with a handsome budget. "You'd credit my shop with the decorating?"

"Of course."

He'd emailed the floor plans, so she showed him several ideas she'd sketched. As he reached to take them out of her hand, she was startled to notice his ring was missing. *What kind of a jerk is he? Does he plan to two-time his wife and make a move on me?* Missy scooted her chair back from where they leaned over the papers, and her demeanor changed from the girl with the hometown style to a brisk professional. "The living room is a good size. It can stand a fairly-large sofa, but too much will make it feel cramped. I'd like to leave space for two chairs pulled up around the fireplace."

Tim was impressed with her professionalism and the exact footage she included, but he was disturbed by the noticeable change in her behavior. "Have I offended you in some way, Ma'am?"

Resolved to be stern, Missy bit back her smile at his old-fashioned politeness. "Forgive me for noticing, Mr. Raines, but your wedding ring seems to be missing today." She raised her eyebrows, and the coal black eyes snapped. *At least he has the grace to blush.*

He stammered, "Miss O'Malley—God, help me out here. Get me out of this mess."

"I'm sure the good Lord didn't put you in this mess," Missy retorted.

"In a manner of speaking, He did, though I doubt you'll believe a word I say, and I can't blame you. You see, my wife died several years ago, and I didn't get around to taking off my ring until last Sunday."

Missy looked at him skeptically, but bright tears shimmered in his eyes. *Either he's telling me the truth or he's good.* "I'm truly sorry, Mr. Raines—Tim— what happened?"

Tim told her his wife and their unborn child had been killed by a drunk driver. She shared the similar loss of her beloved grandparents when she was a young teen and asked him to forgive her for thinking poorly of him.

Tim shook his head, releasing a small laugh. "I told you I wouldn't blame you. I never thought you noticed. I didn't get around to taking it off, although my brother and sister have been urging me to get on with my life. On Sunday, I went up to the altar and left it there."

"Hmm, 'Get on with your life.' Sounds like my brother and his wife, but I'm not sure how to go about doing it."

"I have another confession to make since we are laying it on the table here. I remembered that Tuesdays are your afternoons off and that you were going to Thomas."

"I have to pick up a few items at Mountain Made to finish some projects."

"Would you trust me enough to ride with me? I have an obligation in Canaan, but I'd love to drive to Thomas with you if you can spare me half of an hour."

"Timothy, if you're lying to me about the altar, God Himself will get you." Missy laughed. "It's the least I can do after being judgmental."

"I wouldn't call it judgmental, Miss O'Malley, just cautious. Wise, in fact."

"Please, call me Missy," she said, reaching for the check.

"Company dime. I'll get it." Tim took it from her.

They had a wonderful afternoon. As they drove, Tim heard something overhead and looked up to see a window rolling back.

"Do you mind? Smell the Mountain Laurel!" Missy breathed deeply. "Whenever I come up here, somewhere around Middle Mountain, I feel my cares rolling off my back and down the mountainside."

"I look to the hills, from whence my help cometh," Tim quoted. Missy asked him about his Christian experience. "As a teenager, I went to a church camp one summer with a group from another church. I got enthusiastic about God. It drew me away from my parents at first. We were not an enthusiastic church, and they feared I'd become a fanatic. They saw my behavior change and checked out my church. Now we all go there—my folks, my sister and my brother, and their kids. You?"

"I went to church with my grandparents. After they died, my father—who always drank too much—started drinking even more. He and my brother had a huge fight one night, and he left. I was angry with God. Like you, I went to youth camp and got turned on to God. Mom was glad to find a new church. My grandparents' church was legalistic."

Missy was surprised at how easy it was to talk to Tim, and she confided in him about their struggles to survive after her father left. "We sold several parcels of land so Mom could go to nursing school. I hate having a gas station and a café in front of our property."

"Your mom's a nurse?"

"She's almost got her RN now."

"My mom's a teacher. Dad calls himself a miner, but he got a degree in Mining Engineering at WVU."

Tim turned into a high-end development, apologizing for his need to stop. He invited her inside. He opened the front door of a beautiful home with his key. "Like Ken says, the stuff down there is what we do to make a living, but this is what I love."

Tim's Masterpiece

Missy gasped as she walked into the sweeping, great room, with floor to ceiling windows flooding the hardwood floor with light and the most magnificent fireplace she'd ever seen in the very center.

"Timothy, this is incredible!" She turned slowly in a full circle.

Tim delighted in her appreciation and was touched in a deep place by her use of his name. No one called him by his formal name, but it didn't sound stilted—it sounded...intimate.

"Tim, is that you?"

"Hey, Mike, it's me...and a friend."

A heavy-set older man came from the back of the house. "This place has come a long way since I was here last." Noticing Missy, he took her hand in both of his. "Mike Green," he said.

"This is my friend, Missy O'Malley, from Elkins. She's working with me on a project." Tim pulled out canvas folding chairs for all of them. "Missy is an interior decorator. I've got several catalogues for you to look at to select your kitchen cabinets."

"I like these two," Mike pointed. Missy frowned.

Tim asked, "What do you think, Missy?"

"It's not my business. It's Mr. Green's house," she replied, looking at two other options. "But seeing the spaciousness, the openness in this house, it calls for soaring and open, like this one, or this." She indicated two with glass doors and space for hanging glasses underneath.

"You guys are friends or colleagues?"

Missy laughed. "Only met the guy last week, but he's already putting me to work."

"I was told about her shop, and I'm trying to get her to help me set up the model house in a subdivision my company has built."

"Did you talk all the way up here and tell her your 'vision' for this house?" He turned to Missy. "That's what he calls it, 'his vision.' Call me Mike."

"It definitely is a vision. It's no ordinary house. It's a...sanctuary, a cathedral, a refuge from the world." She walked slowly toward the fireplace, looking up. "The fireplace rises like a steeple through the center of the home." She breathed in deeply and whispered, "It's awe-inspiring." She spun around to face the two men. "When you walk into this room and see it, it takes your breath away. I believe I could stand up in there!"

"How tall are you, Missy?" Tim asked.

"She couldn't be over five feet," Mike guessed.

"I'm five feet, two inches!" Missy retorted. Both men looked at her. "Almost," she muttered. Ignoring them, she returned to the fireplace. The hearth began at around her waist, but she leapt up onto its broad stones. "It makes my Shawnee blood leap!"

"Shawnee—you have Native American heritage?" Mike asked.

"My Pop was mostly Mingo, but he had a lot of Shawnee blood in there. My Gram was Navaho and Cherokee."

"All those Appalachian tribes kind of mingled together," Tim explained, and he rattled off a list of tribes in the large grouping classified as the Appalachian tribes.

"I'm impressed; most West Virginians know little about our original American ancestors."

Tim smiled. "Golden Horseshoe, 1988. Some things get drummed into you until they stay."

"Then you probably know the Shawnees were a warrior tribe. The Mingos were peaceful until pushed into war. They were close to the land. My grandfather could talk the seeds up from the soil. Mom's like that too. Tecumseh was Shawnee—have you ever read Alexander Thom's book *Panther in the Sky?*"

"No. I read *Follow the River*. Loved it. Thom is an excellent historical West Virginia author, Mike. Isn't his wife Native-American, Missy?" She nodded.

"That explains it," Mike commented.

"What?" Missy wanted to know.

"You're as brown as a walnut, and it isn't even July. You don't appear to be the sun-worshipping type like my daughters are. I can't imagine you in a tanning booth."

Missy visibly shuddered, and both men laughed. "You should see my brother. His hair is red, and his eyes are bright green with golden flecks. But his skin gets real dark in the summer. Our dad is Irish, and Jimmy calls himself a Native American Irishman. Poor Daddy couldn't get out in the sun at all. Mom always said Jimmy got the best of both worlds." She jumped down from the hearth. "Now, what are you doing here, Tim? Tell me your plans."

He walked her through the downstairs, showing her the two bedrooms blocked off behind the fireplace on both sides of the house. She looked at the long area between them, against the back of the house.

"Do you have a family, Mike?"

"Divorced. Two daughters in college, one a senior and the other a freshman."

"You'll definitely have families up here. You need these big bedrooms. You even have room for a crib in there."

"Cribs? I hardly see them, and you're thinking of grandchildren? Money, I've got, but my kids have been taken away from me."

"Mike, they'll come to this place. They're adults now, and they'll make their own choices. Trust me. Did you ever see *Field of Dreams?* If you build it, they will come." She hugged him quickly, and he looked surprised.

"Let me see the upstairs. I assume the master bedroom is upstairs?" She went to the foot of the wide staircase running along the western wall. "Can I go up, Timothy?" But she was half-way up.

"Be careful. I haven't gotten any railings."

She looked over her shoulder. "That's fairly obvious." She grinned. "I'll be careful."

Tim came up two steps at a time behind her and watched her turn her head from left to right, surveying the grand openness. "How did you envision this? It's a work of art! Those wonderful windows. I'm in the middle of all creation here. I see heaven!"

Mike called up. "What do you think we should do? I thought two rooms, my study on the left, and my bedroom on the right." He pointed east.

Missy and Tim came back downstairs. "I'd flip that—put your study over there on the east, where the morning sun can stream through those grand windows Tim has installed. Put your bedroom over there." She pointed to the western side. "Aren't you plumbing a Jacuzzi under the west wall?" Tim nodded.

"Who wants a Jacuzzi in a study? Wouldn't you rather have it in the bedroom? You could bask in that relaxation and watch the sunset. Rooms? Mike, you aren't seriously thinking of cutting up that grand space into boxy rooms, are you?"

"How else would you divide it?"

"Let your furnishings do it—it's easy. Put a large sofa or massive desk where you walk into the creative area, with bookshelves surrounding the walls. I bet you have lots of books, don't you?" Mike nodded. "Tim, you need floor to ceiling bookcases along this wall and the back wall, with rolling ladders to get to the top shelves. Oh, it'll be grand!"

"Maybe my study, but what about the bedroom? How would I have any privacy?"

"A huge sleigh bed would do that, with a tall headboard and an oversized width. You're a big guy—don't you want a California King?" She folded her hands in a praying position. "We'll figure it out. Our wonderful woodcrafters in West Virginia could make something. I could get something specifically for this, but please, please promise me you won't chop up this...this cathedral!" She looked up at the soaring ceiling and threw her hands in the air. "Look at the light warming all the wood. I could go for a few screens, maybe, but walls? Ugh!" She shuddered.

Tim shook his head and held his hands up in surrender. "I swear I didn't tell her anything. We talked about other things."

Mike clapped him on the back. "If I had a girl this pretty riding in my truck on a beautiful spring day, I wouldn't talk shop either." Mike explained to Missy that he was a writer, and he was building this house to "stir his creative juices." He added, with a chuckle, "She sure has caught your vision. Bet she won't let me have carpets either."

Missy's eyes got big, and she clapped her hand over her mouth, but it didn't stop her. "Carpet! How prosaic. You can't be serious? Cover this beautiful wood? Timothy, tell him it's got to be wood. A few area rugs about, in front of your couch, beside your bed, but I beg you, no carpet. Who puts carpet in a cathedral?"

"You two are ganging up on me, but I still don't see it."

"I see it, Mike. It'll be grand! So grand that you'll write the Pulitzer Prize here."

"Okay, Missy, give me some more ideas." Mike laughed at her.

"Tim, do you have your laptop in the truck?"

"I'll get it." When Tim returned, she was walking slowly down the hall toward them. While Tim booted up the computer on the kitchen counter, Mike leaned close to his ear. "You need to get a hold on that one, Tim. I bet a little Shawnee warrior blood would be good for a man! Do you think you could handle it?"

Tim kept his eyes on the screen but replied, "I'm definitely going to give it a try."

Missy was chewing on her bottom lip as she drew near. She leaned over the laptop and studied the back wall. "Why are you chopping up that space and creating a hallway? What is this little room? If you ditched this wall..." She made a few swift keystrokes. "Look at that nice space with a beautiful backyard view. Put two doors, one going out to each hallway, and you'd have a huge room. Put two doors on each of the bedroom bathrooms...of course, you'd have to have latches for privacy...add a built-in day bed along the back wall for the kids—make them from the same kind of wood so they'd look like they grew out of the wall. You'd still have plenty of room for the kids to play."

Mike groaned. "I don't even have grandbabies yet, and she's giving me teenagers!"

"But you see, there's your privacy. Even guests need a place to be, a living space of their own. I can see it now, massive doors. I saw some doors like that when I lived in Ohio."

"I thought you lived in Beverly all your life."

"Uh, it was only a few months." Mike asked her where she would find the furnishings, and she told him about her relationships with the local crafters.

Tim looked up from the screen. "One small problem. Your guest living room was the laundry room. Where will we put a laundry room?"

"Tim, I can't believe you'd put a washer and drier in that delicious space. Lookie here." She made a few more keystrokes. "Put the laundry here, by the side door to the slopes. You need a mud room, a place to hang skis and wet ski clothes, and a weather break. Wouldn't that be better? The kitchen is long enough...unless...You aren't a gourmet chef, are you, Mike?"

Amused, he shook his head, watching her and then looking over to Tim.

"Tim, you need a climate break. You're going to tile the kitchen, right? Tile all the way across. See? A long narrow room with a door into the kitchen. Perfect!"

"I like it. We could sure do it. Mike?"

"Blueprints are Greek to me, but I like the concept. Go for it. Look, Raines, finish the place up. I like her. Give her free reins. Missy, furnish it."

Missy's eyes sparkled. "Are you serious? You'd trust me to do it?"

"Look, I haven't got time. I like your wacky ideas. Obviously, Tim does too. Do it."

"Thank you. I'd love to do this wonderful house!"

"Go for it. If I don't like it, I'll pitch it when I get back."

When they pulled out, two hours had passed, and Tim apologized. "I'm sorry. I didn't mean to take so long. I hope you have enough time to get your work done in Thomas."

"Timothy, are you apologizing for gaining me a lucrative contract? I can't imagine having money like that. 'I don't have time. If I don't like it, I'll pitch it.' Who thinks like that?"

"He's a famous author, with lots of books on the New York Times bestseller list. Money's not an issue for him."

"Humph, I should say. Let's get up to Thomas before this place closes." Using her cell phone, she called ahead to say she was late. He stepped on the gas. As they walked around the exquisite handcrafted works of art, the artisans spoke to Missy on familiar terms. She had several pieces waiting for her—a wormy chestnut sideboard, a huge hand-blown glass vase, an entry table, and two coffee tables. Tim offered to take them back in his truck, and several men helped him load them under wraps and tie them down. The vase went in the back seat.

Before she left, she arranged to have one of the woodcrafters call her about Mike's furnishings, and she ordered a few more items, teasing them about hurrying out before she got thrown out.

"Never, Missy! You give us too much business for us to lose you," the chatty lady at the desk said as she rung up the total, but she locked the door behind them, and they walked down the outside stairs.

"I'd say you have some pretty well-heeled clients yourself," Tim noted. "That's expensive stuff."

"But not open checkbooks. Everyone I work with knows what they want, and they give me a price range. I do the leg work." She looked up at him. "Have you been to Thomas before?"

"Can't say that I have. What's there?"

"Let's head over to The Purple Fiddle and see if they have any blue-grass tonight. Probably not since it's in the middle of the week and between seasons, but they have fabulous homemade soups and sandwiches."

They drove into the tiny town, made the long loop around, and came back on the one-way road along the river. Missy pointed out the little café at the end of the block. They lingered over a light supper, and Missy promised to bring him back sometime for live music. "My dad would like this place. He'd be playing here himself."

"He's a musician?"

"Mmm. An amazing one. He can play the mandolin like no one in the world. He can play any stringed instrument, but the mandolin—nobody else in the world can play it like him."

Tim drove back to Elkins way below the speed limit, trying to make the evening last. Their conversation was comfortable, compatible. They shared faith and interests. They fit. Missy seemed to be winding down. She laid her head on the seat back and sang quietly, and he loved her sweet, clear soprano.

"I always was a sucker for an Irish singer," he told her.

"You should hear my brother!"

"I'd like that very much. Do you guys sing together?"

"Sometimes, most often in church. Sometimes at festivals."

"The Singing O'Malleys?"

"No, that's our dad. He plays mandolin, sings, and makes his living picking up gigs. We're plain old Jimmy and Missy, singing siblings."

Twilight was closing in as they pulled into Elkins. "Do you want to go back to the shop, or should I take you home to Beverly?"

"Thanks, but I need my car to get to work in the morning."

Tim pulled up and parked in front of her business. "I'll walk you to your car. When do you want to unload, and where?"

"Oh. Do you have time to run out to Jimmy's? I'll put it in my storage unit."

"That's fine." She showed him the way to Jimmy's garage, beside his house in Elkins.

Tim drove down the long driveway. Jimmy was walking to the house and saw a strange truck. He was surprised when his sister got out...and even more so when a tall man stood beside her.

"Jimmy, this is Tim Raines. We're working together. Got a minute to help him unload some stuff?"

Tim and Jimmy shook hands. "You got room in there?" Jimmy asked.

"I took a bunch out this week," she said.

Tim and Jimmy unloaded the truck, and Jimmy invited them inside.

"I need to get home and feed my dog," Missy said. "But thanks."

Tim took her back to the shop, which twinkled brightly with lights framing her showroom window, revealing a cozy room that anyone would want in their home. He insisted on walking her to her car. As he closed her door, he smiled down at her. "Thanks for a perfect day. I'll call you about going out to the subdivision one day next week."

"I had a good time too, and I love your masterpiece. Mike has a beautiful home."

"We'll put it together; how about it?"

"I'd like that."

Tim closed her car door and patted the window sill. "Lock up now. Be safe." Stepping back, he waved as she pulled out of the driveway. Missy watched him in the rear view mirror as he walked slowly down the drive, and she thought about him all the way home, wondering where this might lead. She fixed a cup of tea and curled up in front of a fire. It was late in the year for a fire, but she loved to listen to the warm crackle and the logs popping, watching the flames dance. She relaxed in front of a fire, and that night she prayed and wondered if perhaps it was time to get on with her life.

Timothy

Later in the week, Tim called to arrange a time to go to the subdivision. Missy thought she would be comfortably ready by Monday evening, after work, and she asked him if that would work. Since he would be at the project all day, it worked out well. She had a busy day on Monday. Some clients were impossible to please, trying to do a mansion on a pup tent shoestring! The phone rang at 4:55, and she muttered, "Close enough," and let the answering machine pick it up.

Tim walked in, and she asked for a minute to get ready. "Have you ever had one of those days when clients change their minds about everything?" She hurriedly ran a comb through her hair and dabbed on a bit of lipstick before joining him in the showroom, where she found him laughing at a woman who was whining on the phone's answer machine.

"You can't please some people. Usually they tell me about it when I have the walls framed in. 'Did I tell you I want an extra two feet in the recreation room?' Or, how about, 'Can we put a half-bath in the laundry?' Of course, it's after the plumbing has been set."

"Teach me to fuss about taking back a couch or a chair. What is this—are you upping the ante, Raines?"

"Why, Miss O'Malley, you sound like a poker-playing woman!" Tim laughed and held open the door, waiting while she locked it. He'd parked the big truck in front of her shop, with the lights blinking. He opened the door, and she attempted to climb in. Suddenly her feet had wings as Tim easily lifted her up.

When he pulled off, she said, "You're going to be with my brother, who taught me every evil thing I know. He's going to help us. Remember the way?"

"Can I get him to sing for me too?"

"I doubt it—you have to catch him in the right mood." She smiled at Tim. "Thanks for the lift. It's a trial being vertically challenged sometimes."

"You are fine. Perfect. And your height has nothing to do with the impact you make."

"What does that mean? Right at the next corner, remember?"

"In less than ten minutes, Mike Green saw your taste, your talent, and your judgment. He's wealthy, but I spent months trying to gain his trust. You had him immediately. Of course, he's a sucker for a beautiful woman." He winked.

Missy ducked her head. Tim was flirting with her! "I was in good company."

"No, he's an artist, and he recognizes another one."

Missy pointed left, but Tim recognized the long hill and had already veered to the fork. "Tim, that house is a work of art. The symmetry, the lines—I wanted to raise my hands and shout to the Lord."

"Let's hope it has the same effect on poor Mike. He needs the Lord in a big way. His wife left him. It was costly and nasty."

"I heard him said he had money but that he'd lost his kids. Sad. We'll have to pray we have a chance to speak into his life. We'll work hard to glorify the Lord in what we do and open the door to speak into his life."

"Amen. I didn't notice the sign the other night." Tim pointed to the sign over the garage. "Who's the 'A' in A & J Garage?"

"Mr. Andrews was the wonderful man who gave Jimmy two chances to start over in life. I don't know what would have happened to Jimmy without him. He loved him like the son he never had, and when he died, he left him the business and enough money to get a start on the building and his house. My brother's the best mechanic in six counties, and he keeps two other men working." She indicated a door to the fourth bay. "When he built this, he added extra space for his baby sister's collection of stuff. Don't worry, it's well sealed—no diesel fuel odors get into the furniture."

Tim set her on the ground, and a red-haired dynamo appeared out of nowhere, hurling his five-year-old body at Missy. "Auntie Missy, where'd ya get the truck? Who is this guy? Can I go with you? Daddy says he is. I want to go. Can I go, please?"

"Whoa, Jamiekins. Hold on...one question at a time. This is Mr. Raines. He's a friend of mine, and we're doing some work together. Tim, this is my nephew, Jamie, Jimmy's boy."

Tim put out his hand, squatting to be eye level with the exuberant child. "Jamie, nice to meet you."

"Tim, have you got a minute?" Jimmy was walking across the yard. "Won't take long. I promised a guy I'd have his truck out tonight. No longer than fifteen minutes. Julie's in the house, and I think she made some fresh coffee for you. Go on in and wait for me."

Missy looked up at him with a question in her eyes, but he was smiling and agreeing. "Sure, I'd love a cup." He followed Missy up the side steps to the house, watching Jamie cling to her hand and chatter.

She pushed open the door and found Julie balancing a fussy Alice Ann on her hip while trying to prepare a salad. The toddler's legs started pumping with joy as she saw her aunt, and she reached out her arms and let out a squeal.

"Work your magic on her. She's driving me crazy!" Julie grumbled.

Walking to the adjoining family room, Missy snuggled the beautiful girl's dark curls. She sat on the couch and blew on her tummy, and the baby was all giggles.

"This here is Mr. Raines, Mom. He's a friend of Auntie Missy's," Jamie announced.

"Good job, Jamie. What a nice introduction. Forgive my manners, Tim. Julie, Tim Raines. Tim, my brother's wife and my best friend since forever."

"Cream, sugar...how do you like your coffee, Tim Raines?" When Julie turned for the answer, she saw Tim smiling at Missy as she played with her niece.

"Hmm? Oh, just cream, please."

"Here you go. Would you take Missy's out to her? She likes a little coffee with her cream and sugar."

"I've noticed," Tim replied.

Julie raised her eyebrows at her friend. "I can sit a minute," she said, and she joined Missy on the couch.

"You can sit here, Mr. Raines." Jamie indicated a chair.

"You've got more manners than both of us, son," Julie praised.

Soon Jimmy stuck his head in the door. "Come on, Miss. Tell the guys what junk you want hauled, and we can have some help before they leave."

Tim smiled at the curly-headed moppet who clung to Missy, giving Missy no choice but to carry her with them. The guys had doffed their work coveralls and washed their hands, which they held up for inspection. Missy laughed and punched at one of them.

"Give it up, Jerry! I see you've learned your lessons well."

Everyone was laughing, and Jimmy explained to Tim, "Missy has a temper, and when Jerry got oil on one of her precious pieces, she threatened to make him pay for it."

"How can an old, used sofa cost so much? That's what I want to know," Jerry complained good-naturedly.

"It was a Duncan Phyfe, Tim," Missy clarified as she walked toward the last door on the building, which Jimmy had already raised. She pointed out a chair, a couch and matching chair, plus another chair, and a coffee table.

"Are these recent things all you need?" Shrugging his shoulders, Jimmy looked at Tim. "It all looks the same to me, but when Missy puts it together, it looks nice. She decorated our house for us on a dime, and we like it. She got most of the stuff from shoppers' news, used furniture stores, and even yard sales."

"We need two lamps and a side table." Missy indicated a table lamp and a floor lamp, and then she begged them to retrieve a rug that was rolled up, way in the back of the building. Grumbling, Jerry and Jimmy moved three dressers and a table to get to the rear of the building.

"You mean this red one?" Jimmy called back.

"Thanks, guys, I really appreciate this."

Tim could tell no one minded doing Missy's bidding.

When everything was secured in the truck, Jerry offered to come help unload.

Missy looked at Tim. "Jimmy and I can get these," he said.

"Thanks, Jer, we can get it from here. You're a peach though."

Alice Ann hung on Missy's neck, and Jamie was hopping up and down, begging to come and demanding to ride in the big truck.

Julie, wiping her hands on a dish towel, surveyed the situation. "Jamie, Mommy and Daddy will take you and your sister in the car."

Alice Ann buried her face in Missy's neck. "No, no, no," she wailed.

Missy apologized to Tim and walked over to the car, murmuring, "Auntie Missy wants you safe, Girlie-girl. You must ride in the car seat with Mommy to be safe, but I'll hold you when we get there. I promise." The child looked up at Missy and let her buckle her seat.

Tim was waiting by the passenger door to help her in the cab, watching Jamie argue with his father about riding in the big truck

"He could ride here with us, couldn't he? We have a middle seat belt."

"Jimmy would never reward such behavior. Gosh, I'm sorry you got stuck with the whole clan. I had no idea they'd want to come along."

Lifting her into the truck, Tim grinned. "I'm a sucker for kids. I'm happy to have them. They seem fun, like my niece and nephews. They love their Auntie Missy."

"I spoil them rotten. Do you spoil yours?"

"They're all I have—of course I do."

"I've been a part of these kids' lives since the day they were born. I was in the delivery room—Julie's been my best friend forever."

"Isn't she the one who used to hide you in her treehouse?"

"She's the one. Their farm abutted Pop's. She was such a part of our family—Jimmy had to marry her."

"They look like they're crazy about each other, and the kids are terrific."

"They give me hope for home and hearth. With all the divorce in our culture, it's comforting to see a couple who'll stick it out. They went through some tough times."

"You'd never know it now."

"Jimmy used to drink a lot after Dad left. He blamed himself because they had a huge fight before he left. He quit for a while, but then he relapsed when...after he started dating Julie. I'd gone to some counseling, and I stood behind her—do you know the concept of co-dependency?"

"Yeah, I do. I guess you learned it in the Al-Teen program."

"Umm," Missy didn't correct him but simply added, "When she refused to put up with it and broke it off, it was the best thing she could've done for him. She'd watched us grow up, and she didn't want to be married to our dad. Jimmy loved her like crazy, and he checked himself into rehab. Once he was clean and sober, he went all over the state looking for a maintenance program. He runs the recovery program in our church, and he hasn't had a drink in fourteen years."

"Good for him. Amy and I were like that. We went through a hard place, worked it through, and nothing but death could have taken her from me." Tim was quiet the rest of the drive. He led Jimmy to the model house and parked in the driveway. His own emotional memories fled when he saw Jamie pile out of the car and head for his aunt.

Alice Ann was waving her arms and screaming a sound that might turn into "Auntie Missy" one day. Missy took Jamie's hand, cautioning him to be very, very careful in Mr. Raines's brand new house. She didn't want him to get hurt or get anything dirty. Tim threw the door key to her.

After the entry and front room were arranged, Missy asked Jimmy to get a package out of his trunk. He came in with a large package wrapped in brown-paper.

"Wait till you see this; this is the icing on the cake!"

"I love the long, low cabinet to divide the entryway. I was going to put it along the wall, and I thought it would take too much space, but you put it on the other side and framed a walkway over the tile. Nice touch."

"Thanks. Did you get the rods I ordered?"

"I not only stopped at JCPenney yesterday, I came here and hung them before I came to the shop."

"Good man! Now, let's get these hung." Missy, who'd been standing and swaying the toddler while directing the men, handed her sleepy bundle to Julie. The baby had her thumb in her mouth and went to her mother, contented, snuggling into the crook of her neck.

Tim got a step ladder from the closet while Missy put the hangers in the pleated folds. Julie and Jimmy exchanged glances, watching the two of them work smoothly and efficiently together, almost wordlessly. They arranged the drapes, stepped back, looked at them, and re-arranged the folds. Jimmy marveled at Tim's patience, saying Missy was picky. "But you see what she sees, don't you?"

"It's not perfect until it's right," Tim agreed. He would suggest something, sometimes point, and she would nod and fix it. They both stood back, looking at drapes, a master stroke bringing the furnishings and the area rug together.

Tim agreed when Missy stood off to one side, surveyed it all, and declared, "Perfect!"

"As soon as my boss sees it, he'll want a bedroom done too. This looks fabulous. We should sell for several thousand dollars more than we projected. He liked your idea for the foyer, and when he sees what you've done with the cabinet, he'll be amazed. If we do as well with the sale as I think we will, I'll take you out to a steak dinner."

Missy laughed. "Be careful; I might hold you to it."

Jimmy draped an arm around Julie and whispered, "That's an excuse. He'd do it anyway."

Missy and Tim gathered up the hammers, the trash, and the level used to hang the pictures on the wall. "Do you want me to catch a ride with Jimmy so you can head home?"

Tim looked like someone had punched him in the stomach. "We promised him a ride in the truck." Jamie jumped up and down, screaming his agreement. "Hush, Jamie, you'll wake your sister," Jimmy said. "Come on. I'll ride in the truck with you."

"Since you've put up with the whole crew, the least we can do is invite you to dinner. Do you have time to join us?" Julie asked.

Tim's face lit up like a prisoner on reprieve. His eyes lit up. "I'd like that."

Jimmy had already buckled Jamie in the seat and was climbing in, so Missy got into the car with Julie. "I can't even reach the pedals when Jimmy drives my car," she complained.

"That's why he drives a truck. He doesn't fit in your car."

"Tim's tall too. He's cute, Missy, and he's obviously smitten. Don't let this one get away. I understand about Jerry, but you and Tim work together like a well-oiled machine. Jimmy is over in the corner saying you're being too fussy, and Tim gets it and fixes it exactly the way you want."

Missy told her about Mike Green's house, what a work of art it was, and how she'd been hired to decorate. "He's still in love with his wife though."

"Tim? Divorced?" Julie asked. Missy explained the tragic accident that took his wife and unborn daughter. "In a case like that," Julie replied, "you never want to take the first love away. It's part of who he is, but it doesn't mean he can't love again." Missy told her the ring story, embellishing her own nastiness until she had Julie laughing at her. "Didn't you feel like the wicked witch of the West?"

"He was kind about it, even apologized. I think he was a bit flattered I'd noticed. I do like him, and we have this big job together. We'll see."

"You are getting too old for that 'we'll see' attitude. Just grab him!"

"I haven't even met his family yet. He could be an axe murderer."

"He is no axe murderer. He's a doll."

"You're married to my brother, thank you very much—I'd better not hear you saying stuff like that!"

"You know I'm a sucker for tall, dark, and handsome."

"You seem to like Jimmy's red curls well enough. You play with them all the time."

Laughing, they pulled into the driveway right behind the pizza delivery truck. "When did you call them?" Missy asked.

"When you were fussing over the drapes. Picky, picky—the guy deserves this!"

Jimmy paid the driver, Julie took Alice Ann off to bed, Missy took the pizzas to the back deck, and Jamie grabbed Tim's hand to lead him to the back yard. They gathered around the table on the deck to eat, and afterward the men tossed the Frisbee with Jamie.

Julie put her arm around her friend. "Look at him. He's a natural with kids. I'm telling you, Missy..."

Missy bumped her with her hip. "Will you shut up, nag?" Missy laughed, but her eyes followed Tim as he ran around the yard, and she shouted encouragement when he dove to catch a low throw.

Unwilling to break up the party, Julie let Jamie stay up past his bedtime, but finally she had to call, "Come on, bub, you have to take your bath and get in bed. School day tomorrow."

Jamie started to whine, but Tim scooped him up and carried him a few steps with his legs dangling, saying, "We kept you up past bedtime. Are you going to fall asleep in class tomorrow? Like this?" He pretended to fall asleep, dropping on the grass. Jamie laughed and turned toward the house. "Race ya," Tim said, and he took off running.

"You handled that like a pro, Tim, thanks," Jimmy said.

"No problem. I have a niece and two nephews myself—my privilege. He's a great kid. Thanks for dinner, and for your help." He helped Missy gather up paper plates and stuff them into a garbage bag. "I guess we'd better let this family wind down. Ready to ride to town?"

They walked downstairs, calling back good-byes. "Are you going back to Clarksburg tonight?"

"No. I have a few ends to tie up at the development tomorrow, so the company is putting me up in a hotel."

"It's early. Would you like to come by my house? Have a cup of coffee? Mom can take me to work in the morning."

"I'd like that," Tim responded. They drove through Elkins, out the winding road to Beverly, east of town. Missy told him about their long bus rides to Elkins High, and Tim told her about going to Virginia Tech to get his degrees in architecture. Two blocks off the main road, through the little town, he turned into her driveway. The house sat on the end of the road, with forest beside and behind.

"Don't you feel isolated? Do you get nervous?"

"Wait till you see the farm where Mom lives, and nothing we can say can get her to move. Beware—I have ferocious protection!"

"Should I be worried?" Tim saw a huge dog bound out of the house and lope to the woods. "What is he, or she?"

"She's a Burnese Mountain dog, sweetest thing in the world, and she's rotten. No protection at all." The dog completed her business and rubbed against Missy. "Ready to eat, girl?"

Maggie recognized the dinner call and turned to the house after pausing to sniff Tim up and down thoroughly.

"I forgot to ask. Do you have allergies? I can leave her outside."

"No, she's fine," Tim said, rubbing her soft neck. She leaned against him. "See, she likes me."

"She likes anybody who'll scratch her. Come on in. Something to drink? Coffee? Tea? I hate that it's too late in the year to have a fire. I love a fire."

Tim stepped into a miniature palace—elegant yet inviting, everything speaking of warmth and welcome, from the over-stuffed sofa to the tiny chairs beside the fire. The fire was carefully laid: a few balls of paper, small kindling, split pieces, and logs, ready for a match.

"My grandfather taught me to always have your fire ready. I told you he was Native-American, right?"

Tim looked at her and nodded. "This is unusual. Where did you get it?" Missy's coffee table was an enormous slab of wood, polished to a fine hue and fitted with legs.

"My brother wouldn't speak to me for weeks when I hauled that thing into the shop. 'This is the last straw. The crazy things you get up your sleeve. I'm not messing with that ugly thing.' I started by myself, a little at a time, sanding and rubbing. One night he came out and grumbled about getting me out of another mess I'd made for myself. I bought him a sander, and this is the result—now he wants it!"

"It's lovely. I like the way you brought out the grain. I hate to set a glass on it."

She laughed. Tim loved the rich, musical sound of her laughter. "We have I don't know how many layers of protection on it. After a ton of coats, I begged Jimmy to please bring it home."

Missy handed him a cup—she remembered he liked it with cream. She tucked her feet up under her and sat facing him. They talked about their families, their careers, and the work they were doing together. Missy told him about several pieces she'd picked up for the mountain home, including a California King bed she'd ordered from a crafter, made entirely of native wood.

Naturally, Tim eagerly accepted her invitation to see her place. In the small bedroom she used for an office, she told him she'd gotten his emails right there. Her kitchen and dining nook were workable and efficient. A bench curved down the side wall and against the back to the side door. Maggie's bed was on the other side of the door. Missy's warm bedroom felt peaceful when Tim walked in, but he sensed she became uncomfortable and turned back to the living room.

"Jimmy calls it my doll house."

"It looks like you. If I'd tried to picture it, I would have come up with something like it."

"I didn't have too much money at the time, so I did what I could. I spent a lot of money on Mom's old farmhouse, but it was paid off, and we could get a home equity loan. I couldn't stand the old place. I changed it, but I'm content here. It's closer to the shop—much closer than the farm. I hate to think of Mom out there by herself, but I'd been away at school, lived in Clarksburg and then Buckhannon, and it didn't seem right to move back there. Mom's super, and we have a great time together, but when you're an adult, you want your space."

Tim told her his parents and his brother urged him to move in with them after Amy died, but he felt the same way. "I felt a burning ache every time I walked into that home, night after night. But I couldn't leave—it was all I had left of her."

Tim's head dropped down and his shoulders slumped. Missy remembered the awful time when she kissed her baby good-bye. Her eyes misted, and she waited in silence.

Tim drew himself up. "Last year I bought a townhouse and furnished it like a bachelor pad. It's masculine. Not homey, like this place. Terri, my sister, took some of the furniture. We sold a lot of it. At first it wasn't like home, but I've gotten used to it."

Missy remained silent, remembering the Christmas she came home without her baby, when her breasts ached and her heart wept. Even now, thinking about it, the wound seemed fresh. *God, when does the pain ever end? For Tim or for me?*

"You're mighty quiet. I'm sorry to be such a downer after our fun evening. I like your family."

"Timothy, I'm honored you shared your pain. The greatest compliment you can pay a friendship is to open your heart. I'm sure Amy was a wonderful woman."

"She was excited about the baby. We waited over five years. We married in school—met in Blacksburg. She was an undergraduate, and I was in grad school. Her family didn't approve of me, and we lived dirt poor as students. We put off our family until we were established."

"How far along was she?"

"Five months. We thought about keeping her on life support to save the baby, but the sonogram revealed she was already dead too."

"Is it cruel or too trite to praise God for the joyful glad reunion?"

"I say that all the time. I never thought I'd marry again. I wore my ring until...well, I told you when I took it off."

"For I know the plans I have for you..."

"...to give you hope and a future," Tim finished with her. "Have you ever thought about marriage?"

"Not really. I've never even had a relationship. It's part of a dysfunctional family—the drive to be self-sufficient. I'll never be dependent, like Mom was. She was young when she and Dad married, and Jimmy came along quickly. I'm determined to make it on my own. She was trapped. If Daddy hadn't left her, she never would've left him. Maybe I'm too proud."

"Does that leave room in your heart for someone, Missy?"

"I'm surrendered to the Lord's will, and I'm content to wait on Him."

Looking at his watch, Tim realized they'd talked until morning.

Missy rose. "Thanks for a lovely evening."

"Thanks for introducing me to your family. They made me feel welcome."

"They like you."

"Your brother is a great guy, and I've never seen more love and loyalty toward a sister. I need to be a better brother."

"Your sister's married. Jimmy looks after me because I'm alone. Mom and his family are all I have. He's older, and he's always been a big guy. He's looked after me all my life. It gets on my nerves sometimes, but mostly it's incredible, to trust in his protection, his love and care."

"I got the feeling on our ride that he wouldn't take too kindly to anyone who hurt you."

"I hope he didn't threaten you."

"Not exactly, but I got the message. I promised him I'd never do anything to hurt you." Tim tucked his finger under her chin and brought her eyes to meet his. "And I make you that promise. Never. I'd never hurt you. I promise."

Missy's glance drifted, but not before Tim saw a look of terror enter them. She caught her breath and stepped back. Struggling to take a breath, she managed to choke out, "Thanks again. Talk to you next week about the bedroom...in the house...if you want me to decorate."

As soon as Tim felt her freeze and move back, he abandoned his plan to taste her lips and turned to the door she'd pulled open for him. "Are you antiquing tomorrow afternoon? I have some comp time."

"No, yes, thank you, but I have to go out with the whiney client you heard on my answer machine. I'll pick Mrs. Andrews up after I close and take her to lunch. Maybe in a relaxed atmosphere she can tell me exactly what she wants for her condo."

"You can make it fun. Good luck. I'll call you." Tim waved briefly and stepped down.

Missy closed the door behind him and leaned her forehead on it, trying to catch her breath. "God, I thought he was going to kiss me. What am I going to do? What do You want for me?" She thought of the Scripture they quoted together—God had a plan and a future for them both. She felt like she was having a panic attack. Her heart was racing, her palms were sweaty, and perspiration beaded on her brow.

Going to her bedroom, she washed her face with a cool cloth and brushed her teeth in the tiny bathroom to the side. The Twenty-Third Psalm popped into her mind, the psalm that she quoted to Jimmy when they found out she was pregnant, the one that she and her mother quoted when she surrendered Gracie.

"Gentle Shepherd, lead me into that rest beside still waters. Make me to lie down," she whispered.

Getting to Love You

Tim climbed into the truck, puzzling over his departure from Missy and her response when he wanted to kiss her. *Somebody has hurt her—badly. She didn't mention childhood abuse, only the drinking, but someone has made her afraid. Jimmy indicated something. God, help me to figure out what it is and to help her. Make me gentle, kind, and patient.*

The next evening, as Tim unlocked his door, he heard his phone ring. He recognized her number and answered with, "So how did your luncheon go?"

"I could hardly wait to call and tell you," she burst out. "You'll never guess! I'm excited. Are you home?"

"I'm glad. I'm home—tell me." Tim tugged his tie loose and sat.

"I picked up Mrs. Andrews, and we went to lunch."
"Wait, Mrs. Andrews, the widow of Jimmy's boss, Mr. Andrews?"

"Bingo! How observant you are. She told me how lonesome she'd been since her husband died and how hard it was to sell her house and close it down to move to something smaller. She asked if I was Jimmy's sister and said he'd been wonderful to her husband when he was dying. He went over every night to put him to bed—Mr. Andrews wouldn't let hospice do it; he wanted Jimmy. I knew he'd led his boss to Christ before he died, but he never mentioned going over there every night."

"You said the man was a father figure to him."

"He was. Anyway, Mrs. Andrews asked me if I was 'religious' too, and I told her I loved the Lord and that Jimmy and I went to the same church.

She said she went to church, but she didn't talk to the Lord the way Jimmy did. Then, guess what?"

"You make it too easy. You led her to the Lord right in the restaurant."

"It was thrilling—I reaped what Jimmy sowed. His life made a deep impression on Lenore. I had to call and tell you. Isn't that cool?"

"Yes, it is," Tim chuckled, "and much more eternally significant than hanging with me—but I missed you."

"I knew you'd rejoice with me. Tim, you're fast becoming my best friend."

"That's something anyway. Did you get her furniture selected?"

"No problem. She was more lonely than picky, and we started at her house, selecting some pieces she loved, and I figured out how to bring them along. I had my measurements—she was surprised what would fit. But I regret the mean things I said about her. What did you do today?"

"Nothing nearly as exciting. I plugged away at the office, completing a proposal, which my boss liked a lot, and catching up on material orders. Scanned our suppliers for sales."

"Timothy, doing excellent work glorifies the Lord. One day you'll speak into his life. We'll tuck him into our prayers for Mike."

Tim rested his phone between his shoulder and ear to free his hands so he could pour a glass of milk and make a peanut butter sandwich. He didn't want to hang up, and they talked for over an hour. Calling back and forth every evening became a pattern, and they both looked forward to sharing their days. Tim figured getting to know each other this way would help build their relationship until he could figure out what caused her fears.

When he was in town the next Tuesday, he called the shop. Missy was in a rare foul mood, working on the books. "Where is that stupid phone?" she muttered, shuffling papers around her desk and finding it under a stack. "Missy's Interiors," she snapped.

"Uh, did I catch you at a bad time? If you've got a minute, I have something for you. Are you at the shop?"

"I am, but the front door is locked. Come around back, where I park."

"I'll be right there."

There was a light tap, and the door opened. "May I come in?" Tim had a file folder in his hand, with something clipped to the front. Surveying her piled-up desk, he said, "You look busy. Am I interrupting?"

"Uh, lunch. I was making a peanut butter and banana sandwich. Want one?"

"Got any jelly?"

"Homemade blackberry okay?"

"Thanks. Make it two if you have enough bread. But first, let me give you this." He showed her a check. "We sold the model for considerably more than we were first planning to ask, thanks to you. My boss was much impressed with your work and wants you to do another."

"Timmy, that's awesome!" Tim thought she might throw her arms around him, but he saw her check that impulse. "I believe I owe you a steak dinner, plus your handsome commission. The buyers want to know if they can buy the furnishings, but I told them I'd have to ask the decorator."

"Your company paid for all that stuff, remember? It's not mine." Missy covered her sudden confusion by making their sandwiches.

"I really like your hair, the way it frames your face. It looks nice," Tim complimented.

"Thanks. I hadn't changed it in forever, and I was tired of the same old look. Mom watched the kids, and Julie and I went together." She handed Tim two plates.

"Where do you eat in here?" Tim looked around the small space.

"Ta-da—lookie here." Missy opened what appeared to be a cabinet and unfolded a table. "Magic!"

"'Lookie here' is right. You are magic, Missy. It's neat." They pulled up two chairs, and when he held out his hand to say the blessing, her small brown one fit in his palm. After the short prayer, he looked up and said, "You didn't sound like yourself when you answered the phone—something wrong?"

Missy groaned. "The inevitable bookkeeping. I hate that part!"

"The company does all mine after I bill it out. That's the good part about working for someone else. What software do you use?" When she told him, he suggested another, one his brother-in-law used. "What you're using is basically a tax program. This gives you room for growth, adding employees, paying benefits, all those complexities. Les is an accountant, and he likes it, says it's user friendly and a non-financial person can use it."

"That's definitely me. I've handled a checkbook since I worked at McDonald's when I was sixteen, but taking out taxes, paying quarterlies...I hate it!"

"Don't you have an accountant?"

"Hey, Mister, this is not some big, swanky place here—only me."

"An accountant would be worth it. You'd end up saving money by maximizing your creative time. He or she would save you money, and you'd be more productive. Do our next model. Work on Mike's house—how's that coming? And I know you have other jobs."

"I like the way you talk, big guy." Missy stood, "I mean...I like your dreams for this little shop."

Noticing her confusion, he smiled to himself. "Can you tear yourself away, or do you need to do those reports today?" He handed her the check. "The boss gave you $1,000.00 for your services."

"What? I hardly think it's worth that much. I picked up a few things while I was selecting for other clients. That's too much."

"You're selling yourself short. It isn't the time—it's the talent, the artistry. Using elegant drapes in a subdivision house; dividing the foyer with the pretty little cabinet. And the entryway itself—it's far more practical, and Mr. Bonner is adding it to all the houses. He wrote the check himself, said you made it more than an ordinary house. You want me to tear it up?" He held up the check between his two hands.

"No! I want to go celebrate. Let's chuck these old books. What are you suggesting? Do you have the afternoon off?"

"I have comp time, remember? Mr. Bonner recommended we go to some Inn and Restaurant overlooking a river for dinner." He patted his stomach. "Not that I could stuff another bite in there after such an elegant repast as you have served me."

Missy snapped a towel at him, laughing. "It must take six sandwiches to fill you up!"

"Maybe in my youth, but that was quite a while ago. I can wait, oh, about an hour or so. Have you heard of this place?"

"Sure, the Cheat River Inn. I know exactly where it is, but I don't want steak. They have the best pecan-crusted trout you've ever put in your mouth!"

"I've never put pecan-crusted trout in my mouth, but if you say so, I'll try anything once."

"You won't regret it. Now, what else can we do? Have you ever been to the trout farm?"

"Trout farm? No, I can't say that I have. You have an exciting array of activities up here in the mountains."

"This is Elkins, West Virginia, remember? It's interesting though. Let's go, and we can drive around the beautiful campground in the National Forest. Are you a camper?"

"No, I can't say that I am, but I'm willing to try. Are you a camper?"

"If I go with Jimmy and Julie and he puts up my tent." She locked up the door behind them.

"That's cheating!" Tim closed the passenger door and walked around his truck.

"I guess it is," Missy responded, "but once I'm there, I love it—the peace and quiet. When the sun's coming up, I walk the river. I'm a birdwatcher. I put so many bird feeders around Mom's farm that she complains that it takes an hour to fill them."

"Are you a morning person?"

"Yep. It's my best time. I'm up before anyone intrudes. I talk to God, I listen to the sounds of His world before they get crowded out, and I hear Him speak to me. I do my best work at about five in the morning."

He groaned. "I knew I'd find something about you I wouldn't like."

"How can anybody not like mornings. You don't like mornings?"

"Let's say they're tolerable after a couple of cups of coffee."

Missy directed him to the turn-off, and they wandered around the trout farm before driving over to the Cheat River campground. The playground was filled with laughing children—maybe it was a field trip. Missy pointed out the trail by the river, and they walked downstream.

Finding a place on the bank of the river where they could sit, they stopped. Tim tore up leaves and idly watched them floating in the current.

"Did you ever play Pooh-sticks?" Missy asked.

"Pooh-sticks?"

"Pooh-sticks. I love to play Pooh Sticks. Jimmy, Julie, and I played Pooh-sticks when we were little, and I play with the kids all the time."

Tim shook his head at her. She loved everything. "You'll have to enlighten me about this game. Is it too complicated for a city boy?"

"No, it's easy. Come on. I'll show you." Missy reached for his hand to pull him up.

Tim put his other hand behind himself and pushed off. "That's a good way to land in the river!"

She dropped his hand and ran lightly ahead. "I'll show you a great place to play Pooh-sticks." She led him to a bridge over the creek. "You have to find just the right sticks—not too heavy, because they'll be slow, but not too light, because they won't have enough weight to pick up speed."

Amused at her seriousness, Tim let her show him the right sticks. They dropped them in the current and crossed the bridge to watch them appear on the other side. "Looks like I won," Tim said.

"Beginner's luck. We have to do it again."

Missy won the next two times, but Tim won six times in a row after-wards. "You must have given me the best stick." He grinned at her. "Is that your stomach I hear growling?" Missy turned a deep tan, and Tim realized she was blushing.

"Yeah, it is. I'm getting kind of hungry. Are you?"

Tim rolled his eyes. "This friend of mine is trying to starve me. She gave me two tiny sandwiches, enough to fill a mouse, and hiked me all over the national forest."

"That's enough, Timothy! Hush," she said, placing her hand on her tummy and giggling as more rumblings came out of it. "Okay, we'll go feed you."

Tim tried to avoid watching her tiny brown hand on her little belly. Those blue jeans she was wearing about did him in. "Since you're in jeans, I guess jeans are fine at this place?"

"You'll fit right in. We can eat on the porch. It's good to get there early. All these campers will be pouring in at dinner time." As soon as they were seated on the porch overlooking the river, the waiter appeared. "We'll have two of the pecan-crusted trout, please."

The waiter, holding a pitcher of ice water, said, "Um, I was going to get your drink orders, but if you know what you want, I can put that in for you. Do you want drinks?" Tim asked for coffee. Missy wanted water with lemon. The waiter scurried off.

"What, Tim? What are you laughing at?"

Tim shook his head, still chuckling. "You. Not 'at' you, just...at you. I love your enthusiasm. You're a breath of fresh air in my stodgy world."

Missy tilted her head to one side, appraising him. "You're not 'stodgy.' You're lots of fun."

"No one has ever said that to me. My brothers call me 'old sober sides,' and my mom kindly refers to me as her 'serious child.' You must be good for me, Missy."

"Gosh, I'm going to have to reappraise my thinking about you. I could tell you're earnest about your work, but that's not a bad thing. Tell me about your other hopes and dreams."

"I want a quiet life...a home, white picket fence, lots of kids running around. What about you?"

She responded with a rueful frown. "Life hasn't afforded me that. My biological clock is ticking away. I always thought I wanted that though."

"You aren't too old—what 30, 32?"

"35, and not getting any younger."

"That means we'll...er, you'll have to get going, although, little as you are, having babies might be hard on you."

"I can have babies fine, thank you very much!" Missy retorted. She looked away, her chin quivering. She fidgeted with her hands, jumped up and excused herself, and went to the ladies' room.

Could you have been any more insensitive, Tim? God, how do I get out of this one?

After more silent prayers and what seemed like forever, he saw her winding her way back to the table.

"Excuse me, Tim," she said quietly.

"It was a tactless thing to say. I had no right. Please forgive me."

"It's all right. It was nothing." Missy looked up with relief as the plates were set down and the waiter refilled their drinks. Tim reached for her hand and blessed the food. She looked at him expectantly. "Now, tell me what you think."

Tim gingerly put a forkful of trout in his mouth, and his eyes widened. "Wow!" he said, eagerly taking another bite.

"I told you you'd like it!" Missy crowed triumphantly.

The rest of dinner went smoothly. Missy's feathers didn't seem too ruffled, but a quiet sadness settled over her, and her usually buoyant enthusiasm drained away, but she was kind and genuinely interested in the conversation. Tim steered carefully away from family and kids. Missy stumbled around, trying to find neutral ground, and asked him if he'd ever been to Seneca Rocks.

"I went once with the Boy Scouts, but I must confess I don't get in this part of the state as much as I'd like."

"Did you go to the caverns?"

"No, we hiked the cliff."

"Pops loved to take us there. I used to cling to his hand in the dark, follow along the stream bed underground, and imagine my ancestors had been in that very spot. Once, he showed the guide some markings on the wall. Pop could read animal tracks and talk seeds out of the soil. I still miss them—Gram and Pops—and I can't wait to see them in heaven."

It was still daylight when Tim dropped her off at the shop. She slid out of his truck and walked to her car. "Wait," he called. "Don't forget your check. I'll get that software at the office supply store and bring it up one day next week."

"I need to get on this. I'll go with what I have."

"What about Saturday? Can I bring it up then?"

"Isn't that out of your way...and a big chunk out of your weekend?"

"I'd like to do it. Les could show me a few things before I come."

"How kind—could you buy me a new brain to tackle this stuff?"

"I'll see you Saturday then. I'll call you on the way."

Missy's Fears

See you," Missy called as she backed out, steering her little Liberty around his big truck and carefully pulling into the traffic. Tears trickled down her cheeks. *Wonder what he'd think if I told him about Gracie. Guess he'd have to reappraise his whole thinking about me. If only I could avoid his dancing blue eyes!*

She reached over and turned on the Christian radio. Praises filled her car, and she sang along. *Funny how God always knows what I need, and when I need it, He provides.*

Glancing down at an incoming number ringing on her phone, she turned it on speaker phone and said, "Hi, Mom, whatcha doing?"

"I've been working in the garden all afternoon, and I just came in. Do you want to join me for dinner? I can make a nice grilled chicken salad. I have some fresh garden greens."

"Thanks. I've already eaten at the Cheat River Inn. I love their pecan-crusted trout."

"Did you drive up there by yourself, or were you with the 'colleague' that Julie and Jimmy like so much?"

Missy laughed. "I was with Tim, you old busybody, and he's coming up on Saturday to bring me some new business software. Maybe you could drop by the shop and pop in...if you want to meet him."

"I have a better idea. The kids are spending the night with me so their parents can have a night out. We could have a picnic here, and you can invite him."

"I'll think about it. We'll see. I'll have to let you know."

"You are too old to have this 'we'll see' attitude."

"Mom, you and Julie sound just alike! You're around each other too much."

"Maybe we've been around you too much, watching you love those children hungrily for years. You've been alone too long. Invite him—it's your turn."

"Maybe. Let's put it in God's hands. We talk every day. I'll invite him. But I have a problem. He was going to kiss me the other night, and I swear I had a panic attack...No, he was a perfect gentleman. He always is."

"You need to take this to Recovery."

"Mom, I went to rape counseling, placement counseling, individual therapy, and group therapy. I'm therapied out, and I'm perfectly fine."

"Obviously not, sweetie. Pray about it."

Tim called on Thursday night. "I hated to miss our call last night, but I got home late from church. Everybody and his brother wanted to chat. Thanks for our lovely day on Tuesday. I had a wonderful time with you."

"Thank you, Tim. It was your dime. Are we still on for Saturday?"

"I picked up the software yesterday, and Les is giving me a cram course tomorrow night. Should I come to the shop?"

"Perfect. Mom wants to know if you could come by the farm afterward. Jimmy and Julie are bringing the kids out to spend the night."

"I'd like that." He asked her about her day, and she asked him about his, and they spent several hours talking.

"My big old mutt wants to go out, and it's past my bedtime. I'd better say good night."

Tim laughed. "Am I keeping you up till the wee hours? Gosh, it's 10:30."

"I have a 9 o'clock bedtime, Timothy." Missy laughed back at him. "See you Saturday."

Missy let Maggie out and walked back to her bedroom. Brushing her teeth, she looked at her reflection in the mirror critically. *Mom and Julie are right, kiddo; you're not getting any younger.* Hearing Maggie, she went to let her in. Maggie circled around on her bed in the kitchen, but she came to the kitchen door and cocked her head when Missy sat on the couch.

"What's up, girl?" Sensing an invitation, the dog came to her, tail wagging. She pushed her head under Missy's outstretched hand. "Maggie, I don't know what I'll do if he tries to kiss me again, but he can't be patient forever." Maggie looked puzzled at Missy's sad tone. She whined and put her huge paw on her mistress's hand. Missy buried her head in the dog's soft neck, weeping.

"God, You said You wouldn't put more on us than we can bear, but this is killing me. I think I love him. What's not to love about him? He's all I could ever hope for in a man. Why am I afraid?" She shuddered involuntarily and looked around. "This is silly! Go to bed, Maggie."

Maggie walked to her mat obediently as Missy turned out the lights in the small living room. She climbed into bed and began to read the psalms. She read long past her bedtime.

Tim called at about 10:30 on Saturday morning. "I'm turning on 33 now. I should be up there in 45 minutes."

"I'll meet you at the shop." Dressed and ready, Missy looked at her forlorn dog. "Get in the car, Maggie. You can go." Maggie barked, wagged her tail frantically, and ran to the door, where she waited, whining. When the door opened, she ran outside, did a quick bit of business, and hopped in the jeep. Missy drove to the shop, booted up the computer, and put on the coffee.

Hearing his truck turn in the driveway, Missy threw her glasses on the desk and ran to the bathroom to run a comb through her hair. She closed the bathroom door and crossed over to the back door. Thinking she looked too eager, she looked around to find something to make herself look busy.

She put her glasses on and called, "Come in," when Tim knocked.

He looked at her a minute before he crossed the room, sitting in the chair beside her desk. "I've never seen you with glasses. You look cute. Do you wear contacts?"

"I only need them when I'm reading or doing close work."

"I like them. I like you, with glasses or without."

She softened under his warm look. "Do you have the software?"

A look of feigned horror crossed his face. "Software, software," he muttered, patting his pockets one after another. When Missy was getting seriously concerned, he pulled the disk out of an inside pocket in his blue jean jacket. "Oh, here it is—I've got it after all." He grinned, and mischief danced in his eyes.

"Timothy Raines, sober-sides, my foot. You're the biggest tease I ever met." Missy pummeled his arm, giggling. "We'll never get to business if you keep that up."

"Is that a threat or a promise?" When Tim looked deep into the deep, dark pools of her eyes, Missy swallowed. He looked like he could lose himself in her eyes. He stopped chuckling and popped the disk in. "I'm going to a picnic today, so we'd better get on it."

After an hour and a half, Missy had entered several worksheets of data by herself. She threw her glasses on her desk, announcing, "I've got it. Let's get out of here. The farm is calling my name, and I'm starving! You hungry, Tim?"

"Not really. I grabbed a breakfast sandwich at Sheets in Weston."

"At 10:30? You ate breakfast at 10:30? Morning is over by then."

He looked at her. "It suits my schedule fine, thank you, Ma'am. You morning people don't get it, do you?"

"I haven't had a bite since six, and you've worked my butt off!"

"6:00 A.M? On a Saturday? There must be some law. Maybe it's a sin. The Eleventh and great commandment is this: Thou shalt not get up before 9 on Saturdays."

"Shut up, Timothy!" Missy laughed. "I can't miss my mornings. Do you want to take two cars and follow me out? If we take your truck, you'd have to drop me off on the way back, and you'd have to let Maggie ride in your truck."

"In my infamously clean work truck?" Tim opened the truck door. "Come on, Maggie."

The dog looked at Missy with a question in her large brown eyes. "It's okay, girl, get in." Maggie lay down on the back seat. "I can make her ride in the back, Tim."

"It's fine. Your mom's is out beyond your place?" Tim turned east. "You think Jimmy and Julie are already there?"

"I'm not sure. Jamie had a little league game. Mom usually goes, but I bet she's cooking up a storm. She likes to show off for special people."

"That's a nice category to be in."

"I can't help it. My brother seems to have said all sorts of nice things about you, and Julie likes old sober-sides."

"I knew I was going to regret telling you that." Hearing a horn, he glanced in the rear view mirror. "They are right behind us."

Turning in her seat, Missy waved. "Gosh, I hope Alice Ann is asleep in the car seat. She'll be a bear if she doesn't get a nap."

A few minutes later, the two trucks turned into a large circular drive. "Holy smokes, where is the little farmhouse? This is some place."

"Didn't I tell you I helped Mom remodel a couple of years ago?"

"You did. Where is the original structure?"

"I'll show you. Come, Maggie. We're at Gram's." The dog was obviously at home here, and she ran toward Missy's mother, stopping and sitting at her feet. Alice ruffled her fur, and Jamie ran over to Missy, hollering about his base hit.

"Mind your manners, young man," Jimmy admonished as he lifted the car seat out of the truck.

"Good afternoon, Mr. Raines," Jamie said politely. "Now can I have my hugs, Auntie Missy?" She picked him up, getting dirt from the baseball field on her jeans.

"Missy, he's going to break your back. He's almost as big as you are," Julie fussed.

"Not quite, are you, tiger? I can still carry my boy." But Jamie squiggled down and took off for his grandmother.

"Nice to have you along, Tim," Julie said. "Come meet Alice."

An older version of Missy approached, wiping her hands down the sides of her jeans in a gesture already familiar to Tim. She put her hand out. "Welcome."

"Thanks for inviting me, Ma'am," he responded."

"So, Gram, whatcha got to eat?" Jamie asked.

Julie was half-way up the steps, with Alice Ann asleep in the car seat. "Jimmy, would you do something with your son?"

The guys were laughing heartily, and Tim ran his fingers through the boy's red curls. Missy announced that she, too, was hungry, and she knew

Jamie was since he had just played baseball. Dropping a hand on his shoulder, Alice told the boy what was waiting on the table.

Family

Tim followed Missy up the stairs as Missy opened the door, and Julie put the baby in the crib, car seat and all, in the back bedroom. The family gathered around a beautiful wood table in the large dining area off the kitchen. Automatically, hands stretched out and linked together while Jimmy said a blessing.

With two hands, Jamie lifted a bowl of green beans to Tim. "Nobody makes better green beans than Gram. But Auntie Missy's potato salad is better."

After everyone had eaten, Missy said, "I'll hold off on cake. Tim wants to see the house."

"I see what you've done here," Tim said, looking at the area where the new kitchen-dining area was enclosed from the old porch. "It's hard to see, but you must have enclosed a porch, right?"

"You should have seen her. She had men out here with jacks lifting up the whole front of the house and building a new foundation."

"You have to do that, Jimmy, to set it square. And you added those windows?" Large windows surrounded the dining area, and at the side of the kitchen, there was a garden window.

"We gutted the small kitchen, incorporated the old porch, and made it all open into the great room. We rebuilt the fireplace and set in the large bay windows. See all Mom's feeders out there?"

"My feeders?!" Alice protested. "But I do love sitting here and watching all the beauty and my birds. Go, show him what else you did."

Missy took him through the house, putting her finger to her lips as they looked in where the baby lay. The others stood, plates in their hands, watching and listening. Missy explained how she enlarged Jimmy's bedroom, the master bedroom, and the hall bath, putting the laundry room in the bathroom. Tim nodded, pointed, and murmured his agreement as he asked questions. Heads together, he leaned down to catch what she said.

Tim saw her mother and Julie whisper, and he rejoiced to overhear them say, "Didn't I tell you, Alice? We couldn't have asked for anything more perfect for her!"

"I've never seen her happier, Julie, but she's troubled. I fear a relationship won't be easy for her."

Overhearing, Tim wondered about that. *Why would a relationship be hard for her?*

Jamie headed down the hall after his aunt, but Jimmy waylaid him. "Let's go catch some salamanders. We'll get the buckets." Grabbing his daddy's hand, the lad skipped to the barn.

Returning to where the ladies were putting the dishes in the dishwasher, Tim said, "Mrs. O'Malley, your daughter has done a top-notch job here, and I hope I never have to make a living as an architect in this town!"

"Please, call me Alice. She was much impressed with your beautiful work in the house you're building in Timberline."

Tim saw the slight darkening of Missy's complexion, which he had learned to recognize as a blush. She was caught bragging on him!

"You timed it perfectly," Julie said. "We're finished up here, and the guys have gone off to fetch the buckets."

Alice Ann cried, and her grandmother pushed the younger women aside. "I'll get her. You go help catch salamanders."

"Catch salamanders?" Tim asked. "Is that anything like Pooh-sticks?"

Julie laughed so hard she had to sit down on the steps. "Missy, only you!"

"What, Jules, what?"

"Just, just..." And off she went into gales of laughter. "Imagine playing Pooh-sticks with a grown man!" She ran across the meadow hollering, "Jimmy, can you believe your sister taught Tim to play Pooh-sticks?" Jimmy looked back at Missy and shook his head, laughing.

"I'm sorry, Tim. I guess that was pretty stupid." She looked down.

"Don't let them mess with your head. I had a lovely time." Missy shoved her hands in her pockets and kicked a stone. He stopped. She stopped too, looking up at him with a frown. "Honest. I mean it. It was a perfect time. I liked playing–" But a chuckle slipped out.

Missy chased him across the meadow.

Jamie shouted, "Mr. Raines, are you gonna catch salamanders with us?"

Jimmy and Julie lay back on the bank, rolling with laughter. Wiping his eyes, Jimmy said, "I'm afraid this mountain family is too much for you, Tim."

"You'll have to show me how to do this, Jamie." Noticing that the boy and his aunt were in the water barefooted, their pants legs rolled up, Tim sat on the bank, pulling off his shoes and socks. "I wish you'd let that child call me Tim."

"How about Mr. Tim?"

Jamie held his hand up. "Come on, Mr. Tim." Missy was pattering in the creek, turning rocks over.

"Auntie Missy is the best salamander-catcher in the whole wide world," Jamie announced, spellbound as she scooped one up in her small brown hands and put it in the bucket, which she handed to Tim.

She pointed. "Here, Jamie, right here. Get it! Get it." Quick as a wink, she placed a salamander in Jamie's outstretched hands for him to put in the bucket.

Tim looked across the meadow. "Is that your farm over there, Julie? Missy told me you had the next farm over."

"Daddy sold it off years ago when it got too much for him. He's passed away now, but it was a perfect life, growing up here in the country."

"You have some nice woods behind your house," Tim commented.

"Not too bad, for in town," Jimmy responded. "It works well for the business. You can't put a garage in the middle of nowhere."

Alice was coming toward them, carrying a blanket and a toddler. Julie jumped up and spread the blanket on the grass.

At a shout, Tim looked to see Jamie holding up a fat salamander. "Ain't that the biggest you ever saw, Gram?"

"Isn't, Jamie. Isn't it?" Alice corrected.

"Well, isn't it?"

"I do believe it's the biggest salamander in the whole wide world."

Tim grinned at Missy, her little brown feet hopping from one rock to another. "Not only are you one fabulous Pooh-sticks player, you are also the best salamander catcher in the world!"

"I'm not going to teach you to catch salamanders, Timothy. You beat me at Pooh-sticks seven times out of ten." She kicked water up at him. Alice looked confused, and Jimmy and Julie dropped back on the blanket, holding their sides and laughing.

"He did, Mom. I think he cheated somehow."

Laughter is contagious, and Tim joined in as he reached for her hand. "Missy really and truly selected the best sticks for me." He pulled her up on the bank.

"Thanks, Tim. I'm glad somebody appreciates me."

"Come on, Tim. I'll challenge you to a game of horseshoes, if that's not too rural for you." Jimmy hoisted Julie up. Alice Ann had already gone to Missy, and they were chattering away as they walked back to the house. Jamie and Alice carefully poured the water and the salamanders back into the stream.

"Listen, man, I'm a coal miner's son. I've been playing horseshoes since you were knee high to a grasshopper."

"You're not that old, Tim. Yes, Ma'am." Jimmy did as his mother bade him, leaning to pick up Missy's tennis shoes. "I wish I had a dollar for every shoe Missy's lost in this creek."

"We'd be millionaires! Do you remember the time...?"

"The pink pair, with the bows. I thought she'd cry her heart out."

"You came back that night with a flashlight and found them."

"I didn't want the old man to beat her when he found out."

"Your dad never laid a hand on Missy," Julie said.

"No, he didn't."

Tim watched Jimmy closely, but he was quiet as they continued to the side yard. Soon they were in a lively game, and Tim was good. Jimmy, not used to losing at horseshoes, hollered, "That's cheating, Raines. You've got to be cheating."

"What's the matter, Mountain Man? Somebody getting the better on you?"

Julie and Missy headed back to the house. "I thought you and Jimmy were going to have a special night out?"

"And miss all this fun? Catching salamanders. How about a good game of Pooh-sticks?"

Missy shoved her friend with her hip. "It seemed appropriate at the time." Which sent Julie into further spasms of laughter. "Cut it out, Julie!" She looked at Alice as they stepped onto the porch. "What do you think, Mom?"

"About Tim? I like him, and I guarantee he's no axe murderer."

"You guys better quit talking behind my back."

The men came up the stairs, and Tim announced he had to let Jimmy win the second game. "He's into this. I didn't want to make an enemy for life."

"I beat you fair and square!" Jimmy protested.

"It's true, I must admit."

"Anything left to eat around this place?" Jimmy asked.

Alice rose from the swing and carried the baby into the house. Missy and Julie were putting the noon leftovers on the table. After supper, the children caught fireflies, and then Jimmy bathed Jamie while Julie cleaned Alice Ann in her mother-in-law's bathroom. Jamie never wanted to go to bed, but he agreed he would if Missy read him a story. Sitting on the couch with her arm around him, she began. "One day in the Hundred Acre Wood, Winnie the Pooh and Christopher Robbin looked about to see what they could do on this beautiful day. Finding Eeyore and Piglet, they decided to go to the river."

Alice was smiling. Tim leaned over and whispered, "I can guess where this is going." She patted his hand. Missy finished story about the imaginary friends' game of Pooh-sticks and carried Jamie to bed. Looking at her when she returned, Tim said, "You never give up, do you, Missy?"

With the kids settled, Jimmy pulled out some board games. They played several, laughing and enjoying themselves thoroughly until Missy announced the time. "It's only an hour past your bedtime, Killjoy," Jimmy teased.

"Tim has a long way to go down the mountain, Jimmy, and tomorrow is Sunday."

"That usually follows Saturday. Almost always." Missy threw a couch pillow at her brother, who ducked, and it hit Julie instead. "Tim, why don't you just stay over?" Jimmy invited. "You could come to church with us in the morning."

Tim looked at his jeans. "I might get away with jeans, but these seem to have—What is this...salamander juice?—on them."

"Jeans are fine, and we can get those washed and dried before morning. Jimmy's bound to have something back there that you can wear tonight," Alice assured him.

Missy sat and watched the back and forth, feeling set up. "Suit yourselves. I'm going home," she announced, standing up.

Tim grinned at her. "It's five miles back. Want a ride?" Missy looked confused, and Julie and Jimmy suppressed giggles. "I don't know what I'm going to do with the whole lot of you!" Missy pretended to be angry, but she couldn't quite pull it off.

"Pull me up, Miss," Tim pleaded, reaching out his hand. She slapped it away, laughing then, and even Alice laughed as Tim lumbered his way up from the chair. He opened the door, bowed at the waist, and announced, "Your chariot awaits, Madame."

"Shut up, Timothy," she said as the door closed behind them. "Honestly, I don't know who's worse, you or Jimmy." The laughter trailed behind them as the couple went down the steps.

"What did I tell you, Mom? Isn't he terrific?" Jimmy asked.

"He is—as terrific as this beautiful daughter you gave me," Alice answered. "And he fits right in, doesn't he?" Alice hugged her son and went into the kitchen. Tim must have dropped Missy off and came straight back, probably not wanting her to wait up to wash his jeans. The door was open, and he came in to find her doing something for the next morning's breakfast. She handed him a stack of clothes. "Jimmy found you an old pair of sweats. You

171

can change in the bathroom and pop your clothes in the washer." She heard the washer and was pleased to see him come back to the kitchen and sit. "Coffee?" she asked.

"No, I'm good, thanks. Missy seemed tired. She's an early to bed, early to rise kind of person, isn't she?"

"She always has been, even as a baby. Jimmy slept late, and I worried after she was born. She was up with the sun, but she never fussed. She played with the sunbeams in her crib. Never was much trouble, Missy wasn't. Ian used to walk around with her on his hip, trying to keep her awake so she'd sleep in, but she'd conk out in his arms every time. He was good with the babies, Ian was."

She looked down, remembered she'd been rolling out dough, and returned to her task. "Missy goes full steam all day, every day, never stops. It wears me out to watch her."

"Are you like that, Mrs. O—Alice?"

"I was when I was young. Ian used to say I'd changed, but I was tired a lot. Two babies close together. And I was...depressed, I guess. Has Missy told you her father is an alcoholic?"

"Yes, Ma'am, and Jimmy indicated some abuse?"

"Ian had a temper when he was drinking, but he never hurt Missy. She was his golden girl, his heart. Jimmy covered for her a lot, so he took the brunt of it."

"Jimmy is a great guy."

"He's come a long way. Julie and Missy helped us straighten him out after..." Alice seemed at a loss for words.

"She said she'd learned a lot about co-dependency at Al-Teens," Tim offered.

"Al-Teens? We did pray about it and arranged what they call an encounter—our pastor, his boss, me, Missy, and Julie confronted him one night. He adored Julie and didn't want to lose her. He went to a rehab program down in the southern part of the state. Now he runs the Recovery Program at our church. I heard the washer go off, Tim. Put those clothes in the dryer, and we can go to bed."

"Yes, Ma'am." Tim started out of the room but turned back. "Did you ever divorce him?"

Alice smiled at Tim, but she had a sadness about her. "No. I never thought to divorce. I never stopped loving him. I pray every night he'll come home to me. If he doesn't, I'll go to my grave loving him."

Tim's heart broke, looking at her. If he'd known her better, he would have pulled her in for a hug. "I'll join those prayers, Alice."

"You do that, Tim. I'll count on it." She brushed her hands together and led the way down the hall. "We put you here, in Missy's old room. Alice Ann is in here, but she sleeps like a rock. Would you rather sleep on the sofa?"

"I don't mind sleeping in there. I sleep in my niece's bedroom sometimes."

"You're a comfortable guest and welcome anytime. Good night."

Tim slipped into the bedroom without turning on a light. He stopped by the crib. Moonlight spilled over the baby's cheek as he stood, gazing down. "Father," he whispered, "please let it be Your will for me to find my way into this family. What wonderful folks they are. They seem to have no bitterness after all they've been through. What a mighty God You are, Healer, Deliverer, and my Savior."

Tim dreamed of a little girl, who tilted her head up at him and patted his cheek. She looked exactly like a miniature Missy. He smiled in his sleep and slept peacefully in her old room.

He felt Alice Ann staring at him when he opened his eyes. He propped up on his elbow and whispered, "Hey, Girlie-girl." Hearing Missy's word for her, she began to crow.

"I told you she was awake, Jimmy. Go get her before she wakes him."

"I'm awake," Tim called through the door. He lifted the baby out of the crib. When she came readily to him, he was pleased. He gave her to Julie and wasted no time getting ready. Alice told him she'd drive her own car and suggested he go get Missy. He needed no persuasion.

On the way, he wondered if he should have called ahead, but when he turned in, Missy was outside playing with Maggie. "You're all ready to go. You look nice—that's a pretty dress."

Missy twirled around. "You like it? I bought it because Jimmy and I are singing today. Come, Maggie, I've got to go to church. Have you eaten, Tim? I've got a Danish inside."

"No, but I'd take coffee if you have it." Tim walked in behind her, watching the full skirt sway around her little hips. The flame orange dress suited her brown skin—if only she wouldn't look at him with those doe eyes!

Missy guided him to the church. They arrived early, and she introduced him around. Jimmy walked across the fellowship hall. "Julie's got nursery. We can go on to class. She'll be in later; she has the Sunday school hour." Tim sensed that Missy was cautious and that he needed to hold himself in check, so he didn't take her hand. But it was fast becoming difficult.

Julie did hurry to meet them in the sanctuary, sitting between Jimmy and Alice. Tim sat on Alice's other side, with Missy by the aisle. When it was time for the offertory, Jimmy slipped down the side aisle, and Missy walked up the middle. They met at the stairs going up to the platform. Jimmy took her hand, giving it a slight squeeze. At first she glanced at Tim, but she listened to the music, closing her eyes and lifting her voice to the One she adored. First Missy sang, and Jimmy echoed. On the chorus, their voices mingled as one. Closing together, their voices soared, and Missy's hand was in the air. Tim realized he was holding his breath.

Alice leaned to whisper, "They sing beautifully together, don't they?"

"I've never heard anything quite like it," Tim whispered back.

Julie beamed at Jimmy, and Missy flashed her bright smile at Tim. "Pretty song, isn't it? Jimmy wrote it."

Tim nodded mutely and found himself unable to concentrate on the sermon with her warmth beside him. He reached for her hand, pleased when she took it. As they walked into the sunshine, Alice invited him back to the house, but he declined. "It's my niece's birthday. Mom said they'd hold dinner for me, but I need to hurry back. Maybe some other time?"

"Another time," Alice promised. "Bye, Tim. I'll take Missy home." She slipped away to let Missy and Tim say their goodbyes.

"Mom asked for a turn. She said if I'd spent the night here, she wants you to come down next Tuesday for the Fourth. Their community by the lake has nice fireworks."

He held his breath, waiting for her answer. "I'd like that. Call me." Tim let out his breath and dropped a kiss on her forehead.

Missy invited her mother to her house for lunch. They rode in silence.

"You're going to have to tell him, you know?"

"I know, Mom. Do you think it'll make a difference?"

"No, not really, if he's the man I think he is. He's crazy about you, Missy."

"Let's pray. His eyes are so blue, like the sky on a summer day, and when he looks at me—" Missy's voice drifted off. "I'm scared. You said it's my turn, but what if it isn't? I don't think I could stand losing him. I talked to Jimmy, and I'm going to meetings. I messed up the first time, blurting out the whole story about Grace. Jimmy assigned me a sponsor, Mary, Ken's wife. He said she'd be perfect, and we've started to meet once a week."

"That's wise. Do you ever have the horrible dreams you used to have?"

"Not in years, but I'm scared of him. I know it's silly, but when he touches me, I freeze. I can't keep putting him off."

"That's why you must tell him right away. He's not a young man, and he won't wait forever while you turn away. He needs to understand. We'll pray. Julie, Jimmy, and I—we'll keep praying. Gram would say, 'God makes a way when there is no way,' remember? He'll see you through this. I need to be at the hospital at three. I'll drop you off and go change."

"Bye, Mom. Thanks." Missy leaned over to kiss her. "I love you."

"Love you back, Girlie-girl."

Tim Knows

When Tim called, he told Missy he'd come get her, but she said not to be silly. He gave her directions to his condo, and she had no trouble finding it. They planned to go to Lake Floyd together. His parents lived several miles west of Clarksburg. After he showed her his small apartment, they went out to his truck.

Missy had butterflies in her tummy as they drove. "You have a nice place, but I'd put your small desk under the steps and put a comfortable chair in the living room. Where do you relax?"

"I'm not there much. Are you offering to help me fix the place up?"

"I'm such a busybody. Forgive me."

"It's part of who you are—you see how to make things better. We'd better get a move on. Mom and Dad are eager to meet you."

"That's scary."

"Be yourself. They're going to love you. I promise." He turned into the neighborhood, looping around a man-made lake that was glittering in the sun. His parents' driveway was shaded by towering pines and lined with azalea bushes. She didn't say a word but clung to his hand as he led her into the house. They came into a large, open house overlooking the lake. Tim's brother and his wife, his sister and her husband, and all the kids swarmed Tim. He made introductions, pointing at Tom and his wife, Dannie, and then at his sister, Terri, and her husband, Les.

They all chorused, "Hi, Missy." She took a small step backward.

"They won't bite," Tim comforted.

Tim's mother, drying her hands on a towel as she walked in, fussed. "It's not fair to gang up on her. You know this whole rowdy crew. It's a bit much all at once." She held out her hands and took both of Missy's. "Welcome, Missy. You are welcome in our home." Anne Raines beamed at her, and Missy immediately relaxed in her warmth. Soon Tim was on the floor while his niece and nephews crawled all over him.

"Don't tickle me anymore, Uncle Timmy!" the little girl panted, giggling.

Missy watched them play and followed Anne into the kitchen. She was comfortable with helping and felt at home. She carried the overflowing platters out to the long table on the porch. The young mothers were relieved to leave her with it, and she moved back and forth without too much direction. Anne seemed to sense that Missy was feeling her own way around and let her work in silence.

Tim's father came bounding up the steps and swept into the house. "Where's the food?" he roared jovially. "If we don't get his show on the road, I'll be late for my own fireworks!"

Anne gently put her hand on his arm. "This is Missy O'Malley, Tim's friend from Elkins, remember?" Her eyes sparkled as she told Missy that the 'big oaf' was Tim's father, Todd Raines.

Missy looked up into the most mischievous eyes she'd ever seen, which were twinkling down at her. Tim's blue eyes.

"You're most welcome in our home, Missy O'Malley. We've heard all about you." Everyone laughingly agreed, and Tim blushed, shrugging his shoulders. "Okay, that's done. Let's eat." Todd beamed and gathered everyone around to say the blessing.

"Mrs. Raines, you've outdone yourself. Everything looks wonderful!"

"Call me Anne, Missy. I feel like I know you, and thank you for all your help."

Todd peered at her. "She is a little mite of a thing, Timmy, isn't she?"

Missy drew herself up to her full, almost 5 foot 2-inch height, and everyone laughed, a warm, affectionate laugh, and she laughed along. Conversation flowed around her, and she looked from one happy face to another.

"Good meal, Mama," Todd boomed. "I need to finish setting up. You guys better get down to the lake if you want a good seat."

The ladies ran for the powder room, changed diapers, and headed toward the fireworks. As they walked, Tim moved closer to Missy and put his arm around her waist. She stiffened, then made herself relax. She smiled and looked up at him. When she hesitated, Tim kept his arm loose, casual.

"Here, Missy, over here. We're going to sit on the blanket with the babies," Terri called.

"Is this okay?" Missy looked up at Tim.

"It'll be fine. We have several blankets." Tim shook out another one, telling Missy his father was a volunteer firefighter, so he oversaw the fireworks, which were in the middle of the lake, on several rafts that were tied together. Missy sat cross legged on the corner of the blanket, and Tim lay down beside her, propping up on his elbow, his long legs stretched out.

"Why are you all 'T's,' after your dad?" she asked. "You could be Adam, Andrew, and Alice, after Anne. Why not?"

Tom hooted. "Because we are all chauvinist pigs. Haven't you heard? Big Christian family, and Dad's a coal miner."

"Anne doesn't look like a woman anyone could push around."

"Well put, Missy, thank you," Anne said. "They're all mouth, Tom and his father, and they don't scare me a minute. Big teddy bears, both of them. I can hold my own in a classroom of 28 middle school students."

"I've been in that class. She runs it like a dictator," Tom added.

"I don't believe that for a minute, Tom Raines," Missy protested.

Tim was amused. "You have my family pegged in an hour and a half, do you? What am I, dictator, oaf, or teddy bear?"

"Hmm, let me get back to you on that one." Everyone laughed, and Les punched Tim in the arm. Missy was glad when the fireworks started and covered her confusion. Everyone oohed and ahhed until the fabulous display finished with a glorious finale, and they gathered up their things. Tim's siblings headed off to their homes with sleepy babies and one tired little boy. Tim helped, carrying his little nephew and tucking him into his car seat, and then he kissed each one of his niece and nephews goodnight. His mom and dad stood beside Missy, looking at her as she watched him.

"Come on in. We've prepared a day bed for you in our den," Anne invited. Tim got her overnight bag out of his truck, and they walked up the steep stairs to the house.

After they left her, Missy slipped into a jump suit that she brought to sleep in. She knelt beside the bed, thanking God for this home, this family who'd taken her in like a long, lost prodigal. If only they knew! Memories crowded her mind. Too restless to sleep, she wandered out to the porch and sat, looking at the lake. She needed to talk to Tim, and they hadn't had a moment alone. She heard a shower turning off, and shortly afterward, Tim joined her on the porch, his hair still wet.

"I thought I heard you come out here. Everything okay? You need anything?"

"No."

"Penny for your thoughts."

"I have ten dollars' worth, Timothy."

He sat down. "I have time. Do you mind?"

"No, I want to talk to you. There are some things you need to know."

"Oh?"

Missy started to cry. Tim already knew she was like her mother and felt better moving, so he asked, "Do you want to take a walk?"

"I'd like that. Do you mind?"

"Let's go." Tim offered her a hand, and when she got up, he didn't let go. They went down the steps and took the road leading to the pavilion on the lake. He didn't intrude on her silence; he simply waited, holding her hand.

They sat. "Tim," she began, her head down. "You asked me if I'd ever loved anyone. I was honest when I told you I hadn't, but I...but I have had a baby." Tim never loosened his hold on her hand. "She was a beautiful baby. I called her Gracie because she was God's gift to me. I was 17, and I gave her up for adoption. I met her parents. They're wonderful people, and it brought me joy to know how happy they were to have her." Missy rubbed her nose on her sleeve, took a deep breath, and continued, her head still down.

"But I never loved anyone. I was, it was—Jimmy wasn't doing so well at the time. He had some friends over. They were sorry boys, plain sorry. Julie and I worked at McDonald's, and she dropped me off. I went into the house and...they...they raped me. Three of them."

Tim gathered her into his arms and let her cry. He made no sudden moves, only held her in a tender embrace.

Missy sniffed and spoke into the quiet. "Now you know, and if it makes a difference, I'll understand."

Tim rested his chin on the top of her head. "It makes a difference. It makes a huge difference. I thought I loved you. I thought I respected you. Now I know the depth of your courage, the depth of your faith, and I honor you for giving Gracie life and a home. How hard it must have been for you!"

"Everyone thought it was easy—I should want to be rid of a baby that was a reminder of that...that violence, but I never could hold the sins of her father against her, and when she grew inside of me, it was such a miracle to feel her sweet presence filling me up. I loved her, Timothy!" And she wept anew.

"Where was Jimmy when this happened?"

"He was drunk, high, and semi-passed out. He's never forgiven himself. I screamed and screamed. You know how remote Mom's place is. It was violent. They ripped off my clothes and took turns. All of them, more than once." She began to tremble. "They laughed at the blood. I used to wake up at night and be terrified. I thought I could hear them laughing, hear their truck screech out of the driveway. I decided not to call for help. Jimmy was in no shape to drive, nor was I. Mom had gotten her first nursing job. I didn't want to mess things up for her."

Missy told him of her night in hell, washing her sheets, throwing away her clothes, and trying to clean up the house. She let Tim hold her loosely as they sat on the bench together. He turned her in his arms and let her lean back against him as she told him how Jimmy sobered up and met the challenges they faced. "I couldn't have made it without him. Gracie touched her uncle too. He started going to church with us." Missy relaxed in Tim's embrace, telling him about Hope House, Miss Ginny, and Beth.

"Jimmy and Mom came in the day Gracie was born. I called in the middle of the night, when I knew she was making her way into the world. It was an easy birth. She weighed almost seven pounds. It's hard to explain, but God moved right into that room. He was all around us, welcoming the new life He had made. I felt like He and I had done something good—we made a life. I nursed her once and asked Mom to take her to her parents."

"You've lost a baby too, and it was hard."

"It was the hardest thing I've ever done...but also the best. It was like the 'goodest' thing I could've done. I'd met with her parents several times, and they were praying for me and for her. I know they've brought her up with love and all the advantages a poor, unwed, young teen could never have provided." Tim placed a kiss on her brow and tucked a piece of her hair behind her ear. "She's alive, growing to her potential, developing the gifts God has given her, and being a blessing to so many people. But, God knows, going home without her was...horrible. I felt empty, and I cried all the time. It hit Jimmy like a ton of bricks."

"And that's when he started drinking again, and Julie had to break up with him."

"You know everything about the O'Malley family now." They fell quiet.

Tim broke the silence. "Now I know, and it helps, Missy. I've been confused, troubled. We seem to fit, and I do love you. You must know that, and I think you love me too, but then you pull away. Like the night at your house and tonight when we walked to the lake. I feel you stiffen, but now I understand. I told you once before...I promise never to hurt you. I understand Jimmy's protectiveness too."

"I've started to go to Recovery meetings. I told Mom I wanted you to kiss me, but I panicked. I was afraid. I want to love you—I do love you. I'm...I'm... I don't know. I'm scared."

"You take all the time you need. I'll be here. I'll wait. Don't cut me out. Let me be here for you."

"I'd like that, Tim. You're my best friend. Remember the night we talked way past my bedtime?"

"Twice. The night I tried to kiss you and the night after Mrs. Andrews got saved."

Tim tightened his arms around her. "What happened to those guys?"

"One guy died in a drunk driving accident several months later. The biggest guy was killed in a prison fight a couple of years ago. I ran into the youngest guy. He's in the Army. He's become a Christian, and he begged me for forgiveness. He was a kid and got caught up in what the older guys did."

Tim nuzzled the top of her head with his chin. "If I ever met them, I'd lose my Christianity. I couldn't stand it if anyone ever hurt you again." Tim straightened and turned her to face him. "Let's pray, Missy." Holding her hands, he prayed. She prayed, and sometimes their voices mingled together. Tim prayed for her memories to heal, for her trust to grow, and for himself to be worthy of that trust. She thanked God for him, for his acceptance, and asked that she would be able to love him as fully and completely as he deserved.

Tim stood and stretched. "We seem to have a propensity for talking into the wee, small hours of the morning."

Missy stood too. "I'm not a night person. You're corrupting me." She leaned into him, and he placed his arms around her. She breathed in deeply, taking in his scent. Stepping back, she took his hand and looked in his eyes. "Thank you, Timothy."

"When you say my name, I feel ten feet tall. Just my name, the way you say it. I feel like God is calling me."

"You're dear. Thank you for being you."

"You make me a better person. Loving you is a privilege, an honor I can only hope to deserve." She leaned into his side, and he placed his arm around her. This time she didn't stiffen, and he smiled.

Waiting

They spent the summer together, back and forth between the farm and his parents' house. Tim was true to his word. He never pushed her, but sometimes he thought he'd go crazy. One night at the farm, he heard her in the hall after they'd all gone to bed. He found her in a state of terror, but when he went to her, she stumbled backward, begging him not to touch her.

"Can you at least tell me? What is it, Missy?"

"Did you hear anything outside? Trucks on the gravel?"

"No." Tim walked down the hall, flipping on lights. He turned on all the lights in the great room, flooding the house with light. He looked on the porch. "Maggie's sound asleep. Did you have a bad dream?"

Missy was shaking from head to toe. She went to the couch and pulled her feet up, wrapping her arms around her knees and tying herself into a tight knot.

He went to get her a blanket. "Don't go, Tim!" He carried it to her, placing it beside her. She was shaking too hard to reach for it, so he shook it out and eased it over her. "Don't go."

"I'll be right here. How about some hot chocolate? Do you have any mix? I can't make it from scratch like you and your mom can."

"We keep it for the kids, in the cabinet on the left." Tim prepared a cup and took it to her. She reached for it, but her hands were shaking, and she couldn't hold it. He set it on the table beside her. He kept up a light chatter, telling her about his progress on Mike's house and how he longed to work for himself. They'd hoisted the big bed to the second floor before they set the rails, but Mike hadn't seen it yet. He watched her as she began to relax.

"Better?" She nodded. "Let me warm that for you."

Missy sipped the chocolate. "It's almost time to get up. I've kept you up all night. I'm sorry."

"I'm glad I was here. I can't bear to think of you handling this alone. Promise you'll call if you need me again?"

She shuddered. "I haven't had that dream in years. I don't know what happened."

After Tim made her promise, they went to their separate rooms.

When he woke up later in the morning, he went looking for her. Usually he'd find her in the meadow, paddling in the creek, and once, he found her up in a tree. If she hadn't laughed, he never would have looked up and found her. But she was nowhere to be found, and Alice didn't know either.

"What happened last night, Tim? I heard you up with her." Tim described what happened. "I thought I'd leave you with her. I lay in bed and prayed. She had nightmares all the time before she left for Hope House. They wring her out—maybe you should try her room."

Tim opened the door without a sound. She was sleeping the sleep of the dead, but she looked peaceful. His heart swelled with compassion for this tiny girl he loved. When she finally joined them, over an hour later, he and Alice were sitting on the porch swing. Her eyes had deep, dark circles under them, and she looked fragile. Tim was afraid to touch her, but he rose. She stepped into his arms and leaned her head on his chest. "Maybe you should just give up, Tim."

Raising her chin so her eyes met his, he asked, "Where would I go, Missy? You are too much a part of me to ever let you go now."

Watching them, Alice felt tears drip down her cheeks. She tiptoed into the house.

On Monday afternoon, Tim looked at his watch at about 2:30. He drove out to Lake Floyd to have time with his mother before his dad got home.

"Hey, Tim, I wasn't expecting you. What's up?"

He told her what happened at the farm. "She hasn't had that dream in years, she said. I wonder why she had it now."

"I'm no shrink, as your father says, but my guess is that perhaps she had an erotic dream about you, and it frightened her."

"Mom, I'm really careful with her. I haven't done a thing to her."

"I'm sure you didn't. But we women also have dreams when we're in love. She may not even remember, but perhaps her subconscious mind became frightened over the needs her body is naturally experiencing, and it kicked in the old nightmare."

"What am I going to do?" Tim rubbed his hands over his face.

"I don't pray as well as you and your precious Missy. She makes God part of every conversation. But I've bought some books on prayer, and I've been praying. I sense the breakthrough is near. She's better. She takes your hand, and love shines in her eyes when she looks at you."

"Thanks, Mom. I hope so. I never dreamed it would be this hard, but the terror was profound. She shook for forty-five minutes. It was awful watching her like that!" He got up. "I'm going to run before Dad gets home." Anne hugged him and sent him on his way.

Tim didn't see Missy for days, and then he couldn't stand being away. They drove up to Timberline several times, working together on Mike's house. Maggie rode proudly in Tim's truck as if it were her own. They laughed. Missy sang. And Tim prayed. She went to weekly meetings with her sponsor, read books, and kept Tim aware of her progress, which seemed painfully slow to him.

One beautiful Indian summer day, Tim and his parents drove up to the farm. Alice liked them. Missy and Tim had been teasing one another, and she took off, running like the wind.

"She doesn't have any shoes on," Anne observed. "Doesn't that hurt her feet?"

Alice laughed. "Getting and keeping shoes on that child was the only problem I ever had with her."

"She doesn't have any weight to press her feet into the ground," Todd said. "Boy, look at her go!"

"She won both sprint and distance run in track at state her junior year. She never gets winded."

"Tim will never catch her."

"He keeps trying," Alice told her.

"We like your gal, Alice. I asked Tim if she was worth waiting for earlier in the summer, but she is. He told us he'd wait forever if he had to—and then he told us what she'd been through. He said we didn't know how much courage is packed into that tiny body. She's worth the wait. I know that now. And she's revealed the depth of his character. He told me he didn't want my advice. She was God's gift to him, he said, and he'd never let her go, but we had to be patient for her to get through this." Todd's eyes glistened.

"I'm glad Tim told you. She is special, and the joy of the Lord is her strength. Even in the maternity home, she filled the place with laughter and teasing. She led one girl to the Lord, and two others said she carried them through their labors. But, speaking of children, your Tim is wonderful. You brought up a mighty fine son." Alice told them her daughter had been going to recovery meetings and that she was working hard. Then she asked, "Anne, is she anything like Amy?"

"Thank God, no!" Todd responded quickly. "Missy can squeeze ten dollars out of a dime, and Amy spent money like water. We thought she'd bankrupt him, but he did make a fortune on the house she wanted when he finally sold it. The more he gave her, the more she demanded."

"They're not at all alike," Anne added. "Amy was tall and much too elegant—she did love the finer things in life...clothes, shoes, furniture. Amy wasn't—Missy fits. She romps with our family. She's joyous! She's wonderful for our Tim. Even as she's working through her issues, she makes him look ten feet tall by looking at him, saying his name. We never thought we'd hear him laugh again."

"He's never laughed like that, all his life," Todd put in.

"He was always serious—Eagle Scout, Scripts spelling bee, Golden Horse-shoe winner—a brilliant scholar. He had six years at Virginia Tech, full ride, and got two Masters degrees."

The older Raines left after dinner, but Tim stayed the night. Missy rested her feet on his lap, leaning her head back on the couch. Tim held her tiny brown feet in one big hand, rubbing them with the other. "I love your feet, brown Indian princess."

Alice rose suddenly, asking if anyone wanted hot chocolate. In the kitchen, she whispered, "God, if any two people deserve happiness, it's those two wounded warriors. Make it happen, Father."

One weekend, the couple drove up to Columbus, Ohio, to a Hope House reunion. Tim couldn't believe Michelle was the plain, mousey girl Missy described. She was an elegant, handsome woman. She never went back to her parent's home, and she completed her residency at Cleveland Clinic after finishing medical school at the University of Ohio. Candy was now part of a large, exuberant, Hispanic family, surrounded by sisters and brothers. Cathy had a degree in counseling, and her husband was a psychologist. Laura—the cheerleader—earned a degree in Women's Ministry and married a pastor. How far they'd come! But Tim saw the bonds that were forged during their summer of pain and knew these were forever friends.

On the ride home, Missy told him more about Candy, how she'd been abused and impregnated by her step-father. "Joe married her at Hope House before Eddie was born. He wanted his name to be on the birth certificate. He prayed to be like Mary's Joseph and not know his wife until after the birth of the child. I needed to talk to her, and she was a big help." Missy held up some books. "She bought these for me. She said she studied before they went on their honeymoon."

Tim raised his eyebrows but didn't say a word. "Do you think we could stop by Wheeling and visit Miss Ginny?" he asked. Ginny had retired and lived with her daughter, who was also now retired. Ginny was thrilled and met them with outstretched arms, insisting they stay for lunch. When they pulled out, she pulled Missy close and whispered to her, and Missy laughed.

"What did Ginny say that made you laugh?" Tim looked across the seat before he backed up.

"She told me not to let you get away. I'm trying, Timothy."

"I know, baby." But Tim was weary as Missy continued to work hard at her healing, reading the books Candy gave her. He could kiss her lightly now, and she sat in his lap to snuggle. He prayed constantly for her and waited. One evening, while talking on the phone during their regular evening visit, he asked what she was doing.

"Reading my homework."

"Should I be reading something too?" Missy was silent. "Did I lose you?"

"No."

"Is it none of my business?"

"Timothy, everything is your business. My business is your business. I'm reading the Song of Solomon and a Bible study that accompanies it. Laura gave it to me."

"I haven't read that in a while."

"Maybe you shouldn't right now. But soon," she promised.

The next week, Tim promised to come by the shop to take her to dinner. She was working on a project as darkness fell. Noticing the time, she furrowed her brow. *It's not like him to be late.* She left him a message when his number rang and rang. Another hour went by. She couldn't stand it any longer and decided to go to her mother's. She could wait there as well as she could at the shop. When she pulled in the drive, Tim's truck was there, and she was genuinely puzzled. Going up the steps, she pushed open the door.

Tim looked up, surprised, and glanced down at his watch.

Before he could say a word, her voice sharpened by her concern, Missy asked, "How long have you been here? Didn't you get my messages? I've been frantic!"

Alice spun around and faced her daughter. "You have no right to talk to him like that, Missy. Now stop it!" Missy looked at her, confused, and her mouth dropped open as her mother continued. "You must stop abusing this poor man's patience. You need to get on with this. Years ago, you insisted on an encounter with Jimmy. I'm calling for my own encounter with you, right here, right now."

Tim stood and held out his hand. "It's okay, Alice." But Alice spun around again to face him.

"Don't 'it's okay, Alice' me, Tim. Shut up!"

Missy's eyes got wide. She'd never heard her mother say those words, even in jest, but Alice wasn't joking, and she was far from through. Her voice raised a notch, and she glared at Missy. "Do you hear me, Missy O'Malley? Get on with this! How long will you keep this good man waiting? Get over yourself! You are being selfish, and...and...get on with it." She fumbled for words, finally storming out after shouting, "Poop, or get off the pot, Missy."

She strode down the hall, throwing back, "And don't you darken the door of my house again until you do! I'm tired of being patient with you myself." She slammed the door behind her as she went into her bedroom.

Missy stared after her, transfixed.

"Missy, I'm sorry about this."

"I've never seen her like this, never in all my born days. What did you say to her, Tim?"

Before he could answer, the door popped open, and Alice leaned into the hall. She put her fists on her hips and screamed, "I mean it, Missy. Get out, and when you come back here, I want this done. Do you hear me? Now, get out!" She pointed to the front door. "Get out of here, Missy Emma O'Malley!"

"Yes, Ma'am," Missy mumbled, moving toward the door. Tim was shaking with laughter by this time. "What's going on?" Missy asked.

Tim crossed over to her. "I guess..." He shrugged. "I asked Alice for help. We prayed. To be honest, this is getting awfully hard on me. I love you so much, Missy."

Hot tears stung Missy's eyes. "I'd better get out of here before she tosses me out on my can. I believe she means it." They heard crashing and breaking as Alice threw things in her room. The door opened again, but she didn't come out into the hall. She looked at Missy furiously, and shouted, "And if you drive this precious man away with your stubborn selfishness, don't come crying to me. I'll slap you silly, Missy O'Malley." The door banged shut again.

Tim reached out his hand. "Look, I'm sorry. This is my fault. I didn't mean to cause all this. Let's go to dinner."

Missy looked at him with tears streaming down her face. "She's right, Tim. I'm sorry. I need to go home. We can go to dinner another time." She pushed open the door and trudged outside and down the steps. Tim picked up his coat and followed her into the winter night, but she got into her Jeep without a word. Edging past his truck, she pulled out of the driveway.

Tim shrugged on his coat. He shook his head as he got into his truck and muttered, "You've done it now, Raines. You've blown it. You've probably lost her forever." But he couldn't cry anymore. He'd cried all afternoon, and all his tears had been wrung out of him. He drove through Beverly and didn't even see the lights of Elkins as he continued west. He begged God, pleaded with Him, even railed at Him. He remembered the still small voice that spoke to Elijah, and he fell quiet, hardly daring to breathe. Silence filled the truck. He turned north on I 79, and a thought popped into his mind. *Some kind only come out by prayer and fasting.*

Tim had never fasted much, but he knew as clearly as he'd ever heard the voice of God that this was what he was supposed to do. He sat at the little table in his apartment and looked up that Scripture. He read it, and it seemed to shout at him. He cross-referenced other passages on fasting. "Okay, God."

The funny thing was, the next day he wasn't even hungry. In fact, his senses were sharp and keen. He worked from home, and by noon, he had completed two proposals that he'd been stuck on for a week. He hardly thought about Missy, but when he looked at his watch, he automatically reached for the phone to call her. He picked up her message from the night before, listening to her concern. He started to dial her number but checked himself. He wasn't supposed to call. He turned his phone off. Running his fingers through his hair, he waited for the still small voice, but no thought came to his mind. Sighing, he walked across the living room and flipped on the TV, listening to the news for a while. He turned it off and sat in the big recliner Missy had given him for his birthday. He put his head between his knees and prayed. In that posture, he prayed for hours, and he still wasn't hungry. Wondering what Missy was doing, he went to bed at the unheard-of hour of nine o'clock, but he felt peaceful and calm. A new faith swept over him as he gently placed Missy in their heavenly Father's arms, and he slept well.

* * *

Early the next day, Missy called Jimmy. He didn't answer. She called Julie. No answer. She called the hospital. Her mother would be on the floor after seven. She wanted to tell her she was right. It was time.

"Hey, Cynthia. I thought you were off today. Can I speak to Mom?"

"They called me in because she called in sick. You'd better check on her, Missy. She's never sick."

Missy knew she couldn't do that. Unlike her usual morning, she hadn't eaten as soon as she got up; she hadn't even had a cup of coffee. *I know what I'll do. I don't have anything pressing. I'll call myself in sick and declare a fast day.* She read her Bible, talked to God, and even read a book on prayer and fasting. By nightfall, she hadn't heard from a soul. A day never went by without talking to her family or Tim, but she was fine. A calm determination swept over her, and she slept well.

The next day she went to the shop. She was still not hungry. At one, she put on her coat and drove over to her sponsor's house for her weekly appointment—they met when Mary's daughter went down for her nap. She pulled into the drive and saw Julie's car. *Today. This is the day.* She turned off the motor, leaned her head on the steering wheel, and breathed a prayer. "Lord, help me. Let's do this."

Missy wandered into the large den and looked out the window overlooking her beautiful West Virginia Mountains. They looked sad. After a glorious fall, the trees stood bare, lifting their empty branches to the sky. "I will lift up my eyes unto the hills, from whence cometh my help." Didn't Tim quote that to her once?

Mary entered the room silently, sitting beside Julie on the couch. They linked hands.

Missy said, "Mom's right. It's my turn, and we need to get on with it. Is she okay? I haven't talked to anyone since Tuesday."

"We've all been fasting." Julie looked at her friend closely. "Even Tim, and nobody told him. Let's deal with this. A good Christian man loves you, and he's waiting."

"I want to love him with all I have, all I am, and I can't," Missy whispered.

"Of course you'd cringe at a man's touch after you were so violated, Missy. I was sexually abused by my step-brother from the time I was eight years old until I was in my teens. When I finally went to my school counselor, I was put into a foster home. I fell in love with Ken, but I struggled for years with intimacy. I shook at his touch. Poor guy. I loved him, but I was repulsed by the whole idea of sex. I give to you what God has given me, Missy."

"You got over it?"

"I did. Our marriage is solid and exciting now. I know you love Tim. I've heard you talk about him. I've seen you with him."

Julie hugged her husband's sister, her best friend. "We've prayed for years for you to love and be loved. God has brought you through many trials, and when He begins a work, He completes it. He kept you in the tree house. He kept you at Hope House, and He brought Tim to you. He'll deliver you today. Today is the day of salvation, Missy."

"He gave me strength to trust my baby to her parents."

"Let's lay hands on this child of God," Mary said. "She's suffered long enough."

Missy was circled by love as the women prayed. "Father, I offer Missy the comfort You've given me. I lay hands on her in full confidence that what You've done for me, You'll do for her." The women prayed to God for her deliverance and spoke to the forces of darkness, commanding them to loosen her and let her go.

Missy looked up through her tears. "I choose to go forth with joy and walk out my deliverance."

Driving home, Missy asked God for two things: may Timothy be in range in the mountains, and may he be close. With a trembling hand, she pressed speed dial one.

"Hey, Missy, what's up?"

"Where are you?"

"At the moment, I'm about 20 minutes out of Elkins. I thought I'd run up tomorrow and see how the carpeting was coming in the next model, and I hope you can come with me."

"I can't tell you how glad I am. Could you come to my house? Now?"

"Missy, My Love, your wish is my command. I can't refuse when you ask me to come to you."

"Have you had supper, you nut?"

"I planned to get a sandwich from Subway and head for my cold, lonely hotel room."

"I'll have soup and a sandwich waiting. We need to talk."

"Missy, please, marry me. Don't say no. We'll work through this together."

"Timothy, miracles are happening. I can't wait to see you."

Missy hurried home, let Maggie out, warmed up some soup, and made sandwiches. The early night of winter darkened the room, but she kept the lights dim, lighting the fire and setting out candles. She knelt in front of the big chair she'd bought for Tim. "God, I come to you in faith, believing—You are able to do exceeding abundantly, above all I can ask or think. Your promises are yes and amen. Your desire for Your children is for us to walk in love and freedom. The marriage bed is undefiled. You created us to be sexual beings and designed us for joy. I want to give and receive that joy with Tim."

She heard the doorbell, and her heart leapt. She opened it and drew Tim into the warmth of her home. Closing the door behind him, she took his coat, hung it up, and stepped into his arms. She lifted her face and kissed him warmly. He looked down, his eyes crinkling at the corners. Her tummy lurched.

"This is a nice welcome...and certainly worth the drive!"

"Go sit in your chair, and I'll bring you dinner. First, read this." She handed him a small newspaper, folded to an article and a picture. She went to the kitchen to pour his soup into the waiting bowl and picked up the sandwiches.

"What do you think?"

"Amazing. She must be your Grace. She looks like a female Jimmy, and all the dates line up. Her speech is intelligent, sensitive, and powerful. No wonder she took first place. Her closing poem made me cry: 'My mother who bore me'—that's you! Aren't you proud?"

"I did make the right choice. She does look like Jimmy. Julie will help me show it to him. You see the date on this *NRLNews*? I've had it lying around for months, but I happened upon it yesterday, when I needed it. It was like closure for me. Go ahead and eat, and I'll tell you about my meeting with Mary today."

Tim prayed, and Missy told him how she prayed to love him the way God intended, the way He so beautifully created them. "I want to give you all of me." Missy's throat closed.

Tim put his spoon down carefully beside the bowl, studying her face. He didn't say a word, but his eyes misted. He waited, praying in his heart. A slow, sexy grin turned up his mouth. The fire popped, setting off an explosion of sparks, and Missy felt a warmth flood her belly. She moved the tray off his lap and set it on the table so she could snuggle. They listened to the pinecones pop and watched the tendrils of flames curl around the logs. Tim nuzzled the top of her head and loosely circled his arms around her, sensitive to the limits they experienced. She leaned her head back, gazing steadily into his blue eyes, loving them and loving him.

Gently, hesitantly, he leaned toward her. She pulled his face down to meet her own. Their kiss was warm, and deep, and lingering, and it left them both breathless. They kissed again, and her response became more eager. Tim met her, measure for measure, with all the pent-up months of longing.

They broke apart, and Tim rearranged himself awkwardly on the chair. "If you're going to keep this up, we have to get married soon!"

"I've been thinking that it should happen before Christmas."

"Honey, that's less than three weeks!"

"I'm a professional. We don't need a big wedding. Two weeks...if you can talk your family into coming up to Elkins this close to Christmas."

"You watch! They thought I'd never get married again. They've been praying their hearts out for this moment. They kissed again, and Tim said huskily, "I'd better leave while I still can. I can wait two weeks for the promise of your sweetness."

Their heavenly Father looked down on His creation. He saw everything He had made, and behold, it was good.

Epilogue

Tim and Missy were married in two weeks and two days. They waited for a weekend. Tim's family took up one whole wing of the hotel, and the reception took place at the farmhouse. Missy sang "Love Me Tender" to Tim, and when her voice broke, Jimmy stood beside her to help her finish.

A stranger watched the bridal party and the guests that were coming and going from the diner across the street. Watching Alice, who was without a coat, he whispered, "Put on your coat, Darlin,' or you'll freeze."

The waitress didn't hear his words, but she asked if she knew them. He told her he wasn't from around here, but he mentioned that the family seemed very popular.

"Oh, everyone loves Missy O'Malley. When I got knocked up as a teenager, she convinced me to carry my baby. The jerk's long gone, but I still have that precious son. He's seventeen now and going to college. She handed him the bill, and after he left, she picked up a $50.00 tip.

The stranger blew his nose into a handkerchief and gave a wave as he slipped out the door. He pulled into a nearby gas station, and as he started to pump gas, the pastor from Missy's church asked, "Ian? Ian O'Malley?"

Pulling his hat lower, the stranger said, "I'm not from around here."

* * *

The couple spent their first night in the Dollhouse. Missy was quiet, and he put his hand over hers. "You okay?"

"Perfect, Timothy."

He pulled into the driveway and helped her out. At the front door, he swept her into his arms. "How gallant is it for a man to carry his bride over her own threshold?"

"This will do fine until we outgrow it."

Missy disappeared into her bedroom while Tim waited in the living room. She reappeared in a pale yellow gown, with blue flowers set around a low neckline.

"Do you want to sit out here a while?"

Shy but steady, Missy came toward him, shook her head, and took his hand, leading him to the bedroom.

They honeymooned at Mike's house. In the mornings, he awoke to her singing and found her curled up on the couch beside the tree. Often, he carried her back upstairs...even Christmas morning had to wait. He gave her a diamond ring, and she gave him a nice camera and lens, which he put to excellent use taking countless pictures of his favorite subject.

Gracie's Poem

CHILD OF CHOICE

I am a Child of Choice.
My mother who bore me
Could have chosen to ignore me.
She gave the life I have before me.
I'm so glad she chose.

I am a child of choice.
My mother who taught me,
In nets of love she caught me.
With love, she trained (and fought) me.
I am so glad she chose.

I am a child of choice.
My heav'nly Father made me.
His Son's life paid for me.
Ever beside He has stayed me.
I am so glad He chose.

Thrice chosen I am, and why?
I have a divine plan before me.
My life is His purpose for me—
Many days are yet before me.
I am a child of choice.

Now I must choose to pay
The debt of love I owe them.
My own love ever bestow them,
And in every act to show them,
The child of choice I am.

The last of the Hope House books, tentatively titled *Michelle Meets her Match,* will be coming soon.

About the Author

CHARLOTTE S. SNEAD holds a BA in Psychology from Duke University and a MA in Social Work from the University of North Carolina. Oak Tara published three of her books: *His Brother's Wife* in 2012, *Recovered and Free*, and *Invisible Wounds* in 2014. She later received Jan-Carol Publishing's Believe and Achieve Award for her novel *A Place to Live*, the first of a scheduled five-book series. While working on the remaining books in the series, *Always My Son* and *Go for the Honey*, Charlotte published her first children's book, *Deano the Dino Goes to the Doctor*, in 2018.

Charlotte married her husband, Dr. Joseph Snead, in 1962. They raised five children and a foster daughter and now proudly grandparent ten boys and one girl. One of their children and four of their grandchildren are adopted.

In keeping with her strong belief in and celebration of the joy of marriage, family, and writing, she maintains a blog at www.charlottesnead.com, which has the tagline "Sacred Passion—It's God's Idea." Please feel free to contact her there.